Gods
Behaving
Badly

Gods
Behaving
Badly

MARIE PHILLIPS

JONATHAN CAPE
LONDON

Published by Jonathan Cape 2007

2 4 6 8 10 9 7 5 3 1

First published in Great Britain in 2007 by
Jonathan Cape
Random House, 20 Vauxhall Bridge Road,
London SW1V 2SA

www.randomhouse.co.uk

Addresses for companies within The Random House Group Limited can be found at:
www.randomhouse.co.uk

The Random House Group Limited Reg. No. 954009

A CIP catalogue record for this book is available from the British Library

ISBN 9780224081313 (Hardback edition)
ISBN 9780224081320 (Trade Paperback edition)

The Random House Group Limited makes every effort to ensure that the papers used in
its books are made from trees that have been legally sourced from well-managed and
credibly certified forests. Our paper procurement policy can be found at
www.randomhouse.co.uk/paper.htm

Mixed Sources
Product group from well-managed
forests and other controlled sources
www.fsc.org Cert no. TT-COC-2139
© 1996 Forest Stewardship Council

FSC

Typeset in Dante MT by Palimpsest Book Production Limited,
Grangemouth, Stirlingshire
Printed and Bound in Great Britain by
Clays Ltd, St Ives plc

For MY PARENTS

# One

One morning, when Artemis was out walking the dogs, she saw a tree where no tree should be.

The tree was standing alone in a sheltered part of the slope. To the untrained eye, the casual passer-by, it probably just looked like a normal tree. But Artemis's eye was far from untrained, and she ran through this part of Hampstead Heath every day. This tree was a newcomer: it had not been there yesterday. And with just one glance Artemis recognised that it was an entirely new species, a type of eucalyptus that had also not existed yesterday. It was a tree that should not exist at all.

Dragging the mutts behind her, Artemis made her way over to the tree. She touched its bark and felt it breathing. She pressed her ear against the trunk of the tree and listened to its heartbeat. Then she looked around. Good: it was early, and there was nobody within earshot. She reminded herself not to get angry with the tree, that it wasn't the tree's fault. Then she spoke.

'Hello,' she said.

There was a long silence.

'Hello,' said Artemis again.

'Are you talking to me?' said the tree. It had a faint Australian accent.

'Yes,' said Artemis. 'I am Artemis.' If the tree experienced any recognition, it didn't show it. 'I'm the goddess of hunting and chastity,' said Artemis.

Another silence. Then the tree said, 'I'm Kate. I work in mergers and acquisitions for Goldman Sachs.'

'Do you know what happened to you, Kate?' said Artemis.

The longest silence of all. Artemis was just about to repeat the question when the tree replied.

'I think I've turned into a tree,' it said.

'Yes,' said Artemis. 'You have.'

'Thank God for that,' said the tree. 'I thought I was going mad.' Then the tree seemed to reconsider this. 'Actually,' it said, 'I think I would rather be mad.' Then, with hope in its voice, 'Are you sure I haven't gone mad?'

'I'm sure,' said Artemis. 'You're a tree. A eucalyptus. Subgenus of mallee. Variegated leaves.'

'Oh,' said the tree.

'Sorry,' said Artemis.

'But with variegated leaves?'

'Yes,' said Artemis. 'Green and yellow.'

The tree seemed pleased. 'Oh well, there's that to be grateful for,' it said.

'That's the spirit,' Artemis reassured it.

'So,' said the tree in a more conversational tone. 'You're the goddess of hunting and chastity then?'

'Yes,' said Artemis. 'And of the moon, and several other things. Artemis.' She put a little emphasis on her name. It still hurt when mortals didn't know it.

'I didn't know there was a goddess of hunting and chastity and the moon,' confessed the tree. 'I thought there was just the one God. Of everything. Or actually, to be honest, I thought there was no God at all. No offence.'

'None taken,' said Artemis. Unbelievers were always preferable to heretics.

'I have to say you don't look much like a goddess, though,' added the tree.

'And what does a goddess look like, exactly?' said Artemis, a sharpness entering her voice.

'I don't know,' said the tree, a little nervously. 'Shouldn't you be wearing a toga or something? Or a laurel wreath?'

'You mean, not a tracksuit,' said Artemis.

'Pretty much,' admitted the tree.

'Times change,' said Artemis. 'Right now you don't look like somebody who works in mergers and acquisitions for Goldman Sachs.' Her voice indicated that the clothing conversation was closed.

'I still can't get over the fact that you're a goddess,' said the tree after a pause. 'Wow. Yesterday I wouldn't have believed it. Today . . .' The tree gave an almost imperceptible shrug, rustling its leaves. Then it seemed to think for a bit. 'So does that mean, if you're a goddess,' it said, 'that you can turn me back into a person?'

Artemis had been expecting this question.

'I'm sorry,' she said, 'but I can't.'

'Why not?' said the tree.

The tree sounded so despondent that Artemis couldn't bring herself to reply, as planned, 'Because I don't want to.' 'A god can't undo what another god has done,' she found herself saying instead, much to her own surprise. She hated admitting any kind of weakness, especially to a mortal.

'You mean that guy was a god too? The one who . . . did this. Well, I suppose it's obvious now. I kind of hoped he might be a hypnotist.'

'No, he was a god,' said Artemis.

'Um,' said the tree. 'Could you do something about that red setter? I don't really like the way it's sniffing around me.'

Artemis pulled the idiot dog away.

'Sorry,' she said. 'So what happened exactly?'

'I was just taking a walk yesterday and this guy came up to talk to me –'

'Tall?' said Artemis. 'Blond? Almost impossibly handsome?'

'That's the one,' said the tree.

3

'What did he say?' said Artemis.

The bark on the tree seemed to shift slightly, as if the tree was pulling a face.

'I, um . . .'

'What did he say?' Artemis asked again, allowing a hint of command to enter her voice.

'He said, "Hello. Do you want to give me a blow job?"'

A blow job. Why did people do these things to each other? Artemis felt faintly sick.

'I said no,' continued the tree, 'and then he said, "Are you sure, because you look like you'd be good at it and I think you'd really enjoy it."'

'I'm very sorry,' said Artemis, 'about my brother. If it were up to me he would not be allowed outside unsupervised.'

'He's your brother?'

'My twin. It's . . . unfortunate.'

'Well, anyway, I just walked off, and he followed me, and I got a bit scared and I started running, and then the next thing I knew . . . Here I am.'

Artemis shook her head. 'This isn't the first time something like this has happened,' she said. 'Rest assured we will be having words about it.'

'And then he'll turn me back?'

'Absolutely,' lied Artemis.

'No need to tell my family back home what happened, then,' said the tree. 'Good. Maybe I should call in sick at work though. I can't really go in like this. I had my mobile with me; it should be around here somewhere. Could you dial my boss's number and hold the phone to my trunk?'

'Mortals aren't going to be able to understand you, I'm afraid,' said Artemis. 'Just gods. And other vegetation. I wouldn't bother talking to the grass, though. It isn't very bright.'

'Oh,' said the tree. 'OK.' Artemis gave the tree time to absorb this information. 'Why aren't I more upset about this?' it said eventually. 'If you'd told me yesterday that I was going to be turned into a tree, I'm sure I'd have been really, really upset.'

'You're a tree now, not a human mortal,' explained Artemis. 'You don't really have emotions any more. I think you'll be much happier this way. And you'll live longer, unless it gets very windy.'

'Except your brother's going to turn me back.'

'Of course he is,' said Artemis. 'Right then, I'd best be getting on. I've got to get these dogs back to . . . my friends.'

'It was nice meeting you,' said the tree.

'Likewise,' said Artemis. 'Bye then. See you soon. Maybe.'

The pleasant look on her face vaporised before her back was even fully turned. The dogs saw her expression and whimpered as one. But they had nothing to fear from Artemis. It was time to go home and find Apollo.

Two

There was a time, thought Apollo, thrusting rhythmically, when sneaking an illicit bathroom shag with Aphrodite would have been exciting. He scrutinised her as she leant away from him against the peeling back wall, one dainty foot up on the stained toilet cistern, her toenail-polish the only paint in here that was perfectly applied. She was exquisite. He couldn't deny that. Simply the most beautiful sort-of woman ever to have sort-of lived, though Helen of the ship-launching face had given her a run for her money. Eyes (thrust), hair (thrust), mouth (thrust), skin (thrust), breasts (thrust), legs (thrust) – he could not fault an inch of her. Though this was hardly an achievement on her part. She was the goddess of beauty after all. But still, thought Apollo, sublime as she was, did she have to look so . . . well . . . bored? True, Apollo was so bored with Aphrodite that he could almost scream. His pride, however, demanded that she did not feel the same way.

'Right, I'm turning around,' announced Aphrodite.

'OK,' said Apollo. At least he wouldn't have to look at that passively indifferent face any longer.

Aphrodite detached herself from him and turned so that she was facing the wall. She arched her back, pointed the flawless ivory spheres of her buttocks at her nephew, and supported herself against the wall with her slender, elegant hands. Apollo reengaged himself and resumed thrusting. Looking down at the back of her head, her glossy black hair curling down over the alabaster slope of her shoulders, he could almost imagine that he was screwing Catherine Zeta Jones. He wondered whether he could persuade Aphrodite to speak to him in Welsh. Just for the novelty. Anything for some novelty.

Apollo wanted out. Out of Aphrodite, out of this bathroom, out of this house, and out of this life. He was sick of London. The family had moved there in 1665, when the plague was keeping property prices rock bottom, and just before the destruction of the Great Fire sent them spiralling upwards again. This had been a typically canny piece of financial engineering by his sister Athena, the goddess of wisdom. At the time, though, he had foreseen that they would never actually be able to sell the house that they had bought so craftily, and he had tried to warn the rest of the family, but they hadn't listened. It was true that he had been known to lie about his predictions just to get his own way, and everyone knew that he didn't want to move to London in the first place, but even so, this time he had been right, and he'd known it from the start. It was putting the property in Zeus's name: that had been the problem. But even he could not have foreseen what would happen to Zeus.

'I was thinking of redecorating my room,' said Aphrodite, interrupting his thoughts.

'Again?' said Apollo.

'I could do with a change,' said Aphrodite. 'I'm sure Heppy won't mind.'

Heppy was Hephaestus, god of smiths and Aphrodite's husband, as hideous as she was beautiful. Treated with contempt by the rest of the family, he nevertheless did all the refurbishment and repairs in the house. As they had been living in the same place for over three hundred years, that was a lot of refurbishment and repairs. Even so, in Apollo's opinion, he could have done with spending more time on things like patching up this damp, crumbling, leaking bathroom, which would be in the interests of the entire household, and less on adding further

7

unnecessary levels of luxury to their bedroom every time Aphrodite had one of her increasingly frequent whims.

'So what are you going to do this time?' he asked her. 'More gold leaf? Hang some diamonds off the chandelier? Get rid of the roses at last?'

Aphrodite looked sharply at him over her shoulder. Even her glare was calculated to be sexy.

'There's nothing wrong with roses,' she snapped. 'No, I just thought I would change them from red to pink again.' She turned back to the wall, picked up a passing cockroach and crushed it between her thumb and forefinger. 'Do that more slowly,' she said.

Apollo obediently changed pace. He thought of thousands and thousands of years of living with Aphrodite, thousands gone, and thousands yet to come – and that was the best-case scenario. And she never changed. Never, ever. But sex with Aphrodite was better than no sex at all. And none of the other gods would sleep with him. If only he could get a decent mortal lover, someone like one of his old lovers in Greece or Rome, who worshipped him and everything that he did . . . but he refused to let his thoughts stray in that direction. It was too depressing. Things had all been so much easier in the years that they were now obliged to refer to as BC.

There was a knock at the door, a distinctive grumbling thumping like the falling of distant bombs. It could only be Ares, god of war: Apollo's half-brother, roommate, and, gallingly, Aphrodite's favourite lover. Apollo paused mid-thrust.

'Can you get a move on in there?' came Ares' voice. 'I've got a Start the War demo this morning, and I need a shave.'

'Bugger off,' shouted Apollo, resuming his activity. 'I got here first, you'll just have to wait.'

'Oh, let him in,' drawled Aphrodite from beneath him. 'He can join us. It'll be fun.'

'Didn't you hear him?' said Apollo. 'He's going out. He doesn't have time for you.'

'Everybody has time for me,' said Aphrodite.

This was almost certainly true. But Apollo felt no need to be sexually outclassed by his brother.

'This bathroom is first come, first served,' said Apollo primly. 'If Ares doesn't like it he can get Hephaestus to build another one. It would be about bloody time that he did. And your frigging new wallpaper can just wait.'

'OK, I'm done now.' Aphrodite orgasmed quickly and tidily, and removed herself from Apollo.

'I hadn't finished!' protested Apollo.

'Well, you should have been nicer to me then.'

Aphrodite stepped over to the cracked enamel bath and switched the shower attachment on, as Apollo watched his tumescence disappear. He limped over to the sink and splashed cold water onto his genitals. Aphrodite had no respect for him. Glancing at himself in the mouldy mirror above the basin, he wondered whether she might think more of him if he had a tattoo.

'I don't believe it,' said Aphrodite.

'I was just *thinking* about it,' said Apollo. 'I wasn't actually going to . . .'

Aphrodite spoke over him. 'There's no hot water. Again!'

She marched over to the door and opened it, sticking her head out into the cold, empty stairwell. 'Who used up all the hot water?' she yelled. There was no reply. She pulled her head back in and slammed the door.

'I hate this family,' she said.

'The feeling is mutual,' said Apollo.

Aphrodite spun around. Apollo was expecting her to bite his head off – possibly literally – but instead, unexpectedly, she had one of her best smiles on her face, the one that looked like dry land to a drowning man, like water in the desert, the one she saved for only the most special of occasions, or, rarer yet, for times when she was genuinely happy. It had been perfected over the centuries to be irresistible. She wants something, thought Apollo, slowly and numbly, but the words refused to take meaning in his head.

'Apollo darling,' said Aphrodite, her eyes suddenly shining with what Apollo couldn't help but think must surely be unfeigned warmth, 'seeing as we've just had such a lovely time together, I don't suppose you could just use a teensy bit of your power to heat up a tiny little bit of water for me? Just enough for a quick, quick shower. You've made me so . . .' and she trailed a delicate finger down between her breasts, '. . . sweaty.'

Apollo blinked twice and swallowed. He told his penis sternly to stay where it was. He waited until he was quite sure that his body and mouth would obey his brain, and then he said, with all the nonchalance he could muster, 'Sorry, but no.'

'Please, darling,' said Aphrodite. 'I'd do it myself, but you've worn me out. You could join me if you like . . .' She stepped closer to him, gazing up at him from beneath the undulating black of her lashes.

Apollo looked down at the ground. 'The answer is still no,' he forced himself to say. 'If you want hot water, use your own power.'

'Suit your fucking self,' said Aphrodite, dropping the smile like a cold, dead fish, and she stepped beneath the icy beam of the shower, pulling the curtain shut behind her with the sharp rattle of a snake.

It was the wrong decision and Apollo knew it. According to everything he'd heard about the place, hell had no fury like Aphrodite scorned. Improbably, though, he felt slightly cheered. Her revenge would be swift and no doubt deadly, but at least it would pass the time.

Three

Once Artemis had returned all of the dogs to their ungrateful owners and accepted her derisory pay, she did not, as was her usual habit, return to the park to catch some squirrels, but instead headed straight for home.

She paused outside the front door. The once-glossy black paint was peeling off in long, jagged streaks, and the knocker, in the shape of a laurel wreath, was so tarnished that it was impossible to tell what kind of metal it had been originally. Artemis always waited a few moments on the doorstep before heading inside, to shrug off the disdainful world and regain her rightful stature. And also because it was the last peace and quiet she was going to be getting for a while.

This time, before she had even opened the door she could feel the elephantine stamp of a heavy beat reverberating in her chest. She pushed into the house against the tidal wave of music and forced her way down the front hall into the kitchen at the back of the house. Her half-brother Dionysus had set up his decks at the kitchen table. Beside him on the floor was a stack of records, and in front of him an empty bottle of wine and another which was a fair way gone. Dionysus was busy cueing up another record, headphones on, a blissful smile upon his goat-like face.

Behind him, Athena was shouting. She was barely audible above the music.

'Have you any understanding of the duties other members of the household are performing at this hour?' she screamed. 'I am undertaking a groundbreaking research initiative in the upper rooms! The amount of noise that you are producing is rendering that task impossible! I would move that your so-called hedonism is merely a mask for deep selfishness!' Athena was getting so agitated that her glasses had steamed up. She didn't actually need glasses, but she wore plain lenses in order to enhance her air of wisdom.

'Have either of you seen Apollo?' said Artemis.

Dionysus carried on mixing (or perhaps scratching – Artemis didn't know the difference). Athena carried on screaming.

'My research is not just performed for the pleasure of it! It is undertaken for the good of the entire deistic community! Including yours, you pickled lump of goat meat!'

Artemis left them to it and surfed the wave of beats back down the hall and into the living room at the front of the house. All of the sofas and chairs in there were torn or broken, so Ares was sitting on a cushion in front of the rickety coffee table, his maps and charts spread out before him, a pair of callipers in his hand. His brow was furrowed: he appeared to be performing some complex calculation. He didn't look up as Artemis came in.

'You need a shave,' said Artemis, standing in the doorway.

'Mmm,' said Ares, without turning his head. 'This War on Terror isn't producing enough casualties. Bringing in Iran is the obvious choice, but I don't think they've got enough firepower yet. I wonder if I could somehow antagonise Japan?'

'Have you seen Apollo?' said Artemis.

'Bathroom,' said Ares. 'Tell him to get a move on. I need a shave.'

'Yes, I just said that,' said Artemis.

'There's always Russia,' said Ares, 'but they've been harder to provoke since the end of the Cold War. Why are mortals so hung up on peace?' He shuffled through his papers. 'Or maybe it's time to broaden out some of the African civil wars?'

Artemis slammed the door and went upstairs to the first-floor landing, where Hephaestus had installed the bathroom in what had been Athena's old study – a decision that had not gone down very well with Athena. Artemis didn't knock. Artemis never knocked. She merely kicked the door open and swept inside.

Apollo was naked and sitting, legs mercifully crossed, on the toilet seat, painting his fingernails with clear varnish. Before Artemis could speak to him, though, the shower curtain was yanked aside to reveal Aphrodite, glistening wet and smiling a serpent's grin.

'Shut the door, would you?' she said. 'You're letting in a terrible draught. Look, my nipples are all erect.' She fingered one as if testing a cherry for ripeness.

Artemis refused to rise to the bait. She knew that Aphrodite delighted in trying to shock her. Instead she grabbed a towel from the rail and threw it to her aunt.

'Wrap yourself up, then,' she said.

Aphrodite caught the towel and coiled it around her hair. Artemis turned away from her and faced her twin.

'I need to have a word with you, Apollo,' she said. 'Is now a good time?'

'No,' said Apollo.

'Good,' said Artemis. 'I was out running on the Heath today, and guess what I found?'

'Two men rogering each other in the bushes?' suggested Aphrodite, who was now perched on the edge of the bath.

Artemis suppressed a shudder. 'I wasn't aware that I'd invited you to join this conversation,' she said.

'You didn't,' said Aphrodite.

'Apollo,' said Artemis. 'Any suggestions of your own?'

'Not a clue,' Apollo said, but he looked a little pale. He knew what was coming, and he rather hoped that he was wrong.

'Allow me to jog your memory,' said Artemis. 'Does the name Kate mean anything to you?'

Apollo was genuinely surprised. 'It doesn't, no,' he said.

'Typical,' said Artemis. 'That makes it even worse. Kate is the Australian mortal that you turned into a tree yesterday.'

Apollo's face went from pale to white. He looked like a statue of himself.

'You did what?' said Aphrodite, rising to her feet. If anything, she sounded even angrier than Artemis felt.

'I . . .' said Apollo. 'I . . .'

'You wouldn't heat up so much as a cupful of water for me, and yet you were willing to waste gallons of your power on transmogrifying some stupid mortal slut?'

'She wasn't a slut,' said Artemis. 'Not with him anyway. I think that was the problem.'

Artemis and Aphrodite shared a rare, complicit laugh. It was the final straw for Apollo, who leapt up.

'It's none of your business what I do with my power!'

'Actually,' said Artemis, 'I think you'll find that it is. It's all of our business.' She stalked over to the bathroom window and yanked up the blind. 'Did the sun come up today?' she said, squinting outward. 'I think it did. Lucky for you.' She closed the blind again and turned. 'Did it come up on time though, or maybe it was slightly late? Is it shining as brightly as it usually does? Is it as warm as it should be? I'm not so sure. Maybe the sun is fading. Maybe it's going out. Because the god who's supposed to be in charge of it is too busy throwing away what's left of his power on inventing a humanoid species of eucalyptus to do his job.'

'Don't be such a hypocrite,' said Apollo. 'What about you? They've just banned hunting in this country you know. And chastity? What kind of an outdated concept is that? It doesn't sound to me as if you're using your power where you're supposed to. Or maybe you're the one who's got none left.'

'That's not fair,' said Artemis, her eyes appealing to Aphrodite to back her up.

'Two words, Apollo,' said Aphrodite to her nephew. 'Global Warming.'

'Don't you start,' said Apollo, spinning to face her. 'Goddess of beauty? That's going very well, isn't it? Aren't you aware that there's an obesity epidemic sweeping this planet at the moment? Is that what you call beautiful?'

'The difference between us,' said Artemis, 'is that Aphrodite and I don't go around wilfully wasting our power on unnecessary procedures just because some mortal won't let us . . . let us . . .'

'Stick it in her,' finished Aphrodite helpfully.

'You mean you don't get caught,' said Apollo.

'You,' said Artemis, ignoring his comment, 'are going to take an oath that you're not going to do anything like this ever again. No more squandering your power turning mortals into trees or anything else like that.'

'An oath on Styx,' added Aphrodite. Oaths sworn on the river Styx were absolutely binding for gods, which was why they hated taking them so much.

'That's not fair,' said Apollo. 'You have no right to make me swear an oath. I won't do it.'

'Fine,' said Artemis. 'I'll just call the rest of the family in here and tell them what you've been up to. Then we can decide democratically what to do about it. If you really think you'll get a better deal from them . . .'

'No, no,' said Apollo, 'don't do that. There really isn't any need for anyone else to know.'

'So make the oath,' said Artemis.

'Hang on, no,' said Apollo. 'You're not making sense, you can't just make me swear an oath like that. None of us know what's going to happen in the future.'

'Not even you?' said Aphrodite.

'Athena might come up with something to make us powerful again,' Apollo continued. 'And what is the point of being powerful if you can't use your power to do whatever you like?'

'Until Athena figures out a way to turn back time, we are stuck with the power that we've got, and when that's used up . . .' said Artemis.

Beside her, Aphrodite's lovely face turned ashen at the thought.

'Face it, Apollo, we're getting old,' Artemis said. 'You just can't go around using up all your power on frivolities. You won't have any left. And we need you. We can't run the world without the sun. You have to cooperate.'

'So I'll cooperate,' said Apollo. He made a move to go.

'That's not good enough,' said Artemis. 'I need a guarantee.'

'Which means you have to swear on Styx,' smiled Aphrodite.

They were between Apollo and the door. He knew that both were stubborn enough to wait there for years, if needs be.

'So what do you want me to swear?' he said eventually.

Artemis took a few moments, then announced gravely: 'Apollo, you must take an oath on Styx that you will not use your power unnecessarily until such a time when our strength is regained.'

'Wait a second,' said Apollo.

'What now?'

'I'm not swearing that. It's a totally disproportionate restriction of my abilities. We don't know what Styx is going to define as unnecessary. She's a river. There isn't a huge amount that's necessary to her.'

'He has a point,' said Aphrodite. 'All she does is flow.'

'OK,' said Artemis. 'This is what we'll do. You'll have to swear not to use your power to harm mortals, unless we get our power back.'

'No,' said Apollo. 'That's not fair either. I might need to harm mortals. Sometimes it's important, you know that, you've had men torn into tiny pieces for watching you get undressed.'

'True,' admitted Artemis.

'Plus, you said yourself we might never get our power back

and I don't think you have the right to make me swear to do anything which could last for ever. All I did was turn one little mortal into a tree. This is getting totally out of proportion. Harming mortals is fun. We've all done it.'

'You still deserve to be punished,' said Aphrodite. 'Artemis, he still has to swear something.'

'I agree.' Artemis thought carefully, then said, 'Right. You will swear not to harm any mortals unnecessarily for a century, or until we get our power back, whichever is sooner.'

'A year,' said Apollo.

'A decade,' said Aphrodite.

'Done,' said Artemis.

Apollo looked sulky, but he knew that he had no choice.

'I swear that . . .' he said.

'On Styx,' Aphrodite reminded him.

Damn. 'I swear, *on Styx*, that I won't cause any unnecessary harm to mortals for the next ten years or until I get stronger again, whichever comes first. Satisfied?'

'Satisfied,' said Artemis.

Four

'So what do you think?' whispered Alice.

The door was shut; there was no risk of them being over-heard. But Alice never liked to speak loudly in case it drew undue attention to herself.

'It's very nice,' said Neil. 'Very tidy.'

He had the reward of Alice beaming at him, her cheeks flushing pink with pleasure and embarrassment.

'When I first started working here it was terribly messy,' she confided. 'The cleaning products were all over the place and some weren't properly sealed. That can be dangerous you know. With children, for example, or pets.'

Neil nodded. It was unlikely that children or pets would find themselves inside the locked cleaning storeroom of a TV studio, but Alice thought of everything.

'And the mops and brooms were just here and there. Here and there,' Alice repeated, with a faint look of horror. 'Now I have a system so I can find everything I need straight away. It's far more efficient that way.'

'They're very lucky to have you,' said Neil.

'Oh no,' said Alice, shaking her head vigorously. 'No no, not at all.'

Neil looked around the room – was it a room, or a cupboard? There was some basic furniture and Alice had described it as her office, but in reality it was narrow, dark and cramped, dominated by neatly stacked piles of cleaning materials, so carefully sorted by size, type and function that it was like being in the archives of a cleaning museum. The air was thick and stale, but not a single dust mote swam around the bare bulb that dangled at a height that would have been dangerously low, had Neil and Alice not both been unusually short.

'Does it get warm in here?' asked Neil. 'Without any windows?'

'Oh, they let me bring a fan,' said Alice. 'It's under the table.'

Indeed, there was a small electric fan underneath the table, unplugged, with its cable modestly curled around it in deference to the month of February, even though the room was already unbearably stuffy. On top of the table, Neil noticed a selection of the small china figurines that Alice collected, adding a homey touch to the room. Last Christmas, Neil had bought her one, a little shepherdess leaning forward to gather up a stray lamb, and Alice had been so happy that he had thought she might kiss him, but she hadn't. But she had put the figurine right in the middle of her mantelpiece, moving aside the dancing fawn that he knew was her favourite, which was almost like a kiss, after all.

'So are you going to tell me what we're seeing yet?' said Neil.

'No,' said Alice. 'It's a surprise.'

'Should we go straight to the auditorium, then?'

'Not yet,' said Alice. 'I'm sneaking you in. Cleaners aren't really supposed to go into the audiences of programmes. It's bad for the company image.'

'I can't believe you would be bad for anyone's image,' said Neil.

'It's just a policy.' Alice looked down and tucked a stray blonde hair behind her ear.

'You're not going to get in trouble are you?' said Neil. 'I don't want to get you in trouble.'

'No, no,' said Alice, looking back up at him. 'Please don't worry. It's OK. Nobody notices me. I'm just the cleaner. And anyway, it'll be fun. I don't usually break the rules.'

'Well, as long as you're sure.'

'I'm sure,' said Alice. She smiled, and Neil felt his heart jump. 'It's nice of you to be so concerned,' she whispered, even more quietly than usual.

They stood stiffly opposite one another as if carrying an item of bulky furniture between them. Their eyes didn't quite meet, and neither made a move to sit. There was only one chair, made of orange moulded plastic, clashing with the sticky yellow varnish of the tabletop that it was tucked beneath. Alice had hung up her cardigan on the back of the chair, the same sensible navy blue that she used to wear when she cleaned the office where Neil worked, before the maintenance had been contracted out to a larger, cheaper company. Then, as now, he had wanted to pick it up and bury his face in it, inhaling deeply, to find something in her smell that would give him some, any, information about this mysterious woman, this enigma that was Alice.

'Do you want to sit down?' said Alice.

'No,' said Neil, 'I was just . . . I . . .'

'Only you were looking at the chair.'

'I was wondering if maybe you wanted to sit down,' said Neil.

'No, I'm fine,' said Alice.

The silence resumed. Neil could see himself reflected in Alice's glasses, a small, mole-like creature with wiry brown hair that stood straight up like a brush. He wondered whether Alice ever thought about him for even a single second when he wasn't around.

Suddenly Alice's face fell. 'Oh dear. I hope you're not going to get bored in here, with only me to talk to.'

'No!' said Neil. 'Not at all. Please don't think that. Actually, I was just thinking the same thing myself. I mean, you, about me. I mean, you getting bored.'

'Oh, no,' whispered Alice. 'I don't find you boring at all, Neil. Not a bit.'

In the kind of novels that Neil sometimes read in secret, this would be the moment when the hero took the heroine in his arms, pressed his lips roughly to hers, and then ravaged her.

'I've got Scrabble on my Palm Pilot,' he said. 'Multiplayer.'

'Neil, aren't you clever,' said Alice, restored to animation. 'And I think I've got –' and now she looked slyly naughty as she rummaged in the big quilted holdall she carried everywhere, 'Yes! Some orange juice.' She pulled out two individual-sized cartons with straws and handed one to Neil. 'It'll be like a party. Only we'll have to sit on the floor unless you want to share the chair.'

Before Neil could say that sharing the chair was fine with him, she lowered herself onto the ground, leaning back against a metal stepladder and pulling her skirt down over her knees.

'Do you want to play with the replaceable blank?' said Neil, sitting down opposite her. Catching the near-imperceptible widening of her eyes, he quickly added, 'Because I don't.'

'Oh good,' said Alice. 'Me neither. It makes the game so unpredictable. And are you happiest with the SOWPODS list of permissible two- and three-letter words?'

'The, ah . . . ?' Neil swallowed. 'Um, of course. Here. I'll let you go first.'

'It's a double-word score advantage,' said Alice.

'That's fine,' said Neil. 'You start.'

He handed over the Palm Pilot and took a long, deep swig of his orange juice.

Five

In a dilapidated Portakabin in the car park of the television studio, Apollo sat at his dressing table, an entourage of nymphs, graces and demigods fussing around him. He was trying to hide it, but Aphrodite could see that he wished he hadn't invited any of them. Being the centre of attention was, of course, something Apollo adored, but the dressing room itself was not quite as impressive as he had made out it would be. And now all his hangers-on had seen it, which meant that he wasn't going to be able to lie about it to the rest of the gods later.

Stacked at one end of the room was an obstacle course of props and possessions related to a programme that wasn't even Apollo's, some wrapped up in splitting black bin liners as if awaiting incineration. Covering the floor was a rough carpet in a dull, office beige, which was coming away at the corners and had worn right through in front of the tuftless patch of faded brown that had once been the doormat. The windows, rounded at the corners like those of a caravan, were made of some kind of double-glazed reinforced plastic, with a light growth of mildew between the two layers that no amount of assiduous cleaning would ever get to. Some of the plastic chairs wobbled; others had no backs. The mirror that Apollo was looking in was carefully polished but cracked, fracturing his beautiful face into something approaching cubism. Even the sign, written in Biro and Sellotaped to the door, had been misspelled: '*Appolo's Oracle*'.

Apollo affected not to notice any of it, but Aphrodite knew him better. 'A little more foundation on the jaw line,' he commanded one of his attendants; but Aphrodite heard his voice tremble, oh so slightly. This was his big debut and he was being housed like second-class vaudeville. It was marvellous.

'Are you sure I can't get you anything?' Aphrodite purred. 'A little nectar, some ambrosia? A bit of hand relief?'

'Maybe later,' said Apollo, not even turning his head. 'I don't want to sweat through the powder. A shiny face is the enemy of the television professional.'

'Of course,' said Aphrodite. 'Silly me. I wouldn't want to ruin your special day.' It was an effort to keep her voice sweet and level. 'I'm so excited,' she continued. 'I can't wait to see you in action.'

She watched his face in the shards of the mirror, wondering if he could possibly be buying this act, but the god was so arrogant that he genuinely believed that she cared two hoots for his stupid, tedious programme.

'You can watch from backstage if you like,' said Apollo.

'Oh, wow! Really?' said Aphrodite.

Then she worried that this had come across too blatantly as sarcasm, so she clapped her hands together in feigned excitement. Another surreptitious glance in the mirror, but there was no need for concern. The cool water of her attention was making him bloom like a flower in the desert. Little did he know that she had a sandstorm planned.

The phone in her handbag began to ring: 'Venus', the Bananarama version. She pulled it out and glanced at the display.

'Sorry darling,' she said to Apollo. 'It's work. I need to take this.' She spoke into the handset. 'I'm so horny,' she said. 'What do you want to do to me?'

'Mum, it's me,' whispered a voice at the other end. 'Eros.'

'That feels good, big boy,' said Aphrodite. She signalled to Apollo that she'd take the call outside. 'Touch me all over.'

She went out into the drizzle, shutting the door behind her.

'Mum, please,' said Eros. 'Don't be disgusting.'

'Oh shut up,' said Aphrodite. 'You're no fun any more.'

'Why can't you get a decent job?' said Eros. 'You could be a model . . .'

'Modelling's boring,' said Aphrodite. '"Stand here, stand there." Phone sex is much more fun. And you wouldn't believe how much mortals are willing to pay for a spot of deep breathing and a fake –'

'Believe me, I don't want to know,' said Eros.

'Don't take that self-righteous tone with me,' said Aphrodite. 'My choice of job doesn't seem to bother you so much at the check-out of Marks and Spencer's. Maybe you should get your own job if you're so disgusted by mine.'

'I have a job,' said Eros.

'What kind of job doesn't earn you any money?'

'You know how important the volunteering is to me,' said Eros. 'I thought you understood that. Money isn't everything.'

'That's easy to say when you're spending mine.'

'The children rely on me,' Eros persevered. 'In fact if I don't leave soon I'm going to miss archery practice. They'll be really disappointed. They don't get a lot of fun in life.'

'You mean aside from breaking and entering, and mugging old ladies.'

'You're not funny,' said Eros.

'I'm not joking,' said Aphrodite.

There was a pause at the far end of the line, and Aphrodite knew something unwelcome was coming.

'Listen, Mum,' said Eros, delivering as expected. 'I've been giving it some thought, and I've decided I'm not going to do it.'

'Yes you are,' said Aphrodite, her voice a red light.

'No. I'm not doing it,' said Eros, driving straight through. 'It's wrong. I've been thinking about it all day.'

'Wrong? Who cares about wrong? You promised me you'd do it!'

'Well, I'm unpromising,' said Eros.

'Breaking a promise is wrong too,' said Aphrodite.

'It's all relative,' said Eros.

'It's not like it's the first time you've done it,' said Aphrodite.

'That time was before,' said Eros.

'Before what?' said Aphrodite. 'No, don't tell me. Before Jesus.'

'I wouldn't expect you to understand,' said Eros.

'I understand perfectly,' said Aphrodite. 'You prefer that upstart carpenter – that thief of faith – to your own flesh and blood.'

'He's a better role model,' said Eros.

'That depends on your point of view,' said Aphrodite. 'From what I remember he didn't have much to say about falling in love or having sex or dressing well or any of the other important things in life. It's all about being nice. Who wants to be nice?'

'I want to be nice.'

'Well then be nice to me,' snapped Aphrodite. 'I'm your mother.'

Silence at the other end of the line. Aphrodite shifted position a bit, so that the falling rain would splash more flatteringly on her top, making it cling to her breasts.

'Where are you?' she said.

'I'm here,' said Eros. 'I'm in the building.'

'Are you wearing the disguise?'

'Yes.'

'So what's the problem?'

Eros mumbled something.

'I'm sorry?' said Aphrodite.

'Whatwouldjesusdo.'

'What would Jesus do?' said Aphrodite. 'Let me tell you something. Jesus was a very good boy. He would do exactly what his mother told him to do.'

'But –'

'Jesus was supposed to be a god, right?' said Aphrodite. 'Ergo, he did revenge. All gods do revenge.'

'Not exactly. He said you should turn the other –'

'What else does your Jesus say?' Aphrodite interrupted.

'I thought you didn't care.'

'Let me see,' said Aphrodite. 'I remember. "Honour thy father and mother".'

'One, that wasn't Jesus. And two, it's hard to honour your father when there are so many candidates for who he might be.'

'That's not very nice,' said Aphrodite. 'You know who your father is. It's your cousin Ares.'

'You can't force me to do this,' said Eros.

'Remember what else the Bible says: "Charity begins at home".'

'That's not in the Bible.'

'Look, I just want you to do this one thing for me,' said Aphrodite in a new, wheedling tone. 'After all the thousands of years that I've supported you. You owe me.'

There was no reply to this, so Aphrodite pressed home her advantage.

'Allow me to phrase it another way,' she said. 'If you don't do what we agreed, I am going to come and find you, and when I do, I am going to pull down your overstarched, permanent pleated, man-made fabric, smart-casual slacks and turn you over my knee, and I am going to give you the spanking of your life in front of your vicar, his uptight wife and the entire congregation of Christian brothers. Does that clarify things for you?'

It wasn't an empty threat. She had done it before. There was a very long silence.

'I wish the Virgin Mary was my mother,' grumbled Eros eventually.

'If you're lucky maybe I'll get Artemis to adopt you,' said Aphrodite. 'I'll be in the auditorium in ten minutes. You know what to do.'

She snapped the phone shut before he could remonstrate any

further. Taking a couple of breaths of cold air to let the pink return to her cheeks, she pasted a smile onto her face and slipped back into the dressing room.

'How are you coming along?' she said to her nephew.

Apollo turned from the mirror. He had so much make-up on that you could have peeled him from forehead to chin and ended up with an exact facsimile of his original face.

'I'm ready,' he said.

Six

They didn't manage to finish the game, but Alice was already almost two hundred points ahead when it was time to stop playing and go. When Neil had suggested playing, he had planned to let her win, but, as it turned out, that hadn't been necessary. It seemed she was a very proficient player, although she insisted that it was luck.

'That's a very clever little machine,' said Alice. 'It's just a shame you didn't have better letters. Hopefully next time it will be more fair.'

Neil caught that 'next time' like a precious butterfly and pinned it on the Alice display in his mind.

They put their empty orange juice cartons into the bin, and Alice led Neil out of the tiny room and locked the door behind them. Then they set off down the corridor towards the auditorium. The walls were painted a rancid shade of green, and fluorescent strip lighting flickered over the concrete floor. The air smelt sharp and metallic, with equal measures of damp and disinfectant. At not quite equal intervals, somebody had put up star-shaped pictures of the presenters who had made programmes there, to add a touch of glamour. Not one of them was famous any more, and a few of them were dead.

'Very clean,' said Neil, and got an Alice smile in return.

As they turned the corner towards the entrance to the studio, they saw a tall young man heading towards them, carrying a large canvas bag and wearing what appeared to be a fake moustache.

At the sight of them, the young man froze, and in response, they froze too.

'Is that someone you know?' whispered Neil.

'I don't think so,' replied Alice.

'We can go back if you like,' said Neil.

'No, it's fine,' said Alice. Her face had the same look of determination that Neil had seen only a few minutes ago, just before she had put down her second seven-letter word. 'I want to go in. You'll like it so much.'

'OK,' said Neil, 'if you're sure.'

They walked on. As soon as they moved, the man in the false moustache started walking too, as if reassured by their decision. They met at the door.

'I'm just another audience member,' said the man. His moustache wobbled as he spoke.

'So are we,' said Neil.

The man – not much more than a boy, really – looked relieved, opening the door to the studio, and they all slipped inside.

Alice had timed it perfectly, almost all of the seats were already filled. Neil, who had never been inside a TV studio before, was surprised by how small it was. It seated a few dozen at most. As they had hoped, all of the other audience members, mostly older women in varying shades of ice-cream polyester with matching ice-cream hair, were chatting happily amongst themselves and paid them no attention as they entered. Beside him, Alice was scanning the room in rapid movements, like a rabbit newly emerged from her warren.

'See anyone you know?' said Neil.

'No,' said Alice. 'The crew must all be busy getting ready by now.'

Neil let go of a breath he hadn't even realised he was holding. The whole outing had been planned by Alice as a special treat for him, and he'd never forgive himself if she got into trouble because of it.

The man in the fake moustache had already scuttled away to a seat at the back of the room, and Alice and Neil found two empty spaces together at the front. Almost immediately, the woman next to Neil offered him a boiled sweet. He chose one for himself and one for Alice: cherry, her favourite.

Neil looked around. They were seated on long padded benches, steeply banked in front of a small stage area which was adorned with a set which had been designed to look like a Greek temple, but on the lowest possible budget. The crumbling columns and supposedly artful pieces of ruin were made out of polystyrene, the vines out of plastic, and the permanent sunset behind them was a construct of red polythene and bare light bulbs. It was clearly visible that the whole arrangement was being held together with safety pins and masking tape.

'What do you think?' said Alice. 'Do you like it?'

'What is it?' said Neil.

'It's supposed to be the oracle at Delphi.'

'The oracle? As in fortune tellers?'

'That's right.'

'Does that mean there's going to be fortune tellers on this show? Fake fortune tellers?'

'I don't know if they're going to be fake.'

'There aren't any other kind,' said Neil. 'Alice, you're brilliant. How did you know I love this kind of thing?'

'You told me.'

'When did I tell you?'

'About a year and a half ago. In the office one day when you'd been watching *Most Haunted* the night before. You said you loved all that fake psychic bollocks. Sorry. But that was what you said.'

'I can't believe you remembered.'

'Of course I did,' said Alice. 'So I was right, then? That you like it?'

'I love it,' said Neil. 'It's perfect. It's . . . it's absolutely perfect. I can't believe you thought of inviting me.'

'Oh, it was nothing,' said Alice. 'Anyone would have.'

'But I wouldn't,' said Neil, 'have wanted to come with just anyone.'

And he let his knee lean against hers for a second.

Behind a faded black curtain that separated the backstage area from the auditorium, Apollo was getting ready to go on. The backstage area was no more inspiring than his dressing room had been. The whole space was cluttered with items of technical junk – cameras, lights, bits of wire with loose flaps of gaffer tape hanging off them. From beyond the curtain he could hear the thrum of conversation from wobbling, ancient voices, sounding disturbingly like teatime in a nursing home. He peeked around the curtain. Just as he'd thought: it was like a basket of overripe fruit, every one of them past their best, and the rot starting to creep. There was actually somebody knitting. Apollo stepped back and looked over to where Aphrodite had perched herself on a huge reel of wound-up cable. He smiled as convincingly as he could muster.

'Nearly time now,' he said.

'Can't wait,' said Aphrodite with a matching smile.

The stage door opened and two sybils, gorgeous rangy blonde demigods who used to be diviners at his temple, came in. He suppressed the sigh of relief that clawed its way into his throat at the sight of them. As far as the production team were concerned, the sybils were just eye candy, a function they would seem to be born to. In reality they were there for their brain power.

Neither of the sybils looked at all happy.

'What's the matter?' said Apollo.

'Did you design these outfits?' said one of the sybils.

'What's the problem?' said Apollo. 'I'm wearing a toga too.'

'Yours covers your arse,' said the other sybil. She tugged at the pocket handkerchief that was wrapped around her but only succeeded in further exposing her breasts. 'See?' she said.

From across the room there was a crackle. Apollo turned and looked. From who knew where, Aphrodite had managed to acquire popcorn, and was taking it out of the packet kernel by kernel, sniffing it appreciatively, and putting it back into the bag. None of the gods ate mortal food, but Aphrodite, a sensualist by nature, just adored the smell of it. Catching Apollo's eyes upon her, she winked, and her hot pink tongue darted out and licked one of the pieces of popcorn. A light buzz of alarm fluttered at the edge of Apollo's awareness. Was Aphrodite enjoying herself just a little bit too much? She still owed him some revenge . . . Was something up? But before Apollo could pursue this line of enquiry, he heard the director's voice in his earpiece, telling him that they were ready to roll.

The opening bars of *Zorba the Greek* boomed over the loudspeakers and, as rehearsed, Apollo swept the curtain aside, stepping forward onto the stage with the sybils close behind. The audience clapped politely but without any noticeable enthusiasm. Apollo took a deep breath and held out his right hand in a gesture of greeting. His script was inscribed on his palm.

'Welcome,' he said, 'to *Apollo's Oracle*, and prepare yourselves for an unforgettable experience of astonishment and wonder . . .'

Eros sat at the back of the room, miserable. It was desperately hot under the studio lights and his moustache was starting to itch. In his pocket he had his mobile phone, set to vibrate; at his feet, the bag with his bow and arrows inside. On the stage in front of him, Apollo – always his least-beloved relative – was delivering some self-aggrandising speech before the action of the show began. Maybe it wasn't too late to leave.

The phone in his pocket vibrated. He checked the message. It was from his mother.

'DON'T EVEN THINK ABOUT IT.'

Down on the stage, things were kicking off. Apollo had struck a pose in the centre of the stage, hands clawing at his temples, head weaving from side to side, presumably to imply that he was chasing after inspiration, in a manner Eros knew to be entirely unnecessary. Meanwhile the sybils had trotted off in opposite directions, each heading for one of the banked aisles, a lascivious cameraman in tow. Though, to be fair to the cameramen, it would be a feat of technical genius not to make the footage a festival of legs, bums and breasts.

'I'm getting something,' moaned Apollo. 'It's coming to me . . .'

As the sybil working his staircase drew nearer, Eros tried to hunch behind his fake moustache, drawing one hand up to cover his face. But she didn't see him, instead stopping a few steps short of where he was sitting, her gaze fixed on a woman in her fifties, wearing a mauve velour tracksuit, with breasts the size of beach balls and solid yellow hair.

'Yes, yes,' said Apollo. 'I can feel something now . . . It's very strong . . .'

Eros was sitting close to the sybil and he had the eyes of an archer, so he was probably the only person in the room other than Apollo to see her fingers twitch.

'You,' said Apollo. 'The beautiful lady in purple. I have a message for you.'

A sound recordist dangled a microphone over the astonished woman, distracting the audience as the sybil's fingers twitched again.

'You lost someone . . .' said Apollo. 'Some *thing* precious to you. A hat.'

This time the sybil's twitch was more of a jab.

'A cat,' corrected Apollo.

The yellow-topped woman gasped and nodded.

'That's right,' she said. 'How did you know?'

'Worry no more,' said Apollo. 'Rest your troubled mind. Little Cliff got locked in a neighbour's garage and he'll be coming home just as soon as they get back from holiday.'

'Little Cliff – that's his name!' said the woman. 'And the neighbours are away. They're at her sister's cottage in Wales. There's no way he could have known that,' she told the rest of the audience. 'It's a miracle!'

The sybil smiled, resting her hands, but Apollo continued.

'Little Cliff says that you mustn't fret, he's fine in the garage, but he's getting sick of eating mice and can you have his favourite ready for him when he gets home?'

'Fish pie! I will, darling, I will. Thank you,' sobbed the woman. 'Oh, thank you.'

The sybil glared at Apollo but he ignored her, instead staggering back a few paces.

'That's it,' he groaned. 'It's gone, it's gone . . .'

The audience burst into applause, all but Eros, who was incensed on behalf of the sybils. It was like the Delphi days all over again. Apollo, always the centre of attention, palming off all of the hard work on everybody else and stealing all of the plaudits. As Apollo staggered across the room at the beckoning of the other sybil's nimble fingers, Eros found his foot stretching out to his bag, stroking the bow and arrows that were concealed inside.

The telephone in his pocket buzzed. His mother again.

'REMEMBER DAPHNE.'

Down on the stage, Apollo was enjoying himself. At first it had been confusing to wear the earpiece, to hear the constant flow of instructions from the director telling him what to say and how to stand and where to look, but he soon realised that it was a lot easier if he ignored him, and so he did. Apollo had never responded well to being told what to do.

Now he was free to improvise. Sure, there had been rehearsals. Sure, there had been a script. Sure, right now he could see the producer, the director, and various other people he had immediately and accurately assessed as being too unimportant to register, making frantic faces at him through the soundproof glass that separated the production gallery from the auditorium. And he could hear the frantic shouting that corresponded to the faces.

'Get those hairy legs of yours back to the cross on the floor and stop waving your arms around!'

But if he concentrated hard enough, the words in his earpiece were just sounds. Who were they to speak to him anyway? Those ignorant ants who called themselves the 'Production Team'. Apollo was not a team player. He was a showman. He had been doing this for ever, since long before their minor island had broken off into the sea.

'We need to go to a break! Apollo, cut to a break!'

Apollo fell to his knees and clutched at the studio floor.

'By the sands of the Aegean,' he cried, letting imaginary grains run through his fingers, 'the future is mine, oh yes!'

Daphne: of course Eros remembered her. Everybody remembered Daphne: she was the reason that Apollo had been giving him dirty looks for the last three thousand years. Apollo had once made the mistake of denigrating his cousin's abilities, and, to prove his strength, Eros had made him fall in love with a beautiful nymph, and made the nymph hate him in return. In fact she had been so repulsed by his overtures that she had persuaded her father to turn her into a tree. It did no good. Apollo would rub himself against her bark, and wear her leaves as a crown, while all the other gods mocked him. For hundreds of years, long after Apollo had got over the heartbreak, every time he suggested doing anything at all, the reply would be: 'I don't know. I don't really fancy it. Maybe I'll turn myself into a tree instead.' In the end, Apollo had started turning mortals into trees himself, just to reclaim his dignity. Daphne, in other words, was a precedent.

Of course, if he had any evidence, any suggestion that Apollo had changed, had discovered a little humility after all this time, he wouldn't dream of –

On stage, his cousin struck a pose, both arms out: 'Cower before my power!' he exhorted the somewhat bemused audience.

Eros's pocket thrummed.

'DO IT,' said his phone.

Eros took one last look at his cousin's arrogant face, and shut his eyes. He knew his vicar wouldn't be very impressed by this, but then again, there were a lot of things his vicar would be shocked by if he was privy to them. He took a deep breath, and began to pray.

Our Father who art in heaven. Hallowed be thy name. Was it acceptable, he wondered, theologically speaking, to pray for forgiveness for something that you hadn't done yet, just before you were about to do it? Or was there something illogical about it? *Thy kingdom come. Thy will be done, On earth as it is in heaven.* Were you only supposed to sin if you didn't know what you were doing beforehand? Or otherwise, how long were you supposed to wait before you noticed? There were still some things he didn't quite 'get' about Christianity, even though he did his best. Most of the time. *Give us this day our daily bread. And forgive us our trespasses, As we forgive those who trespass against us.* Eros opened his eyes. He reached down, unzipped his bag and pulled out the long bow and the quiver of arrows that only he could see. *And lead us not into temptation, But deliver us from evil.* There was nothing wrong with love, after all: God is Love. *For thine is the kingdom, and the power, and the glory, for ever and ever.* Eros let a gold-tipped arrow fly, perfectly on target, plunging right up to the feathers through Apollo's chest and into his heart. *Amen.*

Whoever Apollo looked at next would be the instant object of his most ardent love. Good luck to him or her, was all that Eros could say. He saw the look of love bloom on Apollo's face, followed his gaze to its unfortunate recipient. He reached back into his quiver, pulled out the lead-tipped arrow that induced hatred, fitted the arrow to the bow, pulled back the string and took aim. He took a breath, then another, and another. And yet another. And then he lowered his bow. He couldn't do it. Making people fall in love was one thing. But making them fall into hate . . . No. He would let the mortal's own free will decide what happened next. That's what Jesus would do.

Seven

Sitting squeezed up next to Neil on the narrow studio bench, Alice felt as if she had drunk too many fizzy drinks. She couldn't believe she had done it: she had picked up the phone and called him and invited him to come to the studio and now here they were, sitting right next to each other, him watching the stage intently, a frown of concentration on his face, and her pretending to watch the stage but actually watching him.

This had nearly happened so many times. She had looked at the phone and not picked it up. She had picked up the phone and replaced it. She had dialled his number and hung up before it had rung. The first time she called him and he picked up, she had only been able to ask if she had left her umbrella behind in the café last time they met, which she knew she hadn't: Alice never left things behind and she knew exactly where her umbrella was; it was in the umbrella stand with her spare umbrella.

But finally she had managed it. It had been a Thursday evening after work but before *EastEnders*. Her hand had been so sweaty that the phone danced around in it like a live eel. He had sounded so confident when he answered the phone that all of the breath had gone out of her. It wasn't that they had never met up before: they had been friends for two years now, but their meetings had always been at his instigation, and usually only if he happened to be coming to her area for some other reason. But after their initial chat about work and the weather, not a word of which she had taken in, she had done it: she had invited him to come and see a programme being filmed and, after a short, agonising silence, he had said yes.

And now here they were. They were sitting so close that their arms were touching. The place where their shoulders met felt hot. If she moved her leg slightly to the right, their legs would be touching too. She could smell all of his different scents, the fresh clean shirt he was wearing, the sharp tang of his deodorant, and underneath it, just the slightest hint of the warm wood of his skin. She could feel every breath that he took and she matched them with her own breathing so as not to disturb him. She could almost hear the beat of his heart.

It would all have been perfect, if only that strange TV presenter would stop looking at her so oddly.

For Apollo, the feeling was like being punched in the chest. He gasped like a caught fish, hooked and pulled up onto deck, left to drown on air. The girl, that incredible girl – how could he have never seen her before? Why hadn't she been on magazine covers, on billboards, on every television channel, in every film? She was perfection: fine-featured, golden-haired, graceful, adorable in every possible way. What was wrong with the world? As he watched, she leant towards some hideous rodent-like male who clearly had no idea what he was sitting next to, and whispered something into his base, undeserving ear.

He saw them entwined on the floor in an embrace. Not the girl and rat-boy; that, once imagined, would take longer than the rest of his immortal years to forget. No: he could see himself and the girl. Was it a premonition or just a fantasy? He could see her naked body twisting beneath him, arms above her head, face turned to one side, her back arched upwards, her breasts forcing themselves towards him as she gripped him between her strong, hot, soft, hard thighs.

'Um, Apollo,' said the director's voice in his earpiece. 'Your mouth's hanging open, you haven't said anything for over ten seconds, and you've got, if I can believe camera two, what appears to be an almighty erection. Do you want to take five?'

Somehow he got to the end of the show. He'd actually had to go back to that draughty, rotting Portakabin to masturbate; it was humiliating. He'd wiped the semen that could spawn an entire nation of heroes onto a paper napkin with drawings of snowmen on, left over from Christmas, and hid it in the rubbish bin underneath a copy of the *Evening Standard*. When he came out, there were two muses waiting in the drizzle outside, pretending not to laugh. Not that it did any good; as soon as he got back to the studio, there she was, looking at him with some curiosity now, her lips slightly parted, a small bead of sweat sliding achingly slowly down her neck towards the smooth creamy skin of her breasts. The only thing that could stop the whole embarrassing process from happening again was for him to concentrate all of his attention on thinking about his stepmother Hera and what she had done to their former male neighbour when they'd had a dispute about the precise boundary between their two gardens. That's their former neighbour who had also, formerly, been male.

After the shoot finally came to an end, Apollo tore through the worsening rain back to the Portakabin. He pulled off his toga and threw it to the ground, then yanked on his jeans and T-shirt. He felt sure that the girl would come and see him in his dressing room – the attraction had been so powerful, so intense that he couldn't believe she didn't feel it too. And so she would come here – of course she would – wasn't that what amorous women did? He had seen enough films to suggest as much. He hoped she wouldn't be expecting cocaine, or any of the other apparently indispensable accoutrements of groupie-dom. Only she wasn't a groupie, was she? This was different. This was love.

He looked for a towel with which to dry his hair and, finding nothing, used his T-shirt instead, squeezing the excess moisture out before putting it back on. It was a shame, really, that there wasn't somewhere more romantic for them to meet. Still, that could come later, and at least the carpet, thin as it was, would help make the sex a little more comfortable.

There was perhaps time for a little tidying. He picked up his toga from the floor, folded it roughly and threw the lumpy result onto a chair. Then he started on his dressing table. He was tipping the sludge from two chipped mugs into the sink bolted to the far wall when he heard the door opening behind him. His heart and stomach seemed to swap places. Immediately dropping the mugs into the sink, he wiped his hands on his jeans, moulded his panicking features into an expression of charming, knowing surprise, and turned, saying, 'How kind of you to drop by.'

'No problem at all. You've got coffee on your jeans.'

It wasn't the girl. It was Aphrodite, looking extraordinarily pleased with herself for some reason. She had probably just fellated a cameraman. His face, though under strict instructions not to, fell.

'What's the matter?' Aphrodite continued. 'Were you expecting someone else?'

'Yes,' said Apollo. 'Well, that is to say, not exactly. I mean, I kind of thought, well, there was someone in the audience, who, maybe . . .'

'I thought I'd come and pick you up,' said Aphrodite. 'Everybody else has gone.'

'Everybody?'

'Everybody. Well, they didn't like to linger. It would be unseemly. Like slowing down on the motorway to look at the bodies after a crash.'

'Are you sure that no one . . . No one . . .'

Aphrodite just smiled – not her irresistible one, but something rather more smug.

'Time to leave,' she said.

Eight

The first episode of *Apollo's Oracle* was screened about a week after it had been recorded. Apollo had spent the entire week trying to track down the angel in the front row. He had managed to charm the woman on reception into giving him a copy of the audience list and had roamed London in search of her, banging on doors in increasing desperation, at first inventing excuses for his unexpected visit, later just turning and walking, wordless, away, when the girl that he was looking for failed to materialise. That morning, he had been to the final destination on his list, a squalid bungalow in Forest Gate, only to be confronted by a shuffling old man who had grabbed him by the arm and begged him four times to come in and join him for a sherry. He had tried to shrug him off, but each time he was overcome by a crippling wave of dizziness and nausea as Styx reached out from the underworld and held him to his oath. Eventually he had gone inside, eyes half shut in protection against the kaleidoscope of the carpet, and consented to an hour and a half of photographs of Bill Craven's koi carp, 1965 to present.

And now this further humiliation. Aphrodite had clearly let it be known amongst her relatives that the filming had been a fiasco, as, in a rare moment of togetherness, all of the gods had crammed themselves into the living room to watch the broadcast. Hephaestus had patched up some of the furniture for the occasion, so Hermes, Eros, Hephaestus and Aphrodite were wedged together on the sofa, while the others sat in armchairs or on the floor. Dionysus was busy going around filling up everyone's glasses with his strongest wine. The mood was festive. Hera and Zeus, of course, were not there, nor were any of the gods who lived offsite – Hades and Persephone in the under-world, for example, or Poseidon in his tiny seaside shack that stank, as he did, of fish – but no doubt word would have spread and they too would be huddled around their televisions ready for the show. There is little a god likes more than watching another god embarrassing himself.

'It's very kind of you,' Apollo said, pacing up and down in front of the television, 'to take such an interest in my work, but really there's no need. I'm sure you'll all get horribly bored. I wouldn't want to put you through that.'

'He's too modest,' said Aphrodite. 'Don't listen to him. I've seen it. I know you'll all find it highly entertaining.'

'Aphrodite's right,' said Hephaestus inevitably, to groans from the other gods.

'And don't even think,' said Artemis to Apollo, 'about making the television unexpectedly stop working. You're on sufferance as it is.'

'There's no reason,' said Apollo, 'for me to do a thing like that. It's not that I don't want you to see the programme. Of course I do. I'm just thinking of you and your precious time.'

'Time,' Ares pointed out, 'is the least precious thing that we have.'

'Speak for yourself,' muttered Hermes, always the busiest of the gods.

'Switch it on,' commanded Artemis. 'I don't want to miss the beginning.'

Dionysus hurried back to his seat, swigging from the wine bottle as he moved.

'I'm sure you've all got better things to do . . .' Apollo tried again.

'Switch it on!' The call came from all the gods that time, and

Apollo, conceding defeat, flicked the switch for the television, located the Psychic channel in the distant reaches of the satellite selection – flicking past shopping, dating, pornography and Bollywood – and retreated to the shadows at the back of the room. He considered just leaving them to it, disappearing up to his bedroom or out to a bar, but not knowing what they were saying behind his back would be even worse than letting them taunt him to his face.

It wasn't as bad as he imagined. It was worse. On the day, they had filmed for well over an hour, but the length of the programme was only thirty minutes, so the show had been cut down to fit the slot, apparently in haste, apparently with an axe, apparently by someone who was holding some kind of a grudge against Apollo. Although the first half of the day had gone well, before he had noticed that girl and lost his concentration, hardly any of this footage had been used, aside from the introduction at the beginning. Instead the programme – the badly-shot, badly-lit, crassly-scored programme – seemed to consist almost exclusively of a montage of moments where he stumbled, fluffed his lines, or blinked in confusion into the lights, intercut with long lascivious shots of the sybils' near-naked forms, and the moribund faces of the borderline cadavers that made up his audience.

But that wasn't the worst thing about it. The worst thing was his family's response. They had started out jeering – all but Eros, who had pleaded with his brethren to pray for Apollo's fortitude at this difficult time – though the jeers were modulated to a low volume so that they could all hear what was going on on-screen. But after only a few minutes, the jeers had tailed off and the room lapsed into silence. His was the only voice audible, slightly tinny through the cheap television speakers. On screen he was telling an old lady that she was going to find her lost earrings at the bottom of her summer handbag, but he may as well have been Cassandra, prophesying doom, as he had cursed her to do, back when he had put curses on mortals as idly as sipping nectar off a spoon. On the television screen, his weakness was pulled out of the camouflage of the murky day-to-day, and displayed, naked, undeniable. All of the gods were seeing their future now, and they didn't like what they saw.

Alone, Aphrodite was not hypnotised by the carnage unfolding on screen. Ignored by the others, she leant towards Hermes, her neighbour on the sofa. She pressed her plump lips up against the shell of his ear, enjoying the shiver of lust that passed through his body at her touch.

'You're the god of coincidences, aren't you?' she whispered, running a finger up the inside of his thigh.

'I'm the god of everything nobody else wants to do,' Hermes whispered back.

'Good,' said Aphrodite. Her hand paused, high up Hermes' leg.

She waited a few moments until the camera cut to the girl in the audience whom Eros, on her other side, had signalled was the object of Apollo's unrequited passion. (That it might be less unrequited than Aphrodite believed was a fact that Eros had wisely kept to himself.) Enjoying the wince of pain that passed over Apollo's watching face, she whispered her instructions to Hermes.

'That girl. Bring her here. I don't care how.' Her tongue performed a complex manoeuvre on the inside of Hermes' ear canal. 'I'll make it worth your while.'

Hermes, not trusting himself to make a sound, just nodded. Aphrodite smiled to herself. She was a very hard goddess to say no to.

Nine

In the upstairs room that he called his den, Neil was multitasking. They said men couldn't multitask; they were wrong. They just needed the right equipment. Right now Neil was Instant Messaging a colleague, burning a compilation CD for Alice, and watching the meltdown that was *Apollo's Oracle* on TV.

The den was a small room which the previous owners of the flat had used as a nursery. The contents of it were no less precious to Neil than a baby. He had lined the room from floor to ceiling with shelves and had filled them with everything he held dear.

At the bottom were his comics: starting with the *Beano*s that he had collected as a child, then graduating upwards through Asterix and Tintin books and onwards to the comics he still read, *2000 AD* and *Judge Dredd: the Megazine*, plus a smattering of manga, which he had experimented with for a while before deciding that it was a bit extreme for him. These were all arranged by title and then chronologically, key issues in plastic binders.

Above these were his books. Neil had books all over the flat – he thought rooms felt nude without them, and in any case had so many that they couldn't all be contained in one place – but the ones in the den were his favourites: classic science fiction, fantasy (but only the top-end stuff), and a lot of non-fiction – weighty historical tomes, mostly about war, not all of which he had finished. These were separated into genres and then alphabetised.

Then at the top was his Betamax, VHS and DVD collection. He was most proud of his collection of complete TV series, recorded over almost three decades, each one labelled and dated. Arranging these had proved a particular headache, as he had been torn as to whether to subdivide into format, genre, home-made and shop-bought, but eventually he had gone for a straight chronology, which provided a pleasing overview of his developing tastes, TV history, and the rise and fall in neatness of his handwriting.

The presence of Apollo, even in virtual form, in the haven that was the den was therefore egregiously intrusive. Neil had seen the way Apollo had been looking at Alice on the day of the filming. It wasn't just admiring (which at least would have been understandable); it was predatory. Suddenly the situation had seemed less like good harmless fun and more like lunchtime on the Serengeti. But he knew that Alice was watching the programme at home and would be asking him about it next time they spoke, and he couldn't disappoint her by not tuning in.

HE'S SO FULL OF HIMSELF, he IMd Derek.

Derek was a work colleague whose similar tastes Neil had discovered only after a year of sharing an office, after a casual mention of *Buffy* at a Christmas party, and who was currently watching *Apollo's Oracle* at Neil's instruction.

ALL THOSE TV PSYCHICS ARE, wrote Derek. IT'S PART OF THE FUN.

THIS ISN'T FUN, wrote Neil. LOOK AT HIM PONCING ABOUT LIKE GOD'S GIFT. HE THINKS THE SUN SHINES OUT OF HIS BACKSIDE.

WHAT DID ALICE THINK OF HIM? wrote Derek.

I DON'T KNOW, wrote Neil.

It was a sore point. Had Alice noticed how handsome he was? After the show, he hadn't been able to get an opinion out of her, she just kept asking him if he had enjoyed himself.

HAVE YOU ASKED HER OUT YET? wrote Derek.

DON'T BE AN IDIOT, WE'RE JUST FRIENDS, wrote Neil.

YEAH. SURE.

SHUT UP AND WATCH THE PROGRAMME.

As he waited for Derek's reply, Neil was interrupted by the phone ringing.

BETTER GO, he told Derek, and picked up the phone with his other hand, even as he was still pressing return on his keyboard.

'Hello?' he said.

At the other end of the line all he could hear was crying.

'Hello?' he said again. 'Is everything OK? Mum, is that you?'

'No,' said a pitiful voice at the end of the line. 'No . . . it's me. It's Alice.'

'Alice,' said Neil. 'What is it? What happened? Aren't you watching us on TV?'

'Yes,' said Alice. 'Yes, I am. I was.'

'So what happened?' said Neil. 'What is it? What's the matter? Didn't you see yourself? You looked very pretty,' he dared.

'I did see myself,' said Alice. 'And then . . .'

'Alice, don't worry,' said Neil. 'Whatever it is, I'm sure it's all right.'

'It's not all right, it's not all right.' Alice was actually raising her voice now; Neil had never heard her speak so loud. 'After my face was on the screen, the phone rang. It was the head of the agency.'

Neil felt sick. He knew what was coming.

'He told me . . .' Alice was back at her normal volume now. 'He told me he'd had a call from the studio boss. He'd been watching the programme and he saw me. He told the agency I'd broken the rules, and said that either I went or they'd get in another company. Neil, they've given me the sack.'

'It's all my fault,' said Neil. 'I'm sorry Alice, I'm so sorry. I should never have made you do it.'

'You didn't make me,' said Alice. 'I did it because I wanted to. It's not your fault, that's not why I called. I just didn't know who else to talk to. Neil . . . What am I going to do? I haven't got a job. What am I going to do now?'

Ten

One morning, a week after the broadcast, Artemis got up early to take the dogs out and was astonished to hear voices coming from the living room. None of the gods were early risers – even Athena tended to do her morning reading in bed. The door to the living room was ajar, and Artemis peered around it.

Apollo was sitting on the floor, leaning back against the split seat of an armchair, playing quietly on one of his guitars. His hair hung lank, sticking to his cheeks as he bowed his head, face pale, eyes bloodshot, crooning to his guitar as if to a lover, over and over again: '*Girl, I miss you, I missed you girl. Girl, I miss you* . . .' Meanwhile Aphrodite, fresh and pert, was lying back on the faded velvet sofa – did it used to be blue? – with her delicate feet, crossed at the ankle, propped up on its careening arm. Her head was turned towards Apollo as she watched him with an unreadable look on her face. She had a Bluetooth receiver in her ear and she spoke softly into it: 'Fuck me harder baby, that feels good, oh yes.' It was a peculiarly intimate scene, and Artemis almost felt uncomfortable interrupting. Although not quite.

'What are you two doing up?' she said, stepping into the room.

Apollo looked up briefly from his guitar. 'I haven't been to bed,' he said in a flat voice. 'I just have to get this song right. *Miss you, oh I miss you, girl, I missed you* . . .'

'What's going on?' said Artemis. 'Have you been drinking Dionysus' wine?'

'Just a little bit,' said Apollo. Artemis saw the empty bottle on its side, mostly hidden by the bulk of the collapsing armchair.

'No wonder you look so rough,' said Artemis.

'I'm sure I look better than I feel,' said Apollo.

'That's unlikely,' said Artemis. 'And you?' she said to her aunt. 'You never get up before lunch.'

'That feels good,' said Aphrodite. 'Right there. You've got it, baby.'

'I have no idea what she's doing up,' said Apollo. 'She's been in here talking on that thing all night. I think maybe she gets paid more to do antisocial hours. That's when there's the most demand.'

'Well, if that's the case she could start putting a bit more in the kitty,' said Artemis. 'The house needs damp coursing and she's spending all her money on bras.'

Aphrodite started moaning and gasping, building up in a crescendo, but halfway through, without even a pause, she switched off her phone and said, in her ordinary voice, 'I just thought I'd keep you company. You haven't seemed quite yourself since we watched your programme.'

Though if there was even a drop of sympathy in her, it was hiding somewhere quite impenetrable, thought Artemis, watching Aphrodite sit up and unhook her earpiece.

'Mortals today, they've got no staying power,' Aphrodite commented. 'You barely have enough time to get their credit card details and they've already finished. I said all along that we should have put the pigs in charge.'

Artemis began doing her warm-up muscle stretches. Stiffness: it was a relatively new sensation, and had not really been worth acquiring.

'You know, they cut your tree down,' she said to Apollo, as she lifted and rotated her right knee.

'My tree?'

'That girl. Kate.' Apollo's face was blank. 'The Australian? The

one you turned into a eucalyptus? She was felled. Standard maintenance coppicing. They do it every year.'

Apollo shrugged.

'I'd forgotten about her,' he said.

He picked at his guitar strings, obviously anxious to get back
to his composition.

'Got someone new on your mind, have you?' said Aphrodite.

'It's none of your business,' said Apollo.

'I'll take that as a yes,' said Aphrodite.

'You know your problem,' said Artemis, 'you're emotionally
incontinent. It never stops. It's all . . .' She dropped her voice to
a whisper. '. . . sex, sex, sex.'

Artemis wrinkled her nose at even having to say the word
once, let alone three times and, even worse, whilst doing sugges-
tive lunges.

'At least I don't have to spend all my time running just to get
rid of my sexual frustration,' said Aphrodite.

Artemis refused to dignify this with a response, occupying
herself instead with some arm stretches.

'So come on,' said Aphrodite, turning to Apollo. 'What's she
like?'

'How do you know it's a she?' said Apollo.

'Lucky guess,' said Aphrodite. 'So what's the matter then? Did
she turn you down?'

'She'd better not turn up as a potted plant if she did,' said
Artemis.

'I can't do that any more, thanks to you, remember?' said
Apollo. 'And no, she didn't turn me down. She didn't get a chance
to. She got away before I even had the opportunity to talk to
her. And now I'm never going to see her again.'

Apollo plucked the same mournful melody out of his guitar,
and sighed.

'Oh come on,' said Aphrodite. 'That's hardly the spirit. I'm
sure she'll turn up.'

'I've looked for her everywhere,' said Apollo. 'I don't know where she can be.'

'You've never even spoken to her and she's got you into that state?' said Artemis. 'For crying out loud. You're a grown god, start acting like one. Cooing and weeping over some mortal that you've never even met! Drinking yourself into a stupor! Singing little songs! Consider your dignity, the responsibilities of your station. You're an embarrassment to Olympus. No wonder I prefer the company of beasts. And no, I don't mean it that way,' she added, seeing Aphrodite's mouth begin to open, the lascivious comment poised on her lithe, pink tongue.

'I don't care about Olympus,' said Apollo. 'I don't care about anything. I don't care if the sun never comes up again.'

'Oh, pull yourself together,' said Artemis. 'She's just a mortal. She'll be dead before you know it.'

'Leave the poor boy alone,' said Aphrodite with a smirk. 'Can't you see he's in love?'

Artemis rolled her eyes and left the room. She gathered up her keys and opened the front door. There, to her astonishment, stood a small mortal, about five feet high, blondish, a little dumpy, wearing spectacles. The only remarkable thing about her was that she was standing on their doorstep. Word obviously hadn't spread about what happened to mortals who did that.

'Are you lost?' said Artemis.

The mortal looked at Artemis, then down at her hands, in which, Artemis now saw, a number of small printed cards were clutched. She looked at Artemis again, and then decided that her hands were the preferable view.

'No,' whispered the mortal. It was barely more than an exhalation. 'I'm a cleaner. I was . . . I was . . . distributing some flyers.'

Artemis grabbed one of the little cards out of the mortal's trembling hand.

'There you go,' she said without looking at it. 'You've distributed it. Now leave.'

'What does she want?' came a voice from behind Artemis.

Artemis turned. Aphrodite had come out of the living room, shutting the door behind her, and was now leaning languidly against the wall of the hallway, eyeing the mortal with one eyebrow raised in an elegant arc.

'It's a cleaner,' said Artemis.

'We don't need a cleaner,' said Aphrodite. 'She'd better go.'

'You heard her,' said Artemis to the mortal.

'Artemis does all the cleaning,' continued Aphrodite.

'What?' said Artemis.

'She doesn't really have anything else to do,' said Aphrodite. 'Her other so-called skills are no longer in demand.'

'I do not do all the cleaning!' said Artemis.

'If you hire a cleaner,' interjected the mortal, 'these domestic disputes will be a thing of the past.'

Artemis had almost forgotten that the mortal was there. From the look on her face, the mortal was even more surprised that she had spoken than Artemis was.

'I assure you, we really have no need for a cleaner,' said Aphrodite.

The mortal was not so easily deterred.

'A good cleaner,' she said, 'is an indispensable investment for the busy modern professional.' She cleared her throat and increased the volume by a gossamer thread. 'In this day and age, time is the most valuable asset that you have, so why waste it on chores that you find boring or unpleasant?'

'Actually, we're not really short of time,' said Artemis.

Without appearing even to look down, Aphrodite reached out behind her and picked up a rather surprised rat, that just a moment before had been making its way down the stairs.

'Here, Artemis!' said Aphrodite, holding the squirming rat up by the tail. 'Fetch!'

She tossed the rat out of the front door and past the flinching little mortal. It bounced down the front steps and landed on its back in the street, where it righted itself and scurried away.

'Artemis,' confided Aphrodite, 'is an expert in pest control.'

'I kill for pleasure,' said Artemis, 'not business.'

The mortal started backing down the steps.

'Tell me,' Artemis said to the cleaner, lassoing her with her voice, 'how do you feel about rats?'

The mortal stopped where she was, gulped louder than her speaking voice, but she replied.

'A poorly maintained home,' she said, 'can become a haven for vermin. A good cleaner is the first step towards a pest-free environment.'

'And experience,' said Artemis. 'Do you have any experience?'

'This is a waste of time,' yawned Aphrodite. 'We have all the home maintenance staff that we need in you, dear niece.'

'I have garnered years of expertise cleaning at some of London's biggest and most exclusive businesses,' said the mortal. 'Now I want to bring my skills into your home.'

'Forget it, Artemis,' said Aphrodite. 'You'll never get her past Zeus and Hera. You don't want to get into trouble, do you? Artemis,' she told the mortal, 'is always very well-behaved. She's naturally subservient.'

'Zeus and Hera will never know,' Artemis retorted. 'As long as she can follow instructions. You can follow instructions can't you?'

'You will find me efficient, obedient and quiet –' began the mortal.

'Well, I don't doubt that,' interrupted Artemis. 'Right then. What's your standard daily rate?'

The mortal told her.

'And do you do extermination?'

The mortal's face answered that question.

'What if we paid you that per hour? Would you kill for us

then? It's only rats and a few other small things. Cockroaches, flies. I don't think we have any squirrels.'

'I –' said the mortal.

'And you'll need to come in every day,' said Artemis.

'We can't afford that,' said Aphrodite.

'Yes we can,' said Artemis. 'We'll just have to stop buying food.'

'But I like food,' whined Aphrodite.

'Too bad,' said Artemis. 'It's not a necessity. Having a cleaner is.'

She turned back to the mortal.

'You'll have to abide by certain rules,' she said. 'I'll have a set laminated for you by tomorrow.'

The mortal was looking slightly dizzy. Artemis hoped that she wouldn't faint.

'I –' said the mortal again.

'No need to thank me,' said Artemis.

'I hope you know what you're doing,' said Aphrodite, 'bringing a mor— a cleaner into this house.'

'Thank you for your input, Aphrodite,' said Artemis, 'but I assure you that I know exactly what I am doing. You, the girl, will start at eleven tomorrow. Right now, I have dogs to walk. Goodbye.'

And she swept down the stairs, past the mortal, who was still gaping, and marched away down the street.

Eleven

Alice still wasn't sure that she'd actually agreed to take the job, and yet here she was doing it. She didn't like rats and as it turned out she liked killing them even less: which was illogical but no less true for that. Her life was turning into a series of paradoxes (*paradox*, lovely word for Scrabble) and it had all happened seemingly without her consent. She was making more money than she'd ever made, she was desperate to quit and yet some kind of magnetic force seemed to pull her legs out of her bed in the morning, to wash her, dress her, feed her and present her on the cracked, mossy doorstep where she'd wait for admittance without ringing the bell – this was one of the Rules – while every single day she wondered why, exactly. Her feelings on the matter seemed as irrelevant as those of a chess piece. But it had been her decision. Hadn't it?

The first day had been strange and from then on things had only got stranger. At first she had thought herself lucky when, on the very first day of looking for a new job, she had not only been offered one, but at a far higher rate of pay than she had made with the agency. It was Neil who had suggested that she go freelance: he had been outraged at her sacking from the agency and pointed out that there was no need for her to give up a percentage of her takings when she could just as easily find work by herself. When she had protested how deeply uncomfortable she felt initiating conversations and talking herself up, Neil had drilled her on communications strategy and helped her come up with a sales spiel. It was really far too kind of him: she knew he had far better things to do with his evenings than waste them helping her out. But he had insisted; had even claimed, nonsensically, that he felt guilty about her losing her job.

The uneasy sense that lucky wasn't quite the word for it had begun the moment she had turned up at the house the next day and the door had opened just as she raised a finger to press on the scratched brass bell.

'Never knock or ring the bell,' said the woman who answered: Artemis. For two minutes the previous day, Artemis had been the most beautiful woman Alice had ever seen. Then the other woman, Aphrodite, had emerged, and made Artemis look relatively plain.

'How will I get in?' said Alice. 'Should I get a set of keys?'

'No,' said Artemis. 'No keys under any circumstances. Just be punctual. Someone will let you in.'

'What about when you go away?'

'We never go away. Incidentally, another Rule is no questions. And no speaking unless you're spoken to. Do come in.'

Alice followed Artemis over the threshold and into the house.

'Rule number one,' said Artemis as they entered. 'Never go up to the top floor of the house. Rule number two. I am always right.'

Alice murmured assent but her focus was on the state of the house. It was dirty. Alice had expected that; had seen enough through the open door to testify to it most convincingly. But she hadn't anticipated quite how dirty it would be. It wasn't grime so much as sedimentation. Everything: the carpet (she assumed it was a carpet – neither sight nor texture gave much assistance to identifying the substance under the black sludge that covered it), the walls, the windows which let in the barest trickle of mottled light as if through thick grey snow – all encrusted with so many layers of filth that Alice nearly suggested calling in the services of an archaeologist, though that would have involved

her speaking, an activity that both she and Artemis were mutu-
ally opposed to. And anyway, one of Artemis's Rules was No
Suggestions.

Feet sticking to the ground with every step, Alice followed
Artemis from room to room, noting the broken, listing furniture, the ceilings obscured by spiders' webs, the skirting boards
riddled with holes, cosy homes for who knew what. All the while,
Artemis was reading aloud from not one but three laminated
sheets of Rules.

'Rule number twenty-nine. Never let anybody else into the
house under any circumstances whatsoever. Rule number thirty.
You must always dress conservatively – that one's for your own
protection.'

Alice could do little but nod mutely, though Artemis never
turned around to check her agreement or even to make sure
that she was still there and had not fled the house entirely.
Artemis, Alice realised, was the kind of person who assumed
that her commands would be carried out. That kind of person,
Alice knew, was the kind of person whose commands always
were carried out, so they never had to doubt this perfect feed-
back loop. Alice was not that kind of person.

When they got to the kitchen, Alice nearly vomited. To her
credit, Artemis seemed at least a little embarrassed.

'Well, yes, I do agree,' she said, though Alice had not ventured
any kind of opinion except that which could be read into an
involuntary spasm, 'that the source of the rat problem is probably in here. But I'm sure when you've cleared away most of the
decomposing foodstuffs it will seem far less daunting. Shall we
head upstairs?'

Alice should have walked away at that very moment but she
had not. Trying to figure out why yielded nothing. It was like
trying to look at something that wasn't there.

*　　*　　*

59

On the afternoon of the third day she met Apollo. The worst of the rotting objects had been put into a legion of reinforced garden-strength bin bags and loaded onto a truck sent round by an obliging environmental health department (calling in outside help was against the Rules too, but as the call had been made from her home, and nobody had actually crossed the threshold, it seemed to be an acceptable and necessary risk). She had laid down traps and poison next to each of the gruyere-like holes that made up the house's multi-storey mouse-park, and emptied the traps, several times each. She was standing in the living room, twirling spiders' webs around a broom as if making a giant candy floss, when the door had opened and he had walked in, trailing an acoustic guitar.

She recognised him immediately from the TV show, but, mindful of Artemis's instructions, couldn't say anything, even if she had wanted to. His reaction, meanwhile, was nothing short of bizarre. (*Bizarre*: another lovely word.) Apollo stared. The guitar fell, unnoticed, from his hand. He reached over to his forearm and gave it a long, hard pinch. Alice didn't want to look at him but felt it would be rude to look away. She prayed for the ground to open up and swallow her whole, but it didn't. Instead she felt herself blush under his scrutiny. She remembered his staring from the show, before. Maybe he had something wrong with his eyes.

'What are you doing here?' said Apollo eventually.

'Artemis hired me,' said Alice, repeating what she had been told to say if questioned. 'I am the new cleaner. If you have any problem with this, speak to Artemis. You're permitted to sack me, but only if you swear on sticks that you'll do all the cleaning from now on yourself.'

Apollo reacted to this as someone might had it just been proved that the earth was made of blancmange.

'Artemis hired you. Artemis! That's impossible! How does she know you? Nobody knows you but me! Has she known you all along?'

'No,' said Alice. 'I came to the door.'

'But I don't understand,' said Apollo. 'How did you find me?'

'Oh no, I didn't,' said Alice. 'I didn't know you lived here.'

Apollo struck his hand against his chest and held it there.

'The Fates!' he said. 'We haven't always seen eye to eye. At last they bow to my superiority! What's your name?'

This was the first time anyone from the house had asked Alice's name.

'Alice,' said Alice.

'Alice,' repeated Apollo, rolling the word around his mouth as if tasting it. 'Alice. Such a poetic name. So sweet and yet so strong. Really, it is a beautiful name, especially considering that it contains the word "lice".'

'Thank you,' said Alice.

'And you're the cleaner?'

'Yes,' said Alice.

'What a noble calling. They say cleanliness is next to godliness. Don't you wish that were true?'

The collar of Alice's shirt stuck to the side of her neck where she was sweating. She wanted to pull at it – actually, she wanted to push past him and run away as fast as she could out of the room – but she couldn't move.

'I don't know what you mean,' said Alice.

'Of course you don't,' said Apollo. 'You're virtuous, aren't you, Alice? I can see that. Virtuous . . .'

His eyes looked dreamy for a moment, then snapped back into focus.

'What are you doing?' he said. 'Put that thing down. Sit down.'

'I can't sit down,' said Alice. 'Artemis said . . .'

'Oh, fuck Artemis,' said Apollo. 'You mustn't listen to a word that old witch says. She's not the boss of me or anyone else and she certainly shouldn't be the boss of you. Would you please put that broom down right now and sit. Sit!'

Alice jumped, dropped the broom and sat on the very edge

61

of a wooden armchair which had lumps of black grease on it that looked oddly like boot polish. Apollo sat down on the floor in front of her, unpleasantly close. She drew her feet a little further under the chair.

'Tell me something, Alice,' said Apollo. 'What did you think of my show?'

This put Alice in an awkward position. The two things she hated most in the world were lying and hurting people's feelings, and here she was, apparently forced to do one of them. She thought about it for a while.

'Your assistants were very pretty,' she said in the end.

'Not nearly as pretty as you,' said Apollo.

Alice pushed herself back as far as she could go, until she was sitting bolt upright. She could feel her spine trying to climb up over the back of the chair.

'I don't want you to judge me on the basis of this house,' Apollo said. 'It wasn't always like this. We were . . . famous once. Back in Greece. And in Rome – Italy. Everyone knew who we were. People were different then. They believed. The adulation, the fame, it was like – well, it was worship, really. We lived in a palace – I wish you could have seen it, Alice! The fountains, the pleasure gardens, nymphs gliding gracefully through the forest – I never looked at them, of course. We had everything. Everything! Can you imagine it?'

He appealed for a response with his eyes.

'It sounds nice,' said Alice.

Satisfied, Apollo continued, his voice taking on a darker timbre.

'Then times changed,' he said. 'We went out of fashion, we fell from grace. I can't tell you the details, it's all still too fresh. It was a long way to fall, Alice. It hurt. This degradation around us – it only reflects the pain inside. So that television show – it was like balm. Recapturing something I thought I'd lost for ever. Can you understand that, Alice?'

Alice, as ever, could not lie.

'Not entirely,' she said.

'Of course not,' said Apollo. 'How could you? Innocent child. How old are you?'

'Thirty-two,' said Alice.

'Thirty-two! Barely even born,' said Apollo. 'Alice, may I confess something? We've only just met and already I feel a connection to you. This conversation – it's moved me more than I can say. We're like twin souls. Do you feel it too, Alice? Do you?'

Apollo put his hand on her knee. Alice jumped up from her chair and seized the broom. For a moment they both thought she might hit him with it, and were equally astonished by this prospect, but instead she just held out the cobwebby end towards him.

'Spiders,' she said, as the spiky brown things seethed in the grey. 'I forgot. I need to take them outside. And then it's time for me to go home.'

Apollo looked stricken. Alice actually thought he might cry, and it suddenly occurred to her that he must have been drinking, or even taking drugs – all of these TV stars did. The thought was reassuring: none of this was anything to do with her, and when he came down, if that was the right expression, he would forget all about it.

'Will you ever come back?' said Apollo.

'Oh, yes. Of course I will,' said Alice. 'I'll be back tomorrow. I'll be here every day.'

A smile dawned on Apollo's face like sunrise after a dark night.

'Then there's no need for us to rush into anything,' he said.

And Alice began feeling nervous all over again.

Twelve

Sundays were dog-free days for Artemis, but she always did her run on the Heath all the same, going faster and further since she didn't have those soft-toothed mutts slowing her down. This was power: the strength of her limbs, the pounding of the turf beneath her feet. She needed that feeling. Passing a newsagent that morning, she had heard a snatch of radio news: campaigners (idiots, the lot of them) were trying to bring about a ban on the shooting of game. She was losing her grip on the world. She would not lose her grip on herself.

The mood in the house had been subdued since the screening of the appalling television programme her twin brother had insisted on being a part of. He had made a fool of himself. There was nothing new in this. Gods were always tricking each other into looking foolish; if they didn't, the world would probably stop turning because they would be too bored to keep it going. But Apollo had made a fool of himself in public, before the eyes of mortals (assuming any of them had bothered to watch), without anyone else's involvement as far as she could tell, and it had been quite obvious that there was nothing he could do to stop it. Artemis wondered just how long it had been since he'd had a clear premonition of the future. It used to be almost impossible to shut him up about them. And yet the sybils apparently still retained that ability. And they weren't even gods! Running up a grassy slope, Artemis almost tripped on a root. There had been a time when they hadn't been gods either. The Titans had been in charge once, but they had weakened, and the Olympians had exploited that weakness. Despite herself, Artemis couldn't help but imagine the world under the control of the sybils. It would be a lot pinker than the world was now.

She shook her head to rid herself of the image. The sun was shining, and Artemis could feel herself beginning to sweat. Spring was coming yet again – soon Persephone would be home. She pulled a face. She hoped that they wouldn't have to have Persephone sleeping in their room again this year. She would have a word with Athena, make sure that she crammed even more books than usual into their space, making it impossible to squeeze the spare mattress onto the floor. There simply wasn't enough room for all of them in that house. Fortunately, Persephone had been making her visits to the upperworld shorter and shorter. Long ago, when Zeus had banished her to the underworld for every winter, he had bound her to a minimum yearly period to be spent underground. At the time, there had seemed little need to set a maximum limit. Of late, Persephone had begun taking advantage of this loophole. Artemis suspected she only came back when she and Hades argued, and eventually, she supposed, Persephone would stop coming back at all.

Walking up the road to the hated house after her run, stretching her limbs out and cooling down, Artemis saw Eros lingering on the front step, wearing a smart suit, his hair neatly combed. She waved, and he waved back. She and Eros got on much better these days than they used to – ever since he had discovered morality, something the rest of her siblings could do with a little more of.

'What are you doing?' she called out, as soon as he was within earshot.

'I just got back from church,' Eros called back. 'Beautiful service. I love the solemnity of Lent.'

Artemis nodded in agreement. She sometimes wondered

whether she would make a good Christian herself, though she couldn't quite bring herself to even feign worship for a mortal – it would be like worshipping a slug.

'Did you forget your key?' she said as she approached the steps.

'No,' admitted Eros. 'I just didn't fancy going in. I don't suppose you want to go for a walk? Delay going back in for a bit. It's a nice day.'

'It is a nice day,' agreed Artemis. 'OK. Why not? It's not like I've got anything better to do.'

Eros skipped down the steps and they both turned away from the house with some relief, and began walking in the direction of the High Street. There was a gentle, pleasant breeze and the light of the sun reflected brightly off the windows of the buildings that they passed. Artemis was glad to see that Apollo could still get something right.

'So,' said Artemis as they walked. 'What do you think of the new cleaner?'

Eros put his hands in his pockets, looked away from her and began to whistle.

'Nice little girl, isn't she?' Artemis continued. 'I hired her myself, you know. Frankly I couldn't carry on living in that filth for another moment. And though I say so myself, the improvement has been . . .'

But she caught a look in Eros's eye which suggested that he might be more receptive to her true feelings than the lie she was about to concoct.

'The improvement has been cosmetic,' she said. 'The house is cleaner, but what difference does that make when we're all still living in it?'

'You're right,' said Eros. 'She does her best, but it'll take more than Flash wipes to clean the rot out of that place. Still, she's more resilient than I thought she would be.'

'What do you mean by that?' said Artemis.

66

'Oh,' said Eros. 'Nothing much. Just . . . nothing.'

He crossed the road and she followed on behind, matching his pace again when they reached the other side. They walked along in silence for a while. There were dogs around, on leads, and Artemis tried to catch their eyes, hoping to detect some wolfish spark, some indication that they knew their heritage, but they were all the same – fat, lazy, dull. There was no point. No true dog would allow itself to be tethered to a human anyway.

'I really wish I'd met him when I had the chance,' said Eros.

'Who?'

'Jesus.'

'Is that what you were thinking about?'

'What were you thinking about?'

'Dogs.'

Eros laughed. 'Well, each to his own.'

'Or her own.'

Eros nodded. 'Or her own,' he said. 'I just wonder . . . what was he like? Was he anything like they say he is, in the Bible? Or was it all just made up later? I mean, obviously he didn't come back from the dead, hardly anyone ever does and we would have known about it . . .'

'Unless one of us sneaked him out.'

'Or he found his own way back.'

'No. Then he would have just been a ghost like the others.'

'So if he didn't do that, was the rest of it all made up as well? I wish I'd known him. It's such a waste. When I think, we were just down the road in Rome, living it up, having orgies –'

'Not all of us were having orgies.'

'And all that time he was right there, living this incredible life –'

'Or not.'

' – that would have such an impact on the rest of the world – even on us. And we had no idea.'

'He's just down there,' said Artemis, 'in the underworld, with the rest of them. Probably keeping a low profile, all things considered. Just think of all his dissatisfied customers.'

'It's not his fault,' said Eros. 'He never wanted to be a god anyway. That's why he does a much better job of it than the rest of us.'

They had reached the High Street now, and it was the busiest it had been since Christmas. Mortals, it seemed, still worshipped the sun, and came spewing out of their boxes to greet it the moment it so much as winked at them. They strolled aimlessly, talking and laughing – to each other or alone, on phones – abandoning the heads-down march they adopted over the winter, when they'd stride with great purpose, fighting the wind and rain. And the shops were busy, doors open, inviting, whilst the mortals inside them paid homage to their other great object of worship – money. No wonder Hermes was always working. There was a time when being god of money had seemed to be a rather minor posting, quite the short straw. Lately he never stopped being in demand.

'And it's not just Jesus,' Eros was saying. 'When you think about all the dross that mortality has produced . . .'

He swept his arm, taking in the scene before them, and sighed.

'And then there are the few, few greats – and I've missed so many of them. In my field alone – would you believe I never met Casanova?'

'You mean he managed all that by himself?' Artemis shuddered.

'He was naturally talented. And Byron. Apollo was always trying to introduce me, and I was always too busy. Next thing I knew he was dead. They all die so soon. I never get used to it. They're gone in the blink of an eye. You always think there'll more time but there never is.'

'You could visit,' said Artemis. 'If you asked Persephone, she might take you down there.'

'Have you ever been?' said Eros.

'No,' said Artemis. She felt cold suddenly. 'Have you?'

Eros shook his head. 'I wonder . . .' he said. 'I wonder what it would be like to be dead.'

Artemis stopped walking. She felt an unfamiliar sensation in her chest – a tightness and a kind of fluttering, and beneath that, a churning in her stomach. Her hands and feet tingled almost painfully, and she felt dizzy. After a few moments, she recognised the feeling as the very start of panic.

'Don't you ever think about it?' said Eros.

'Never,' said Artemis. 'What would be the point?'

'It could happen,' said Eros.

'No,' said Artemis.

'It could.'

Eros led her to the window of a shop, where a skinny plastic dummy, limbs as hard and smooth as bones dried in the sun, posed, hip jutting forward like a missile, in a two-inch ripped skirt, electric-blue fishnet tights and a sheer blouse, unbuttoned to reveal the shiny, tactile fabric of the lacy bra beneath. He didn't bother to comment.

'I keep hoping,' said Artemis.

'What about if you gave up hoping? What then?'

'It's all right for you,' said Artemis, walking away from him down the hill. 'People still fall in love. You've still got a reason to live.'

'I don't know about that,' said Eros, catching up with her. 'I don't think people are that keen on love any more – real love, the complicated stuff. They like romance and sex – sorry – and when that runs out it all looks a bit too much like responsibility and then they quit.'

'So what are you saying?'

'I'm saying that they don't need us any more. They don't want us. They're forgetting about us.'

'I know all that.'

'And our power won't last for ever . . .'

'I need to sit down,' said Artemis.

'Sorry,' said Eros. 'How about this bench? We can smell the pancake van from here.'

Eros took her arm and sat her down. Artemis breathed deeply, and after a few moments she began to enjoy the scent of bubbling butter and melting sugar. She wondered what it would taste like, how it would feel in her mouth, going down her throat. Would it really do her so much harm to try?

'Maybe,' said Eros, 'it wouldn't be so bad.'

'Eating?' said Artemis.

'Dying.'

'I don't want to talk about this any more.'

'Listen, though. Just imagine it. The peace of it. Being somewhere else. Away from all this. Not having to be responsible for anything.'

'But you're the one who's always being extra responsible, for fun.'

'That doesn't mean I don't get tired.'

'I can't imagine not being responsible,' said Artemis, 'not being in charge. It's all I've ever done. It's all you've ever done. Don't tell me you think you'd rather be dead.'

Eros squinted up the road into the sunlight for a few moments without replying.

'If you knew you only had a hundred years to live,' he said eventually, 'what would you do with the time you had left?'

In the street in front of them, a car rear-ended another, and the two drivers got out and started shouting at each other, as all the cars behind them hooted their horns, in no way speeding up matters, but making the waiting much less pleasant for everyone involved.

'I would move out,' said Artemis.

Thirteen

Two weeks after Alice had started her new job, Neil took her out for a celebratory cup of tea. He chose a cosy little café he hoped she would like, small and low-ceilinged with kettle steam on the windows, quiet enough so that she wouldn't feel over-whelmed, but just noisy enough so that she wouldn't feel self-conscious that her voice could be overheard by the next table. He arrived early, chose a seat near the back, so that Alice wouldn't have passers-by looking in at her, ordered a coffee and settled down with the *Telegraph* crossword to wait for her.

He didn't realise how much time had passed and was engrossed in a particularly tricky anagram when her soft voice saying hello made his heart leap. He jumped to his feet to greet her, nearly knocking his coffee over when he leant across the table to kiss her five millimetres from her cheek.

'How are you?' he said. 'Did you find it OK? I hope you didn't have to travel too far.'

'Oh no, it was easy,' said Alice, taking the seat opposite and pulling off her bobble hat. 'Crustacean.'

'Sorry?'

'Scarce Tuna? Crustacean.' She pointed at his anagram.

'Right,' said Neil.

'It's probably easier upside down.'

'What do you want to drink?' said Neil. 'Do you want a cake?'

'I don't know,' said Alice. 'Are you going to have any?'

'We could share some,' suggested Neil.

'Ooh,' said Alice. Her hair was tied back and Neil noticed that when she went pink it travelled all the way up her neck to her ears. 'That would be lovely,' she said.

The waitress came over and Neil ordered a cup of tea for Alice, and a slice of cheesecake with two spoons.

'So how's the job going?' said Neil.

'Oh, it's fine,' said Alice.

'What are the people like?' said Neil. 'Are they nice to you?' Alice hesitated.

'I don't know,' she said.

'What do you mean you don't know?'

'It's hard to tell. I'm sure they are being nice, in their own way.'

'What do you mean?' said Neil.

'Well, with some people, it's easy to tell when they're being nice,' said Alice. 'Like you, Neil. You're nice all the time. You think about people and what they might like and then you do it and that's nice. I mean, I don't want you to think that— I'm just saying that— that's how it seems to me . . .'

Alice suddenly appeared to be much more interested in looking at a small burn hole in the chintz tablecloth than in looking at him.

'And they?' prompted Neil.

'I'm sure they don't mean anything by it,' said Alice, 'but they don't really, um, notice other people like most people do. So when they're nice, it's sort of by accident.'

'That doesn't sound great,' said Neil.

'Oh no,' said Alice. 'They're fine, really. I don't want to be mean . . .'

Alice stopped talking as the waitress arrived with the tea and cake. When the waitress had gone, she resumed.

'I think they do their best,' she concluded.

'So you haven't told me very much about them,' said Neil. 'Who lives there? Is it a family? Flatmates?'

Alice hesitated again.

'I'm not really supposed to talk about it,' she said.

'What do you mean?' said Neil.

'I can't tell you.'

'Why not?' said Neil.

'I don't know. I'm not supposed to talk about not being able to talk about it.'

'Can't you tell me anything?'

'No. Nothing.'

'But no one will know,' said Neil.

'I don't want to get into trouble,' said Alice, looking away.

'I'm sorry,' said Neil. 'You don't have to tell me anything. It has nothing to do with me. I'm sure I wouldn't find it very interesting anyway.'

Alice didn't reply.

'Not that I don't find you interesting,' said Neil. 'That's not what I meant. I just meant . . . it's none of my business.'

Still no answer. Neil wished he'd never raised the subject. He hoped she wouldn't leave.

'Just forget about it,' he said. 'Please. I'm sorry I mentioned it. Why don't we have a game of Scrabble? I've got my Palm Pilot. We could finish that game we played on the day we went to the TV show. I've got it saved.'

To his dismay, this suggestion seemed to upset Alice even more, and she fidgeted in her seat, red-faced. Of course: he shouldn't have mentioned that day, the day he had got her sacked.

'I'm sorry –' Neil began.

'Apollo lives there,' Alice blurted out.

'What?' said Neil. 'Apollo? Apollo from the TV show? Where?'

He squinted out across the room towards the street, half expecting to see him sauntering along the pavement, with his perfect body and his perfect face and his perfect sodding hair.

'In the house,' said Alice. 'The house where I work. I'm not supposed to say anything but it felt like I was lying when I didn't.'

'You clean Apollo's house? You work for Apollo?'

'Lots of people live there,' said Alice. 'He's one of them.'

'You work for Apollo,' said Neil again.

'Why?' said Alice. 'What's the matter?'

'It's just he didn't strike me as very, you know, honest.'

'That's his job,' said Alice.

'Even so,' said Neil. 'It does reflect on him as a person.'

'But I thought you liked that kind of thing. The programme, I mean.'

'Of course I do. It's just, well, I thought he was more dishonest than most of the presenters I've seen. He's shifty. And arrogant. And I'd rather you weren't working for someone like that.'

'It's kind of you to be concerned, Neil,' said Alice, 'but there's nothing for you to worry about, I promise. He's really very sweet, and he's always been very nice to me.'

'I thought you said none of them were nice.'

'He's the nicest.'

'You're too trusting,' said Neil. 'You have to look beyond the façade.'

'I think he's just misunderstood,' said Alice. 'I'm sure you'd like him if you met him.'

'I'm sure I wouldn't,' said Neil. 'Who lives there with him? His wife? His children?'

'I can't really say,' said Alice.

'You've told me he lives there now, you may as well say with whom.'

Alice shook her head.

'Tell me if he's married at least.'

'I don't think he's married,' said Alice. 'I'm sorry. I can't say anything else. I shouldn't have said anything at all. Can we play that game of Scrabble now?'

Neil got out his Palm Pilot and set up a new game but all he could see was Apollo's smug face, and all he could hear was Alice's voice: *He's really very sweet. He's the nicest. I think he's just misunderstood*. He hadn't forgotten the way Apollo had looked at Alice that day at the studio, and he didn't like this turn of events at all.

Alice, for her part, couldn't concentrate on the game. There was plenty she wanted to tell Neil about, but she couldn't. Apollo, for example. She could understand why Neil didn't like him – Neil was much more clever than she in certain ways, and he knew why pretending to be psychic was wrong, even though she couldn't quite see what was wrong with cheering up old ladies who have very little left to live for. But she had seen quite a different side to Apollo after that first, odd meeting. He would follow her around the house as she cleaned, telling her all about himself, or sometimes singing her songs (which were very good, really), which he'd composed on his guitar. At first, it was true, she had found this deeply disconcerting, and worried about how to respond. But her being tongue-tied didn't seem to bother Apollo, he just carried on regardless. It was quite sweet of him really, to keep her company like that. It was almost like having the radio on. And after a while, she began to suspect that Apollo – who was such a handsome man, and so talented and successful – was actually quite lonely, and it made her feel good to keep him company too, even if she could never think of a thing to say to him.

She would have liked to ask Neil's opinion on Aphrodite too, if only she could have. She couldn't quite figure Aphrodite out. When she was cleaning, Alice liked to keep herself to herself and to respect the privacy of her clients, but the people in this house didn't seem to have much of a concept of privacy, and so Alice sometimes saw too much. She particularly saw too much of Aphrodite, who was often to be found walking around in the nude, or having some quite unpleasant conversations on her mobile phone. And even after only two weeks it was obvious to Alice that Aphrodite was having affairs with all of the men who lived in the house, and while this was understandable, given how beautiful she was, Alice, who tried hard not to judge others, also found it distasteful.

The most unnerving thing about Aphrodite, though, was how she had reacted the first time she had come across Apollo and Alice talking (or rather, Apollo talking and Alice listening). She had stood very silent and still, studying them intensely as if she had just discovered two rare but shy animals in the forest, and then suddenly she had started screaming and shouting incoherently, kicking, punching and smashing things. Alice had burst into tears, and Apollo, who hadn't reacted at all to Aphrodite's outburst, had started as if waking up and hurriedly put an arm around her which just made her feel even worse, and she had run away and locked herself in the bathroom and wouldn't come out until Artemis came to tell her that locking herself in the bathroom was forbidden. But the next time she had seen her by herself Aphrodite had been calm and kind and had acted like nothing had happened, and Alice had almost thought she'd dreamed it, only once in a while she'd catch Aphrodite staring at her with vitriol in her eyes, particularly when she was talking to Apollo. It couldn't possibly be the case that Aphrodite was jealous of the attention Apollo was paying her; Alice was hardly a candidate for an affair with a man like that. So it must have been that Aphrodite had some kind of personality disorder, and that she should think charitably towards her, but that didn't make working in the house with her any easier, and Alice was feeling a bit guilty about that, and more than anything she would have loved Neil's advice as to what to do, but she couldn't ask for it.

So there were Apollo and Aphrodite, and Artemis – who was rather more of a hands-on boss than Alice was used to – and Eros and Hermes, both of whom looked at her with a good deal more curiosity than she was comfortable with, and Ares, who always put her in a bad mood for some reason, and Hephaestus, who was so very ugly that she felt sick every time she saw him and this made her feel like the cruellest, most shallow person alive, and she always wanted to say nice things to him so that he wouldn't realise what she was thinking, and she couldn't, because he never spoke to her first, and Dionysus, who made her nervous because he was always drunk, and the other two women, Athena and Demeter, who ignored her so completely that it was almost like noticing her – all of these people who were so perplexing and who she couldn't talk about. She tried not to judge them: they were Greek after all, and all families had their own ways. She was sure outsiders would find her family equally odd: her parents often ate cereal in the afternoons, and sometimes they would spend an entire day speaking only French, just to practise. And yet there was something about this family which filled her up, and, forbidden and unable as she was to find any way to let them out, they became like a wall inside her. And Neil was on the other side.

She looked at him over the table in the café just as he was looking back at her, and she thought she saw the beginning of suspicion in his eyes. And even as she opened her mouth to tell him all about the family – who cared about the Rules – the words seemed to die on her tongue, and even as she resolved that on Monday she would hand in her notice, she knew that she would stay there for as long as they wanted her to.

Fourteen

'So, what do you think?'

The corners of the estate agent's mouth were both pointing upwards, so Artemis assumed that he must be smiling, but she couldn't understand what there was to smile about.

'Is this it?' she said.

'No, no, of course not.'

The corners of the estate agent's mouth yanked upwards again, and he straightened his tie. Artemis noticed a line of peachy-beige foundation forming a circular stain around the collar of his shirt.

'There's the bathroom as well. Which I already showed you.'

'Was that a room?' said Artemis.

When the estate agent had unlocked the grille that shielded the front door – to protect the occupant of the flat, wondered Artemis, or the other inhabitants of the listing, draughty block? – and forced open the door itself, gouging yet more out of the black crescent scoring the peeling, patterned 'vintage' (according to the agent) linoleum, they had stumbled straight into an entrance hall that featured – was this normal for mortals? – a limescale-encrusted toilet and a mouldy, dripping shower.

'Think of it more as an atrium,' suggested the estate agent.

Artemis pulled aside the faded floral curtain on the one cracked window. Down below in the car park, she watched as a group of schoolchildren kicked a smaller child who was lying curled up on the ground in front of them, shielding its head with its hands. She dropped the curtain.

'Does the flat have any outdoor space?'

'There's the – ah – communal courtyard,' said the estate agent.

At the expression of interest on Artemis's face, he indicated the window.

'Oh,' said Artemis.

She took another look behind the curtain. One of the children had detached itself from the group and was now filming proceedings on its mobile phone.

'What about pets?' said Artemis. 'Could I have a dog?'

The estate agent glanced around the room. There was only a tiny strip of floor between the single bed, the three-legged chipped veneer wardrobe, the stainless steel sink and the almost-straight shelf that held up the microwave and the electric hotplate.

'Pets,' he confessed, 'are forbidden in the lease. The damage they cause . . . It reduces the value of the property. Although,' he added, with optimism that belied the death in his eyes, 'I'm sure you could have a goldfish without any objections. Or a budgie. So long as you kept it in its cage.'

'I'm really looking for somewhere I could keep a dog,' said Artemis. 'A big dog. Somewhere with a garden it could run around in?'

The corners of the estate agent's mouth faltered.

'I, ah,' he said. 'I fear that might be . . . on the amount of rent that you're quoting me . . . unless you were able to find a small amount more . . . I would describe it as . . .'

'Difficult?' said Artemis.

'An impossibility.'

When she got home, Artemis couldn't face the house, this place that seemed doomed to be her home, so she went straight out into the garden. Outside, she found Demeter, who as goddess of the earth and fertility naturally took care of the plants. In a wide-brimmed hat and gardening gloves, carrying a small trowel and fork, she was examining the bushes and flowers that filled the beds edging the unsatisfactory scrap of lawn.

Ignoring her, Artemis lay down on the grass and shut her eyes. It was too cold, really, to be outside, but right now this was all she could cope with. The hard points of the grass stems prickled her face like tiny needles. She breathed in. The earth smelt cold and metallic, the sun's rays still too weak to sweeten it. The grass, though, smelt fresh and wet and bright. The ground held her body. It's not so bad, here, she tried to tell herself. It's not so bad. From the house, though, she could hear the sound of raised voices, Aphrodite and Eros, having an argument, as they seemed to do with increasing frequency of late. Aphrodite, yelling. Eros, growling defensively. And then, on cue, the sound of shattering crockery. Artemis tried, with little success, to blank it out, to pretend it had nothing to do with her, but she couldn't. A wave of misery washed over her. It didn't look as if she was going to be getting her own place any time soon. She was stuck with them all. Maybe she could pitch a tent and live out here.

Suddenly Artemis heard screaming from much closer by. Her eyes were open and she was on her feet in a split second. She looked around to see who was being hurt, and whether she should defend them, or join in. It was Demeter. She was standing at the back of the garden, where a high yellow brick wall divided it from the neighbouring plot. She had her back to Artemis and, after her scream, had broken into racking, dry sobs, her shoulders heaving like the spasms of a vomiting cat. Artemis ran over.

'What happened? What's going on? Are you . . .'

Artemis couldn't finish – ill, hurt – the suggestions were terrifying, impossible.

'It's dead,' choked Demeter, turning. 'It's all dead.'

She held out her hands – she had removed the gardening gloves, and Artemis was shocked to see the deep gnarls in her ageing skin. She was holding the dry, crumbling remains of a climbing plant.

'The clematis,' Artemis recognised.

'I couldn't keep it alive. I couldn't save it.'

'But . . .'

'This is what I do. I nurture. If I can't do that . . .'

'Maybe that mortal on the other side of the wall poured weed killer on it. He's always hated us.'

'My hair's going white,' said Demeter.

'Come inside,' said Artemis. 'It'll be all right. Come inside.'

She took the dead clematis from Demeter's hands and dropped it on the ground, then put her arm around her shoulders and steered her back into the house.

'I'm dying,' sobbed Demeter. 'I'm dying.'

To her surprise, Artemis felt a little bit jealous.

Fifteen

It wasn't hard for Neil to find the house. Alice had told him where she was working when she had first got the job – it was only later on that she had become so secretive. Walking up the road towards it he didn't have to check the house numbers to know immediately which one it was. Alice had mentioned to him how dilapidated it had become, but it was worse than he had imagined. It was literally falling down – without urgent attention, he doubted it would last more than another few years. He was shocked and upset that anyone would let such a wonderful building get into such a state of disrepair. He had experienced a similar feeling only last week, looking at a recent photograph of Brigitte Bardot. So he was feeling quite indignant as he marched up the cracked, uneven steps, lifted the heavy, gleaming door knocker – it was Alice's job to polish it, no doubt – and rapped it hard, its sonorous reverberations echoing through the house. Frankly he was surprised that the lintel of the door didn't collapse from the force of it.

After a few seconds, he heard footsteps approaching and then the door creaked open halfway. He opened his mouth to introduce himself, possibly even to offer his services as an engineer, but the link between his brain and his tongue seemed to have been severed as cleanly as if someone had taken a knife to it. On the threshold before him stood the most beautiful woman, not only that he had ever seen, but that he would ever have been able to imagine. Once, years ago, he had come home from school in tears because Marissa MacKendrick had refused to kiss him, saying – and he remembered this precisely, indeed relived it often – that she would never touch an ugly, spotty, skinny-arsed spoddy minger like him if the survival of the species depended on it. His mother had taken him in her arms – and he must have been devastated, because he had let her – and told him, not only that little Miss MacKendrick was a stuck-up cow and so were her parents, but that nobody was perfect, that Marissa probably secretly hated her feet or her ears or her belly, and that one day, when gravity had taken its toll and her husband had left her for someone prettier and younger, she would realise that beauty was only skin deep and that she should never have spoken to him that way. It had been scant comfort at the time, and he had suspected even then that his mother was wrong or lying, and now here was the proof, standing in the doorway in front of him: this woman was perfect, there was no way that she hated anything about herself, except, perhaps, the view in front of her eyes right now, and in fact beauty was not 'only skin deep', sometimes it was every-thing, absolutely everything.

'Fuck off,' said the apparition, with bruising inevitability.

'I –' said Neil. 'Hello. I. Um. Hello. Is Alice? Um.'

'Alice?' said the apparition. Her face was perfectly hewn stone.

'I'm a friend of Alice's,' Neil managed to say. 'Your cleaner.'

The woman looked at him appraisingly, as if trying to calcu-late his exact weight.

'What kind of friend?' she said.

'A close friend,' said Neil. 'She's my best friend.'

'Are you in love with her?'

'I'm sorry?'

'Are you in love with her?'

There was something about this creature which made Neil give the reply that he had never given anyone, least of all himself.

'Yes,' he said.

It was as if he had cast some kind of magic spell. Like clouds lifting after a storm and revealing the blessed face of the sun, she broke into a smile, the smile to end all smiles, and Neil's face creased into an imitative grin, making him, he knew, look like an unspeakable idiot, but there was nothing to be done. But, seemingly undisgusted by his imbecility, the beauty opened the door fully, in a gesture of magnanimous welcome.

'Come in, come in! I'm Aphrodite. It's such a pleasure to meet you! Any friend of darling Alice's is a friend of mine.'

Neil stepped over the threshold into the house. He tried to imagine Alice and this Aphrodite being friends, and failed. Aphrodite, he had to admit, was the more beautiful. But Alice had more class.

'We don't,' Aphrodite said in a stage whisper as she led him down the front hall, 'usually let strangers into the house. We like to keep our privacy. But you're hardly a stranger are you? You're more like family. Let me find Alice for you. She's probably with Apollo somewhere.'

Neil followed Aphrodite up the stairs, trying to keep his eyes away from her bottom, bouncing ahead of him like two hard-boiled eggs dancing a tango. He was beginning to think that this impromptu visit was not such a good idea.

Up until the moment that he had got here, his reasoning had seemed infallible. There was something wrong with Alice. That much was obvious – it was particularly obvious to him when he was trying to work, trying to watch TV, trying to read, trying to sleep, trying to have a conversation with anyone other than Alice, or trying to have a conversation with Alice. And it had started when she began working in this house. He had no idea what the matter was but he knew that there was a matter, and he had come here to find it. What the matter might actually be – or worse, who – and how on earth he was going to do anything about it were questions that were only just entering his head right now as he trailed Aphrodite's perfect buttocks up the stairs.

'Do you know,' said Aphrodite, tossing her silky hair as she looked alluringly over her shoulder at him, 'I think they must be in Apollo's bedroom. I'm sure they won't mind us disturbing them there.'

'No,' said Neil. 'I mean yes. Let's disturb them.'

'It's just over . . .' said Aphrodite as they reached the first-floor landing, but she was interrupted by the ringing of her mobile phone. 'Oh, I'm sorry, I need to get that. There,' she finished, pointing at a door, ajar to their right. 'Hello big boy,' she breathed into the phone. 'I'm so wet. What do you want to do to me?'

Neil nearly swallowed his tongue. Aphrodite gave him a wink and a little wave, then turned her back.

'That sounds really sexy,' she resumed, into the phone.

With some effort, Neil turned away from her and walked towards the door that Aphrodite had indicated. From the other side of it, he could clearly hear two voices laughing – a male voice, and Alice. This made him feel queasy, but he forced himself to believe that at least she sounded happy and that was all that mattered. But then he heard her say, 'That's enough, please,' and the male voice say, 'Come on, just one more,' and suddenly she didn't sound that happy and he remembered why he had come. He pushed the door to the room open and strode inside, as manfully as he could.

The first thing he saw was Alice, standing at the window in a housecoat, a duster in her hand. When he saw her, he couldn't believe that only a moment ago he had been (he had to admit it) drooling (but only slightly) over Aphrodite. She was still laughing, he was relieved to see, but he could also see anxiety in her eyes and he knew that her protests were not feigned. The individual to whom those protests were directed was Apollo, wearing not a toga but jeans and a T-shirt, who was sickeningly more handsome than he remembered, and who appeared to have been taking photographs of Alice using his mobile phone. Alice, Neil knew, absolutely hated having her photograph taken.

'Leave her alone,' said Neil as loudly as he dared.

'Neil, what are you doing here?' said Alice.

'Yes, "Neil", what are you doing here?' drawled Apollo.

Neil really didn't like the way Apollo said 'Neil'.

'What are you doing taking her photograph?' said Neil.

'It's OK, Neil,' said Alice. 'I said he could.'

'She said I could,' said Apollo.

Alice had never let Neil take her photograph.

'Neil, it's really nice to see you, but . . .' Alice tailed off. 'I'm not really supposed to have friends round.'

'No, she's not allowed any "friends" round,' said Apollo.

'You didn't tell me that,' said Neil. 'I just came by . . .' He couldn't actually think of a reason. 'Would you stop repeating everything that she says?' he said to Apollo instead.

'Well, it's very nice to see you,' said Alice. 'It's very sweet of you to have come. Why don't you wait around a bit? I'm nearly finished here and then maybe we can go and have a cup of tea.'

'You heard her,' said Apollo. 'It's nice to see you. Now get lost.'

'He's just joking,' said Alice.

Apollo smiled at Neil in a way that didn't seem all that jokey.

'It's really nice that you two have met at last,' said Alice. 'Apollo, Neil is really interested in your TV programme. That's why we came to see it in the first place.'

'Is that right?' said Apollo.

'Yes,' said Neil. 'Or at least I was interested in it before I saw it.'

'I was interested in humans 'til I saw you.'

'Actually,' said Alice, 'maybe we should leave straight away. I was early this morning so I'm sure Artemis won't mind.'

'Oh, no,' said Apollo, 'please don't rush off. You've only just got here, "Neil". Stick around for a bit. I'd love for you to meet my brother. I'll just go and get him. Why don't you take a seat?'

Apollo left the room and shut the door behind him. Neil refused to sit.

'We should go,' he said. 'Don't you think it's a bit odd that he wants me to meet his brother?'

'I think it's just his way of being friendly,' said Alice. 'He is a little bit, um, unconventional, but he's really very kind underneath it all. Anyway we can't go now when we said we'd stay. Let's wait 'til he gets back, then we can leave.'

'OK,' said Neil, 'but as soon as he gets back I'm going.'

Still feeling tense, Neil looked around, not entirely convinced that the room wasn't bugged or booby-trapped. It was a shared bedroom, divided unofficially but decisively down the middle, each side with its own rickety single bed and tipsy wardrobe. The side of the room he was standing in was marked by a small potted bay tree and several musical instruments on stands – all variations on guitars and harps, many of which seemed to be antiques. The pictures on this side of the room were reproductions of Renaissance paintings – or at least, he assumed they were reproductions – mostly consisting of representations of Greek mythology and the god – but of course, he was that arrogant – Apollo.

The other side of the room was quite different. While the bed he was standing by had been made in haste, the other one's khaki bedspread had been straightened with great precision, not a crease on it. The walls displayed an extraordinary collection of army memorabilia, with every possible space taken up with uniforms, flags, medals, replica firearms – he hoped they were replicas – and maps and charts of famous military campaigns.

'Which side of the room is Apollo's?' he said.

'This side,' said Alice.

'So the guns belong to his brother?'

'Ares, yes,' said Alice.

'I think we should go right now,' said Neil, 'before we get shot.'

'Oh, Neil,' said Alice, 'you're so funny.'

The door to the room opened again and Apollo came in with a tall, muscular, shaven-headed man with a face like a bullet.

'"Neil",' said Apollo. 'Meet my brother, Ares.'

'Hi,' shrugged Neil.

'What do you want me to meet him for?' said Ares to Apollo. 'I'm busy. There's a skirmish in South East Asia that I need to escalate.'

'It'll just take a few minutes,' said Apollo. 'If you stay, I promise I'll polish your medal collection for you for ten years.'

'Fine. What do you want me to do?'

'Nothing,' said Apollo, 'just wait here.'

'Well,' said Neil, 'it was nice meeting you, you've both been more than welcoming, but we really must be going.'

'Why?' said Alice. 'Because you said so?'

'But I thought you wanted to go,' said Neil.

'You didn't think,' said Alice. 'You just assumed.'

Apollo smiled at Ares, who rolled his eyes.

'Oh, I get it,' he said.

Ares slouched over to the wall by the window in his half of the room and squatted down on the ground, took a huge knife from his belt and started picking the dirt from under his finger-nails. Apollo sat down on Ares' bed with his hands on his knees and grinned over at Neil.

'What are you looking at?' said Neil.

'Don't talk to him like that,' said Alice. 'You're in his house. You should treat him with respect.'

'Respect? You are joking, right? Why on earth should I respect him?'

'Everybody deserves respect, actually,' said Alice. 'Though I wouldn't expect you to understand that. You're the most cynical man I've ever met.'

'I'd rather be cynical than believe everything anyone ever tells me. There's nothing clever about being gullible just to be nice,' said Neil.

'What's that supposed to mean?' said Alice.

Neil wasn't sure what it was supposed to mean. He just knew that it suddenly felt very important to say everything he could to make Alice feel small.

'It's not surprising,' he said, 'that you'd take his side, seeing as he likes to manipulate the vulnerable and weak.'

'Who are you calling vulnerable?' said Alice. 'I'm surprised you can even spell the word.'

'Oh don't start attacking my intellect,' said Neil, 'just because you're good at board games. At least I've got a proper job and don't just stand around hoovering and flirting all day.'

'Flirting!' said Alice. 'I wasn't flirting! I never flirt!'

'You were flirting with him!' said Neil, pointing at Apollo.

'I was not!' said Alice.

'Were too! Don't deny it! I can see you blushing!'

And indeed that tedious tide of redness was yet again rushing up Alice's neck and flushing her face. She looked ugly, he thought, wattled, like a turkey.

'Anyway it's none of your business,' said Alice. 'What are you even doing here? You can't just turn up at my place of work and start insulting my clients! Who do you think you are?'

Alice was actually shouting now. Neil had never heard her shout, not ever. It had not been worth waiting for.

'Actually,' said Neil, waggling his head, 'I think you'll find that that poncy, self-important idiot is not, in fact, your client, but your boss.'

'Well, even more to the point, then,' Alice waggled her head too. It was incredibly annoying when she did it. 'I'd never come round to where you work and be rude to anybody there, whether it was your client or your boss.'

'You wouldn't be able to,' said Neil. 'They took your security pass away when you stopped cleaning my office.'

Alice reeled back as if she had been slapped.

'So is that what this is all about then?' she said.

'Is what what this is all about?' said Neil.

'You look down on me because of my job,' said Alice. 'No wonder you've never made a pass at me. You're too scared of getting your hands dirty.'

'That's not true,' said Neil.

'Yes it is,' said Alice. 'You do. You look down on me.' Alice sounded more sad than angry.

'I do not look down on you,' said Neil more gently.

'Yes you do. You think your work is so much more important than mine, because you're a clever engineer and I'm just a cleaner.'

'Don't think that, Alice,' said Neil. 'Never think that. I have so much respect for you and for what you do. I couldn't do it. Really.'

Alice half smiled. Apollo shot a desperate look over at Ares, who nodded, and shifted slightly on his feet.

'Although,' said Neil, feeling his anger return to him in a burst, 'when I say that I couldn't do your job, obviously technically I could, I just couldn't face actually doing it. You couldn't do my job, we both know that. It takes years of careful training. What kind of training do you need to wield a toilet brush?'

Alice was speechless so Neil took the opportunity to press home his advantage.

'But just because you don't have any education,' he said, 'doesn't mean you need to bolster your self-esteem by flirting with the likes of him.'

Alice's jaw actually dropped as he spoke. Seeing this, Neil felt a peculiar stab of achievement. Beat that!

'Well thank you for your comments,' said Alice. Rage had definitely returned to replace sadness in her tone. 'I'm not feeling at all patronised now. But just so you know, I do actually have an education. A university education as it happens. I have a first class degree in linguistics. I happen to clean because I like cleaning.

It gives me time to think. Something that you, apparently, choose not to do, most of the time.'

Something inside Neil grabbed his stomach and squeezed. He knew a lost argument when he saw one.

'I think it's time for you to go,' said Alice.

'I don't want to go,' said Neil.

'Too bad,' said Alice. 'I want you to go. And don't call me. I'll call you. Maybe.'

Neil realised that Alice, Apollo and Ares were all staring at him, Alice in fury, Apollo in glee, and Ares with a look, oddly, of quiet satisfaction.

'Right,' said Neil. 'I'll be off then. Lovely to meet you all.'

'Goodbye,' said Alice firmly.

So that was the last he'd be seeing of her then. Good riddance. He had no idea what he ever saw in her in the first place.

And that feeling lasted all the way out of the room, down the stairs and out of the front door, until the moment that it slammed behind him and he suddenly found himself standing alone on the cold, hard pavement, and he burst into tears, wondering what in God's name had just happened to him.

Sixteen

Upstairs in Apollo's room they heard the front door slam. A small cloud of plaster fell from the ceiling.

'Well if you don't mind, I'll be off too,' said Ares, standing up and making his way to the door.

Apollo followed him out.

'Thanks, Bro,' he said.

'Actually it was quite fun,' said Ares.

'Oh, by the way, I was lying about the medals.'

'What?'

'I'm not going to polish them. You didn't make me swear on Styx. See you later.'

'You're a rancid little shit,' said Ares, but he didn't sound too angry as he sauntered down the stairs.

Apollo went back into the bedroom. Much to his delight, Alice had sat down on the bed, and was crying. Apollo sat next to her and put his arm around her shoulders. This time she didn't run away to the bathroom. Still, he had to time this carefully. He told his erection to wait.

'There, there,' he said. 'He's not worth it.'

'I don't understand,' Alice wept. 'I don't know what just happened. Who were those people? That wasn't Neil. That wasn't me. I never argue with anyone.'

Apollo was mesmerised by the water coming out of her eyes. Tears were a mortal thing; gods produce nothing when they cry. He reached a finger over and touched one of the wet trails snaking down her face. Alice flinched away.

'Sorry,' Apollo said. Slow down, he told himself. 'I'll get you a tissue,' he said. He looked around. 'Though I don't know if we've got any.'

'I've got some downstairs in my bag,' said Alice.

'I'll get it for you.'

'Thank you,' said Alice. 'You're being very sweet.'

Though he didn't like leaving her side, Apollo went down-stairs and quickly found Alice's handbag, alongside her coat, which he rubbed against his face and body, relishing the smell of her. He slung the bag over his shoulder and headed back towards the stairs, thought better of it, and went into the kitchen instead.

Sitting on the bed in Apollo and Ares' room, Alice wiped her nose on the back of her hand, took a deep, trembling breath, and told herself firmly to stop crying. She tried to piece together what had happened, but none of it made any sense. She had been in a normal, cheerful mood. Apollo had been all over-excited about his new phone and she hadn't discouraged him, not really. Maybe that was her fault. She examined her conscience: had she been flirting? No. She knew she hadn't. Then Neil had arrived, out of the blue, and she had been pleased to see him – she was always pleased to see him; though a little self-conscious that she was grubby, and wearing a housecoat, and stank of bleach, which was exactly the state she didn't want him seeing her in, in case he thought less of her . . . Which of course was a silly thing to think, because that was how they had met, so how could he think less of her? Only wasn't that exactly what had happened, what their argument had proved?

The door to the bedroom opened and Apollo came in carrying her handbag and two glasses of wine. He put the bag on the floor and sat down beside her on the bed.

'Here you go,' he said, holding out one of the glasses. 'I thought you might need this.'

'Oh no,' said Alice, 'I couldn't possibly. I don't really drink alcohol and it's terribly early.'

'Go on,' said Apollo. 'Just a little bit. It'll do you some good, I promise. And Dionysus will be horribly upset if you don't. He makes it himself.'

'Really?' said Alice. 'I thought he was a disc jockey.'

'DJ, viniculturist, clubbing entrepreneur . . .'

Apollo proffered the glass again and this time she took it. She had a little sip.

'Oh dear,' she said, 'that's very strong.'

'I don't think it is,' said Apollo. 'We drink it all the time.'

'Oh well,' said Alice. 'I suppose I'm just not used to it.'

She drank a little bit more. Apollo reached down to the bag at his feet, opened it, got out the tissues and handed them over.

'There you are,' said Apollo.

Alice took a tissue out of the packet and blew her nose, embarrassingly loudly.

'Sorry,' she said.

'That's OK,' said Apollo. 'Go on, have a good old blow.'

Alice did as she was told and then folded the tissue and put it up her sleeve.

'Feeling any better?' said Apollo.

'A little,' said Alice.

She took another sip of the wine. It seemed to be going to her head already, but she was probably just dizzy from all that crying.

'I'm very sorry for how I behaved,' said Alice.

'You don't need to apologise,' said Apollo. 'I don't think you did anything wrong.'

'Oh but I did,' said Alice. 'You see, I'm just not like that. Not like that at all. Poor Neil! I do hope I haven't hurt his feelings too much.'

At the thought of it, Alice could feel herself begin to get tearful again, and she drank a bit more wine to steady herself.

'If you did, it's only what he deserves,' said Apollo.

'Don't say that,' said Alice. 'He's really a very nice man and he really cares about me.'

'He didn't sound very nice to me,' said Apollo. 'He didn't sound like he cared very much about you either.'

'Well, no,' said Alice. 'I suppose not. Not just then. Something must be wrong. I do hope he's OK.'

'You worry about other people too much. You should worry about yourself.'

'Oh no,' said Alice. 'No, no, really, not at all.'

She squirmed in embarrassment and as she did, her knee brushed against Apollo's on the bed beside her. The touch gave her a little shock – a pleasant shock. She drank a bit more of the wine. It was very more-ish; she had no idea that Dionysus was so accomplished.

'We've been friends for quite a long time now,' Alice explained, 'Neil and I, and I just think I owe him the benefit of the doubt, because really he's not usually like that. He's never spoken to me crossly before, never. Oh, except –'

She broke off, confused.

'Except what?' Apollo prompted, letting his hand rest on her arm for a moment.

'Well, last time we met up he seemed a bit funny – just not like himself. He wanted to know all about the house, this house, and I couldn't tell him, you see, and then he got a bit . . .'

'A bit what?'

'Just a bit funny.'

'Well,' said Apollo, 'I didn't find him very funny just now.'

'No,' said Alice. 'No, I don't suppose he was.'

Alice's head felt cloudy and she shook it to try to clear it.

'Dear me,' said Apollo, 'you've finished your wine. Here, why don't you have mine.'

Apollo held out his untouched wine glass and exchanged it for Alice's empty one. As he took her glass their fingers brushed against each other and she felt herself shiver. This didn't seem quite right. She blinked, had another drink. Then she thought for a few moments about the argument, replaying it in her head. It was no better for the remembering.

'Oh!' she said suddenly. 'I'm so, so sorry. I haven't even apologised to you for the things he said to you, those terrible, rude things! I am so sorry that he spoke to you like that.'

'You don't need to apologise to me,' said Apollo. 'He's not a family member, is he? He's not your boyfriend.'

'No . . .'

'So what he says is nothing to do with you. It doesn't reflect on you at all. In fact I should be thanking you, for defending me.'

'Oh no,' said Alice. 'Not at all. I hardly defended you . . . I should have defended you more. You haven't done a thing wrong. The things he was saying . . . Accusing us of flirting. As if we were flirting. We aren't flirting . . . are we?'

Alice looked up at him with the question, and at that moment the wine glass was removed from her hand and she found herself being kissed.

'Oh,' she said, as Apollo moved his lips from her mouth to her neck. 'I suppose we are.'

It wasn't as if Alice had never had sex before. She'd had a boyfriend back at university, a scientist who talked a lot and assumed that she wanted him to make all of the decisions for them both. In three years she didn't think he'd asked her a single question. The relationship had ended when he'd got a job in America and assumed that she was coming with him. It was only when she arrived at the airport without any luggage that he had started to suspect, and then all she'd had to do was to point out that she didn't have a ticket, wave him through the departure gate and say goodbye. She hadn't heard from him since.

And there was absolutely no reason why she shouldn't have sex with Apollo. She was a single, independent woman with no ties. He was, undeniably, an attractive man, and his hand running up the seam of her jeans inside her thigh felt very good. She lay back on the bed, let her legs slide open, put up no resistance as he undid the buttons down the front of her housecoat, reached round behind her back and unclipped her bra (white cotton, no underwiring, *Next* catalogue). But as his head bowed down and the tip of his tongue touched her nipple, a vision of Neil popped into her head and she shot backwards off the bed away from Apollo, her knee smacking hard into his jaw as she passed.

'I'm sorry!' she cried, holding the sides of her housedress together. 'I'm so sorry, Apollo. Are you OK? I didn't mean to hurt you. Oh, I am sorry. But I can't do this. I have to go.'

'But you can't go!' said Apollo. He was sitting up on the bed, rubbing his chin, his trousers absurdly undone. 'I love you!'

'Oh dear,' said Alice. 'I'm sorry. Do you? I'm really sorry about that. But the thing is, I don't love you.'

'Yes you do,' said Apollo. 'You have to. Didn't you hear what I said? I love you.'

'Yes,' said Alice, 'I'm sorry, I did hear. But the thing is it has to be both people who love each other. I really should go home.'

Alice quickly did her housecoat up, her undone bra flapping against her sides, and took a step towards her bag. Apollo grabbed it and hugged it to him.

'Oh,' said Alice. 'Apollo. Could I have my bag please?'

'No,' said Apollo.

'Please,' said Alice. 'I really need it to go home.'

'No,' said Apollo again. 'You're not going home.'

'Well, no, I think I am going to go home now, Apollo,' said Alice. 'I'm very sorry. If you won't give me my bag I'm going to go anyway. But I'd rather have my bag please.'

'No.'

'OK,' said Alice. 'Goodbye, Apollo. I really am very sorry, but

I'm sure once you sleep on it you'll realise that it's for the best.'

Alice walked towards the door, but Apollo leapt up and grabbed her waist from behind.

'You can't leave,' he said. 'I forbid you!'

'Please let go,' said Alice.

Apollo just gripped tighter.

'You're hurting me!' said Alice.

Instantly, Apollo's hands flew off her as if she had given him an electric shock. He staggered back a pace, then lifted one hand and stared at it as if he had never seen it before.

'Oh dear,' said Alice. 'Are you all right?'

'Sorry,' said Apollo. 'I didn't mean to harm you.'

He lowered his hand and looked at her with some kind of indecision.

'Goodbye,' said Alice again and took another step towards the door.

'You can't leave,' said Apollo. 'Please. I'm in love with you.'

'The thing is, I love . . . somebody else,' said Alice.

Apollo threw himself between her and the door.

'I'm not going to let you go,' he said.

'I'm sorry, but you can't stop me,' said Alice.

Apollo refused to move, so she was forced to try to prise him away from the door, but her small body was no match for his muscular frame. She pulled with all her strength but nothing happened. Apollo grabbed at her shoulder, but again, his hand flew back as if it had been stung.

'Damn it!' shouted Apollo.

'Please let me past,' said Alice.

'Can I just ask you something first?' said Apollo.

'Of course,' said Alice.

'Does rape constitute harm?'

Alice's blood turned to ice. She was paralysed, instantly, with fear.

'Well, does it?'

'What?' Alice managed to croak.

She tried to figure out which way to run. The door was the only way out of the room; the window was too high to jump from.

'I'd like to rape you, but would that cause you harm?'

Apollo seemed genuinely interested in the answer.

'Yes,' Alice managed to reply.

She willed her limbs to move. She did not want to die here.

'Oh,' said Apollo. 'Is that why they made it illegal?'

'Yes,' she said again.

'Oh, right,' said Apollo. 'And you're not going to consent to sex?'

'No,' said Alice, a little more strongly this time.

'Well, in that case you'd better go then.'

'I can go?'

'Don't forget your bag.'

When the phone rang, Neil was in his den, playing the kind of computer game that involves committing acts of obscene violence on undeserving aliens, and he was losing.

'What is it?' he barked.

'It's me,' came the voice, wavering at the other end. 'It's Alice. I'm sorry. Can you forgive me?'

'Of course I can,' said Neil. 'I'm sorry too. You know I am. Please don't be so upset.'

On screen, an alien administered the last rites, but Neil didn't notice.

'It isn't that . . .' said Alice.

'What is it?' said Neil. 'What's happened?'

'I can't tell you,' said Alice. 'Can I come over? I'm too scared to go home by myself.'

'Too scared?' said Neil. 'What's going on?'

'Please don't ask me,' said Alice. 'It's all my own fault anyway.

Please can I come over, Neil? I don't have anywhere else to go. I can't stay by myself tonight. Please.'

'Of course you can. You don't have to ask. You're welcome whenever you like, you know that.'

'Thank you . . . You shouldn't be so nice to me . . . Thank you . . .'

After he had calmed her and put down the phone, Neil changed the sheets on his bed and then made up a bed on the sofa for himself, struggling with mixed feelings that he wasn't entirely proud of. Alice was upset, so he was upset. Alice was frightened, so he was frightened. And Alice had turned to him for help, and that was the best news he'd had in weeks.

Seventeen

Apollo, meanwhile, decided that the only possible response to Alice's cruel rejection of him was to get drunk. He started drinking at home, in his bedroom, huge slugs of Dionysus' wine out of Alice's glass, which still tasted of her mouth. But then Ares came along and asked him how it had all gone, and Apollo, who didn't like looking weak, and particularly didn't like looking weak in front of war-loving Ares, and even more so when Ares had helped set up the situation in the first place, gave a noncommittal answer and went downstairs.

This was even worse. When he went into the living room, Athena was practising a presentation in front of an appreciative audience of empty chairs, and before he could sneak away she grabbed his arm and asked whether she could count on his '. . . prompt attendance at tomorrow's assembly? Your presence,' she stressed, 'is critical.'

'Yeah,' said Apollo, detaching himself, and went to the kitchen in the hope that nobody would be there.

Unfortunately Aphrodite was at the table, sniffing a bacon sandwich and talking filth into her phone. When she saw Apollo come in, she immediately put the hapless caller on hold and looked up at him with a disturbingly knowing expression.

'The cleaner left in quite a hurry,' she said, a sparkle in her far from innocent eye. 'I do hope nothing was wrong?'

'Nothing at all,' said Apollo.

'I thought that Neil was terribly nice. Didn't you?'

'I'm going out,' said Apollo.

Her laughter followed him down the hall and into the street.

Dionysus' nightclub, *Bacchanalia*, was located in a basement down a poorly-lit side street, popular with prostitutes and junkies, somewhere between Euston and King's Cross. It was a dingy, shabby hole, sweaty and cramped, painted an unwelcoming shade of purple and stinking of stale cigarettes and sour booze. That it was able to survive was testament to the combined pulling power of Dionysus' wine, legendary for its potency amongst bohemian alcoholics, and the still-more legendary floorshows that unfolded on the mirrored stage behind the tiny dance floor. In fact, together these proved such a draw that the club was sold out every night, and – given the cheapness of the rent – should therefore have been wildly in profit, but so much cash went into bribing the police and, when that was unsuccessful, fighting court orders and reapplying for licences, that Dionysus barely made any money from it at all.

It was early when Apollo got there, not even fully dark yet, but the queue was already beginning to tail back along the street. Wrapped in a long coat, head down, hands plunged deep in his pockets, Apollo didn't even bother to admire the clientele – women dressed like Warhol-era New York whores, and sharp-suited, sharper-coiffured men in eyeliner – waiting in multi-sexual combinations of pairs and threesomes. Ignoring them all, he marched straight to the front of the queue, where two cold, bored maenads – followers of Dionysus since the dawn of time – stood, wearing little other than a few vine leaves and scraps of fur, holding clipboards and sorting through the crowd, turning away the insufficiently hip.

'Is he in?' he said.

'Who?' said one of the maenads.

'Don't act the idiot,' said Apollo, 'or I'll button your lip. Permanently. You're not mortal. I can still do that at least.'

The maenad, who had the kind of loathing for Apollo that could only come from having slept with him on a regular basis, clenched her teeth and looked at the ground.

'He'll be behind the bar,' said the other maenad. 'Go on in.'

She unhooked the tatty purple velvet rope that crossed the door, allowing Apollo to slip past before she swiftly hooked it up again, paying no attention to the cries of desperate wannabe punters, insisting they were with him.

Apollo went down the narrow stairs, past the small ticket booth, staffed by a heavily-tattooed hermaphrodite who sometimes performed when other acts called in sick, and into the club itself. On the stage were a trio of dwarf contortionists, doing something that would upset Artemis deeply were she ever to witness it. In front of them, a group of girls, including two current faces of top-selling perfumes and an up-and-coming Hollywood actress were dancing together in elaborately-feigned lasciviousness. They were coolly being observed by the rest of the growing crowd, clustered at the bar or seated at rickety round tables on the edge of the dance floor. From these Apollo recognised the editor of a tabloid newspaper, a top-end hotelier and four minor deities.

Apollo walked over to the bar, the filth of the floor sticking to the soles of his shoes. Dionysus hadn't seen him come in. He was busy restocking the bar with bottles of his wine – the club sold nothing else.

'Hello, Bro,' said Apollo.

Dionysus turned.

'Apollo. You look like shit,' he said.

Without waiting to be asked, he uncorked a bottle and poured out a tall glass.

'Quiet night,' commented Apollo.

'It'll pick up,' said Dionysus. 'What can I do for you?'

'I want to get shit-faced and fuck someone. Preferably several people,' said Apollo.

'The usual, then,' said Dionysus.

'I wish it was,' said Apollo.

Dionysus looked sharply at Apollo. If, as he suspected, he was going to have to endure Apollo banging on, yet again, about the appalling unfairness of his existence, he was going to need liquid assistance. After only a second's thought, he decided to dispense with glasses entirely, and started lining up bottles on the bar between him and his brother.

'It's a girl,' said Apollo, once he had started his second bottle.

'A girl?' said Dionysus. He was surprised. It wasn't like Apollo to get emotional over a mortal.

'The most beautiful, amazing, incredible girl in the world,' said Apollo.

'Right,' said Dionysus.

'The fucking bitch whore,' said Apollo.

'Right,' said Dionysus again.

Apollo swigged back a quarter of the bottle of Dionysus' strongest wine in one swallow. He muttered something inaudible into his chest. Dionysus gazed over his shoulder at the stage, where a lithe, shining, nude black man was currently inserting his big toe into his nose.

'Her name's Alice,' said Apollo. 'Isn't that the most wonderful name you ever heard in your life? Alice. Are you listening to me?'

Dionysus snapped his eyes back to Apollo's face.

'Of course I am,' he said. 'Alice. Wonderful name. Yes.'

'I really thought she was the one, you know?' said Apollo. 'The one. I was ready to settle down . . . Me. For a few decades at least, 'til she died. I really thought she loved me. But now I realise that I was just her fool.'

'Mortal women can be like that,' agreed Dionysus. He hoped that this wasn't going to go on for long.

'You're supposed to tell me that I'm not a fool,' said Apollo.

'Oh. Sorry. You're not a fool,' said Dionysus. But you are incredibly boring, he added, silently.

'Bitches. All of them,' said Apollo, returning to his theme.

'I'll drink to that,' said Dionysus.

He uncorked another bottle.

'Alice ...' he mused. 'You know, I think I know somebody called Alice.'

'You do,' said Apollo. 'She cleans our house.'

'Oh, yeah, that's it,' said Dionysus. 'So where did you meet yours, then?'

'No,' said Apollo. 'That's it. That's her.'

'That's her? That's your Alice? The cleaner?'

Dionysus was delighted. This was turning out to be interesting after all.

'You're in love with the cleaner?'

'Don't be such a snob,' snapped Apollo. 'You're half mortal, remember? You're hardly in a position to be making social judgements.'

'Whatever you say,' said Dionysus. 'So what happened? Don't tell me she turned you down.'

Apollo downed the entire bottle before replying.

'She turned me down,' he said, eventually.

Dionysus stifled a laugh.

'The cleaner turned you down?' he said.

'That's what I said,' said Apollo.

'When did that happen?'

'This afternoon,' said Apollo. 'Tonight should have been the most amazing night of my life. At last I'd met her: the one. The one who was going to make all the difference. The one who was going to mean everything to me. And I would have done anything for her, Dion. I would have moved the world. I swear it. But she just led me on ... the bitch. She led me on and then she dropped me like a stone. No, not like a stone. Like a greased fish. That was how desperate she was to be rid of me.'

'The cleaner turned you down,' confirmed Dionysus.

'And I can't even kill her,' complained Apollo.

'And that's what you want to do, is it?' said Dionysus. 'Kill her?'

It was a funny definition of love, in his opinion, but he knew better than to mention this.

'She shamed me.'

Dionysus contorted his face into agreement.

'And she's got this thing . . .'

'Thing?' said Dionysus. 'Like a deformity?'

'Sort of. His name's Neil. Looks like the skeleton of a leaf.'

'A boyfriend, you mean?' said Dionysus.

'Not exactly, but close enough,' said Apollo. He sighed. 'The evil, manipulative witch . . . I'll never meet anyone else like her.'

He took a long, sorrowful drink from the latest bottle in front of him.

'So why can't you kill her?' said Dionysus.

'I made,' said Apollo, 'some stupid vow. On Styx.'

'Oh,' said Dionysus. 'I can see how that would make things difficult.'

'Bloody Artemis interfering again,' said Apollo.

'She does that,' agreed Dionysus.

On the stage behind Apollo, they were bringing out the crabs. People would start fainting soon. Time to wrap up the conversation.

'Never mind, eh?' he said to Apollo, in a brighter tone, suggesting, he hoped, finality. 'Maybe you'll strike lucky.'

'How's that?' said Apollo.

'Maybe she'll die anyway.'

As Dionysus picked up the empty bottles and walked away, Apollo wondered whether to take his comment just as an observation, or as a piece of helpful advice.

Eighteen

Apollo awoke on the floor of the deserted club. That he had been asleep at all was, in itself, a bad sign. That his head felt like someone was standing on it, wearing hobnailed boots, was even worse. Pain was a new and deeply unwelcome arrival in his physical repertoire. Aside from the obvious discomfort, there was also a certain unpleasant irony to experiencing pain: he could use his power to get rid of it, but in doing so, he would weaken himself, thus becoming more susceptible to further pain in future. Standing up groggily, peeling a flyer from his face and picking the cigarette butts off his rumpled, wine-stained clothes, he decided on a compromise, and reduced the agony to merely an insistent, irritating throb, which suited his mood perfectly. Scrabbling around on the floor of the club, he found enough loose change to pay for a bus ride home – he knew from past experience that Dionysus would already have banked the cash from the till, so there was no point looking there.

At the bus stop, the gathered mortals – mothers with kids, pensioners with tartan shopping trolleys, and a clutch of commuters in suits who obviously believed themselves to be wholly superior to the others – all kept their distance from Apollo, huddling together at the far end of the stand and taking no care to hide the disapproval and disgust on their faces. I could kill you all, thought Apollo, with a click of my fingers. I could turn you into nasturtiums, or worms, or yesterday's papers. I could flay you alive, make your eyeballs boil in their sockets, rearrange your internal organs so that your guts were in your mouths and you were shitting out of your armpits. Or at least I could have. Once. Before Artemis had her little bit of fun.

When the bus finally came, the mortals clambered on one by one, but the driver, who had seemed passive-faced and half-asleep, managed to shut the doors before Apollo could get on board, and sped the bus away. Rather than endure the same humiliation twice, Apollo put his sticky change in his pocket and started walking, telling himself that he didn't want to sit in a rattling red tin can full of rotting mortals anyway.

London, that morning, was bleak and dirty, the colour of soot. There were mortals everywhere, walking in the same direction, silent and featureless, like a greasy tide. Apollo walked against them, smacking into shoulders and briefcases as they refused to get out of his way. If they knew who he was, wondered Apollo, knew that he alone was responsible for the sun that shone above their heads, would they even care? He doubted it. One thing about mortals that had never changed was that they all believed themselves to be immortal. He quite liked that about them. It was so arrogant, so optimistic. Like himself, on a better day.

He had hoped to sneak back into the house and into his bed unseen, but as he dragged himself up the front steps, he heard swift footfalls following him up, and he turned to see, of all possible gods, Artemis, dressed in her tracksuit and carrying a handful of empty dog leads.

'Get out of my way,' he growled.

'You're actually in front of me,' Artemis pointed out. 'You're not coming to the meeting dressed like that, are you?'

'What fucking meeting?'

'You know, Athena's thing.'

Artemis squeezed past him and put her key in the door.

'Oh fuck,' said Apollo. 'I'd forgotten about that. Look, can you make up some excuse for me? I don't want to go. I feel like shit. It's a fucking pointless waste of time anyway.'

Without opening the door, Artemis turned to face him. Apollo noted the familiar look of righteous annoyance in her eyes. He braced himself.

'First of all,' said Artemis, 'I would appreciate it if you didn't constantly use that word in front of me.'

'You mean fuck?' said Apollo.

Artemis winced.

'I find it deeply offensive,' she said.

Apollo rolled his eyes.

'Next,' said Artemis, 'you might want to start taking your responsibilities to this planet seriously.'

'What responsibilities?' said Apollo.

'Look at yourself!' said Artemis.

She reached over and picked the plastic wrapper of a cigarette packet off the side of his shirt.

'Where did you spend last night? In the gutter? What kind of an example does that set to the mortals out there who should be looking up to you?'

'It may have escaped your notice,' said Apollo, 'but most of the "mortals out there" would rather not look up to anyone at all, and the people that they do look up to are exactly the kind of people who spend their nights asleep in gutters or nightclubs and not those who go out running before dawn and never have sex.'

'Be that as it may,' said Artemis, 'even you cannot deny that this family is facing an unprecedented crisis. And that Athena might be able to help us. If she can get her words out straight . . .'

'What makes you think I care about this family?'

'I know you care about yourself. And I know you want to get your power back.'

'I wouldn't need to get my power back if you hadn't taken it away from me.'

'That was a democratic decision for the good of everyone. You had been risking yourself . . .'

'Oh, shut up.'

'You had been risking us all . . .'

'Just shut up. Shut the fuck up, you stupid, uptight, don't drink, don't smoke, don't fuck, don't do anything that might almost be interpreted as fun, sanctimonious little fucking virgin. Fuck, fuck, fucking fuck, I've had enough. I'm not going to this fucking meeting, I don't care what happens to the fucking family, you can tell Athena what the fuck you like, just as long as you get out of my fucking face and stay out of it.'

Apollo grabbed the keys, turned the locks and opened the door, then threw them down the stairs and into the street before slamming the door between him and his twin.

'And don't you fucking start,' he muttered towards the door to the living room, where he assumed that other mothball-cunted bitch Athena was already preparing for her tedious, useless meeting.

Shrugging off the insult from Apollo – you could only, after all, be hurt by someone whose opinion you respected – Artemis picked up the keys and let herself into the house. She couldn't deny that he had a point – not about herself, of course, but about the chances of Athena's meeting being a success. It wasn't that Athena didn't know what she was talking about – she had, certainly, a brilliant mind, and a genius for strategy. It was that she was completely incapable of communicating to the rest of the gods any of the ideas that she came up with. Athena may have been designated the goddess of wisdom but, unfortunately, wisdom and clarity are not quite the same thing. Still, thought Artemis as she entered the living room, maybe this would be the time that Athena finally got her message across. It had to happen one day.

Although all of the comfortable chairs were as yet untaken, Artemis sat on a hard wooden stool from the kitchen, which Athena had placed at the far end of the front row. She liked to remind the others that she, at least, was unselfish and prepared to make sacrifices. She watched as Athena put carefully stapled handouts on each of the empty seats, and wondered whether anybody else was actually going to turn up. Athena had made a huge fuss about this meeting, and spent ages rearranging the furniture in the living room into equally-spaced rows, the better that everyone could see her. Watching Athena now – efficient, conservatively dressed, those totally unnecessary spectacles balanced at the top of her strong, serious nose – Artemis asked herself, not for the first time, whether there was actually any need for a goddess of wisdom. She, Artemis, could do the job just as well as Athena did, she had no doubt, and still have time left over to hunt as much as she liked. Of course, Athena liked to believe that she was the most important of all the gods, and Artemis was pretty sure that, in her own head, she was lining herself up as the successor to Zeus. But that was never going to happen. Artemis was determined: never.

The next god to arrive was Hermes, his slim, athletic form encased in a tailored business suit, topped and tailed with his winged helmet and boots.

'Is this going to take long?' he said.

'Is that the first thing you say every time you walk into a room?' said Artemis.

'Well, is it?' said Hermes, ignoring her. 'Unlike the rest of you, I actually have things to do with my time.'

'And don't tell me, time is money?'

'Funny you should say that, but it is,' said Hermes, unable to keep a sulky tone from entering his voice.

He was the baby brother of the family and had always suffered from an inferiority complex, stemming from the indignity of having, throughout his life, been forced to carry everyone else's messages for them, alongside performing endless other duties that the rest of them had considered undesirable and palmed off on him.

'I will,' said Athena, 'of course be delivering the information required in the most concise and apposite manner, but this is a complex issue which affects us all, and I would ask you to treat this meeting with appropriate respect. There's a handout on the chair.'

'Can I just read it and go?' said Hermes.

'No.'

Artemis was not at all surprised to see Hermes select the largest, least broken of the armchairs and sling himself into it, kicking his winged heels over the arm and flicking in a desultory way through Athena's fact sheet. Artemis watched him attempt to conceal a frown of confusion from his face, the same frown of confusion that she had only recently concealed from her own face when reading the same sheet. This did not bode well.

Gradually the other gods arrived and took their seats in order of comfort. Artemis noted that Aphrodite seemed to be in a particularly good mood, which worried her a little. She wondered who had been made to suffer in the pursuit of it. It wasn't Eros, who, sitting two seats away from her, was looking relieved for some reason, or Ares, who had headed straight to the back of the room, taken one glance at the handout, dropped it on the floor, and was now flicking through a ring binder of his own on his knee, making copious notes. Dionysus had cheerily poured Aphrodite a glass of wine when he had arrived, so it couldn't have been him. Hephaestus was sharing the sofa with his wife, whispering in her ear and cuddling her. Demeter was huddled, pale and dishevelled, in a chair in the corner, but she had taken on a ghostlike mien ever since the death of the clematis, and could probably be discounted too. So it must have been Apollo, which would explain his appalling mood this morning. She wondered what Aphrodite had done, and if it was something she should be concerned about. She was so irritated with Apollo, though, that she chose to put it out of her mind.

At the front of the room, Athena cleared her throat, and

everyone reluctantly stopped what they were doing and looked over at her.

'Are all delegates in attendance?' she said.

'Apollo isn't,' said Artemis.

'Can anyone proffer any intelligence pertaining to his absence?' said Athena.

'He was in the club last night,' volunteered Dionysus. 'Drank at least a gallon of my wine, and was last seen snoring with his head jammed underneath a bar stool. I doubt he'll be putting in an appearance today.'

Artemis didn't add anything to this.

'That is entirely typical,' said Athena. 'I informed him only yesterday that this gathering was to comprise a very important dissemination of information. Perhaps we should postpone . . .'

She was immediately drowned out by a chorus of groans and complaints from the rest of the gods, especially Hermes, who knew that he would be in charge of finding another date that everybody could make.

'Very well,' said Athena. 'Hermes, could you ensure that all of the key representations are conveyed to our absent sibling?'

'Will do,' said Hermes.

'Excellent,' said Athena. 'Thus. To commence. If I could request that all gathered deities address themselves to the schemata reproduced on the uppermost sheet of your textual bundle: "Concerning the necessity for increasing the potency of the true gods and goddesses, brackets Olympian close brackets, with additional suggestions for the implementation of organised religion-based solutions within the crowded global multi-faith context".'

Artemis hated it when circumstances forced her to agree with Apollo.

Once Apollo was certain that all of the other gods had arrived at Athena's meeting – an event which could be guaranteed to go on for hours – he left his bedroom where he had been pacing with increasing agitation, and climbed the stairs to the second floor. Whatever happened now would be Artemis's fault. She had asked for it. If it wasn't for her interference, and for her self-important little performance on the front steps that morning, he would have just gone to bed and slept off his hangover; or, rather, circumstances would have been so different that he wouldn't have had a hangover at all. Now she, and the rest of them, could answer to the consequences of her own behaviour.

He followed the second floor corridor down past the clutch of bedrooms to the very end, to the door that led up to the next floor. Nobody had passed through this door for years, in either direction. He persuaded himself that the twinge he felt in his stomach was not fear, and made himself open the door. The handle turned only with some effort, but the door wasn't locked. He pushed the door forward and it opened with a disgruntled creak. Immediately on the far side rose a dim staircase, cobweb-laced and caked with solidified layers of dust and grime. The air was thick and old, unstirred for years. On one of the steps, near his eye-level, a fat, sleek rat observed him; above it, a pair of giant cockroaches were mating on the wall. It reminded him of the state of the rest of the house, before Alice . . . Quelling that thought, he stepped inside, pulling the door shut behind him and plunging himself into almost total darkness. There was a dim light coming from the top of the staircase though, and he followed this, the stairs groaning with each step that took him spiralling upwards to the forbidden top floor of the house.

At the top of the staircase he reached a landing with bare floorboards, a small window, and another door leading off it, plain and unpainted. In front of the door, on an equally plain wooden chair, sat a goddess Apollo had not seen for many years: his stepmother Hera, the sister and wife of Zeus.

They looked at each other. Neither blinked. She had sat there, as far as he knew, for over two decades, unmoving, alone except for a brace of peacocks, currently prostrate at her feet. She had hair the colour of blackmail, a spine as straight as a guillotine, and a face that could sink ships. If she was even slightly surprised, after twenty years, to receive her first visitor, she didn't deign to show it.

'Hera,' said Apollo. 'I won't say it's a pleasure.'

Hera didn't move, her mouth a cold, thin line.

'Let's not waste time with small talk,' said Apollo.

'I'd prefer not to waste time with talk of any kind,' said Hera, 'but I can see you're not giving me the choice.'

'I have some information,' said Apollo. 'Information that you might find –'

'Cut to it,' interrupted Hera.

'Right.' Apollo swallowed. 'It's like this. There is a plot against you in this house.'

'You astonish me,' said Hera. 'I always thought I was such a popular goddess.'

'At this very moment,' continued Apollo, 'the conspirators are gathered in the, ah, living room –' (how he wished there was a more dramatic word than 'living room' – *lounge*, he'd decided, would have been even worse) ' – plotting your doom.'

'And?' said Hera.

She held his gaze. Apollo looked down at the peacocks. They were so uninterested in what he was saying that they had begun pushing a grain of dust back and forth to each other with their beaks, ignoring him completely. He looked back up at his stepmother.

'They plan to kill you,' said Apollo.

Hera shrugged. 'They won't succeed. Is that all you have to say? If so you can leave now.'

'And Zeus.'

'I'm sorry?' For the first time, a twitch disturbed Hera's impassive face.

'They plan to kill Zeus as well.'

'None of you would dare,' said Hera, but she sounded nervous now.

'Why not?' said Apollo. 'That was how Zeus got the job, wasn't it? He killed his father. His father killed his father . . .'

'Zeus is stronger than you imagine,' said Hera. 'He is not ready to die.'

'You look worried,' said Apollo.

'I'm not worried.'

'You sound worried.'

'I'm not worried.'

Apollo waited. Hera's flint eyes darted towards the staircase. Apollo waited some more.

'How do I know you're telling me the truth?' said Hera.

'Why would I lie to you?' said Apollo.

'Why would you tell me the truth?' said Hera.

Apollo considered this.

'Mainly I'm trying to drop my siblings in the shit,' he said.

Now it was Hera's turn to consider.

'Well, I'll admit that does sound like you,' she conceded.

But she didn't elaborate on this thought, and she didn't make a move from her chair.

'If you think,' said Apollo, 'that this is just some plan from me to get you out of the way so that I can kill Zeus myself . . .'

An involuntary twitch from Hera's eyebrow confirmed this hypothesis.

'Well, don't worry. It's not. I swear.'

No movement from Hera.

'I swear on Styx,' said Apollo.

Still no movement from Hera.

'OK. I swear on Styx that I'm not here to kill or harm Zeus. Satisfied?'

Hera stood. Only her peacocks knew how long it had been since she last stood, but it was done smoothly, with no creaking or clicking of joints.

'Stay here,' she said. 'Guard him. And Apollo?'

'Yes?'

'If you have any love for him, if you have even an ounce of loyalty left in your raisin of a heart, you will not open that door.'

'Don't worry about it,' said Apollo. 'I don't want to see him in that state anyway.'

Hera reached over and slapped him, hard.

'That's for disrespecting your father,' she said.

Apollo nodded. The loss of pride was worth it, just this once. He could take revenge on her some other time. Gesturing to her peacocks to follow her, Hera swept down the stairs. Apollo smelt the fresh air creep in from downstairs as she opened the door to the main house.

'I'll be back,' Hera's voice called up to him. 'Don't, whatever you do, let him out.'

Then the clean current of air was cut off, and he was left alone, choking in the staleness.

'Two birds with one stone,' said Apollo. 'Well, that was a piece of piss.'

He walked around Hera's empty chair and opened the door to Zeus's room.

Nineteen

Downstairs, Artemis was fighting to stay focused. Athena had borrowed an overhead projector from the university department to which she was affiliated, and was currently executing an intricate design onto acetate which, from what Artemis could make out, was supposed to represent the current market interplay of existing faiths and the – what was it she had said? – 'import strategy for niche exploitation and growth'. It didn't help that she was projecting the import strategy onto their peeling floral wallpaper, so that it looked less like a business plan and more like post-match analysis for some particularly complex piece of jungle warfare. Which at least, yawned Artemis, would have been more interesting than this.

She looked around the room. Aphrodite and Hephaestus were kissing violently – Artemis turned her head away quickly but still couldn't help but notice Hephaestus' hairy hand up Aphrodite's skirt. Eros and Hermes were playing noughts and crosses. Ares was working away at his own file as busily as before. The only people who seemed to be paying any attention whatsoever were Demeter and Dionysus, but it was impossible to tell whether Demeter was hearing anything aside from her own doom-laden internal monologue, and as for Dionysus, closer inspection revealed a discreet pair of headphones in his ears, connecting to some kind of music player in his pocket. Meanwhile, at the front of the room, Athena continued her presentation, but Artemis knew her well enough to spot the desperation in her movements, the note of hysteria in her voice as she tried and tried to put across the information that was so obvious to her but which nobody else could understand. It was no use. Artemis let go of her concentration and allowed her thoughts to drift.

She found herself imagining being dead. Running through the Elysian Fields, not a care in the underworld. She thought of how much her family would miss her when she was gone. How they would finally realise the extent to which they had always taken her for granted. How they would belatedly appreciate the import-ance of having someone specific to watch over hunting, and chastity, and the moon. Maybe they would even come to visit her, and tell her how sorry they were for the lowly way in which they had always treated her. The upperworld would be in a terrible state, of course, but at long last that wouldn't be her problem any more.

Suddenly, without warning, the door of the living room flew off its hinges, spun up and exploded into a million splinters, swirling down on their heads like ash. Simultaneously, fireballs shot to all four corners of the room. Artemis leapt to her feet, to a poised, defensive posture, stool held before her like a lion tamer's chair. There, in the doorway, hair flowing back, streams of flame pouring from her upturned palms, was Hera.

Hera? What was she doing here? She hadn't been seen in so long that the latest rumour had it that Zeus had found a way of turning her into stone.

Hera advanced on Athena hurling balls of fire with every step. 'Ingrate! Traitor! Jezebel!'

Athena couldn't look less like a Jezebel as she held up her aegis with one hand and wiped the steam from her glasses with the other. Hera's fiery missiles deflected off the shield and bounced to the walls where they spluttered and spat. Artemis reflected on the unexpected advantages of having a really severe damp problem.

'Hera,' said Athena from behind the aegis. 'It would appear that you are experiencing a transference of personal, internal distress into externally-focused wrath. Perhaps it would be more appropriate were we to confront your issues through mutual, respectful discussion?'

With a twitch of an eyebrow, Hera flipped Athena upside-down and hung her from the ceiling.

'I hear you,' said Athena.

Now didn't seem to be quite the right time to point out to Hera all the power she was wasting, so Artemis settled back on her stool to enjoy the show. She hoped that it would last. It was a long time since she had seen a fight on this scale. Most of the gods would usually let Athena talk them out of a battle, as her tactical genius meant that she would always win. On the other hand, Hera must have built up a lot of tension sitting alone upstairs for all that time, and she was probably enjoying blowing it off. Maybe that was why she had come down at last; maybe she was just bored. Artemis ducked as a flaming footstool shot over her head, leaving a trail of burning woodworm.

Artemis smiled. She felt a warm glow, not only from the fire doing its best to consume the soggy walls. She had missed Hera. Nobody did rage like Hera, not even Aphrodite on a bad day. Watching her performance was like curling up on the sofa in her oldest tracksuit bottoms, with a bowl of ambrosia, in front of her favourite film (*Clash of the Titans*). It was nostalgia so rich she could taste it. And she had almost forgotten what a pure display of power was like, after years and years of rationing. It would almost be worth doing nothing for a few decades if she could put on a show like this at the end of it.

On the other hand, she supposed somebody should step in, before Hera burnt the entire house down. Not that she would miss it, but they didn't have any insurance. What was really needed was for Ares to take charge – and just as she thought this, she heard him coming up behind her, bustling with purpose.

She watched as he approached Hera and Athena with his maps and his callipers at the ready, a grin of anticipation on his face.

'Ladies,' he said. 'Much as I hate to interrupt your conversation . . . Might I interest you both in a small land war in Asia? Winner takes all.'

There was a pause as Hera considered it. Then Athena's body stopped spinning, the flames began to recede, and Hera's face entertained that most rare of visitors: a smile.

Across the house, two floors from where Athena, Hera and Ares were about to seal the fate of two previously peaceful and unremarkable former Soviet republics, Apollo was standing on the threshold of Zeus's bedroom, blinking into the gloom.

Aside from Hera, no other god had ever been allowed into Zeus's room. Apollo had had no idea what he was going to find in there. Whether, indeed, he would even find Zeus in there – at times he had wondered whether the secret that Hera was so keen to guard was that Zeus was dead.

He wasn't dead. Or at least, Apollo doubted that he was, unless the dead had recently taken to watching television. On the other hand, Zeus – the form that Apollo assumed was Zeus – betrayed no awareness that anyone had come into the room. So maybe it was just a lifeless shell in that bed now, the flickering blue light of the television washing over it, oblivious to the advertisers' siren call to spend the money that it didn't have.

The bed – a single, metal-framed cot heaped with mildewed blankets – was pushed back against the wall on the far side of a room that was otherwise bare. At the foot of the bed was a low wooden crate, and on that crate stood the TV. Aside from that, there was nothing – not a picture, not a book – just dust motes floating in the static air. The only sound was the voice of a falsely cheerful young woman coming from the television, encouraging her viewers to consider the cost-effective style of stencilling when redecorating their bathrooms.

Apollo took a step towards his father. The bare floorboard beneath his foot yelped, and the shape in the bed shifted, turned its head towards him.

'Is that you?' came a quavering voice.

Apollo didn't reply. Instead he walked over to the side of the room, where the window should be. It had been boarded up.

'Have you come for me at last?' called Zeus.

Apollo didn't like to see sunlight shut out of a room. He took hold of the corner of one of the boards, and pulled hard. The rotten wood snapped in his hand. Light poured in now, and Apollo turned to face his father.

'Who is that?' called Zeus, flinching from the sudden influx of light.

'It's me, Father,' replied Apollo. 'Your son, Apollo.'

A short pause.

'Are you here to kill me?' said Zeus.

'No, Father,' said Apollo. 'I'm not here to kill you.'

'I can't see you,' said Zeus.

Apollo walked over to the bed and sat down. The only part of his father that was visible was his face, which was as yellowed and creased as the ancient pillowcase it leant against. His hair had grown long and dirty-white, and hung lifelessly by his head, hardened into clumps. His eyes, though, were sharp and fierce and hard, like blue diamonds. They could cut through anything.

'I am here, Father,' said Apollo.

Zeus reached a gaunt, trembling hand from under the blankets and put it on Apollo's hand. The skin was so pale it was almost grey, stretched so thin over the bulging purple veins that it seemed it might rupture at any moment.

'So,' said Zeus. 'Finally you come to visit me. My own son.'

'Yes, Father,' said Apollo.

'My own son,' repeated Zeus. 'Which son are you?'

'Apollo.'

'Ah, yes. Apollo. My son. The sun.' Zeus laughed or perhaps coughed. 'Have you come to make sure I'm still alive?'

'No, Father.'

'And which one are you again?'

'Apollo.'

'Apollo. The sun. Sun son.'

'Yes. Apollo.'

'And you're not going to kill me?'

'No.'

'Which one is your mother?' said the hole in the face.

'My mother? Leto,' said Apollo.

'Leto. Ah, yes. She was a nice one. A kind one. She loved me, I think.'

'Yes, she did.'

'Apollo. My son.'

There was a silence.

'What were we talking about?' said Zeus.

'We weren't talking about anything. I only just got here,' said Apollo.

'Oh,' said Zeus. 'I don't want you. Where is she?'

'I'm sorry?'

'Where is she? Is she coming for me? Where is she?' said Zeus.

'Where is who?'

Zeus's hand gripped Apollo's, surprisingly hard, then released it.

'I don't know,' he said.

Now Zeus plucked at his blankets, pulling them away from himself, revealing the upper half of his body. There was almost none of him left. All of his muscle seemed to have been eaten away, and his skin sagged loosely off his bones.

'Help me,' he said. 'I want to get out of bed.'

Apollo leant over and pulled the blankets aside. Zeus was nude. His genitals flopped uselessly. Apollo thought of the thousands of women, the goddesses Zeus had impaled on that tube of dead skin, laughing or crying or literally dying of pleasure, their shrieks echoing across continents, new life exploding inside them.

'Lean on me,' said Apollo, and he helped Zeus to sit up.

Together they manoeuvred Zeus's spindly legs so that they were hanging over the side of the bed, and Apollo pulled him upright onto the floor. Zeus stood, trembling, as Apollo pulled his arm over his shoulders and propped him up.

'I can stand,' said Zeus.

He said it, and he could.

'Take me to the window,' he said.

Apollo was astonished to see that Zeus could still walk. With every step he seemed to gain a little in energy. His back straightened, and he did not lean so heavily against Apollo's shoulder. He still shook, though, and was so frail that Apollo felt that, even had he not been a god, he could have lifted him with one hand.

'Look at that,' said Zeus.

Apollo looked out of the window but couldn't see anything of interest.

'The trees,' said Zeus. 'The sky. The clouds. That's mine. All of it.'

'Yes, it is,' said Apollo.

'I haven't been outside in a little while,' confided Zeus. 'I'm not allowed to.'

'That's disgraceful,' said Apollo. 'If you own the place, you should at least be allowed to go out into it.'

He pulled another rotting board off the window, now opening up a space large enough for someone thin – an old emaciated god, say – to squeeze himself through.

'This is England, you know,' said Zeus, gazing out of the window.

'I know,' said Apollo.

'I've lived here . . . not so very long. A few centuries only. A blink in the life of a god. Are you a god?'

'Yes I am.'

'She told me I'm not a god but I know the truth.'

'I'm sure you do,' said Apollo.

'She told me that I was mad, that I had to go to bed for a long time. She said that if I stayed outside I would hurt myself, or someone would try to hurt me. She said my own children would try to kill me. Are you here to kill me?'

'No,' said Apollo. Not this time, he thought.

'So I'm waiting 'til I'm not mad any more and then she'll come to get me.'

'Is that all you do, then?' said Apollo. 'Lie in bed?'

'And watch television.'

'I'm on television,' said Apollo.

'You are?' said Zeus. 'Have you ever been on Doctor Who?'

'No,' said Apollo.

'Oh,' said Zeus. 'I like Doctor Who. He's a god too.'

'I don't think he is,' said Apollo.

A split second later, Apollo found himself bouncing like a tennis ball off the opposite wall of the room.

'Yes he is,' said Zeus. 'He's a god.'

'Sorry,' said Apollo from the floor. 'Of course he is. I was confusing him with someone else.'

Apollo stood up and removed a few handfuls of dust that had stuck to his clothes. His clothes were not having a good day of it.

'Father,' he said.

'Am I your father?' said Zeus, in some surprise.

'There's something I need to tell you,' said Apollo. 'Something important. Something that could threaten your security – everyone's security.'

He walked over to Zeus and put a hand on his arm. The arm was thin, but hard.

'What is it?' said Zeus.

'There's been a mortal in the house.'

'What? When? Now?'

Zeus looked frantically around him, as if mortals were about to start appearing from between the cracks in the floorboards.

'No,' said Apollo, 'I threw her out.'

He gazed out of the window in a show of pensiveness.

'But . . .' he added after a few moments. 'I think she knows too much.'

'Who let her in?' said Zeus.

'Artemis,' said Apollo, turning back to his father. 'She deserves to be punished, of course. But as for the mortal . . .'

'What's her name?' said Zeus.

'Alice,' said Apollo. 'Do you want to see her photograph?'

Apollo got his telephone out of his pocket and showed Zeus one of the pictures he had taken of Alice, the one where her face showed most clearly. When he was sure Zeus had got a good look, he took the phone back.

'Of course,' he said, 'it's entirely up to you what you do with this information. I wouldn't dream of influencing your decision in any way.'

Twenty

Afterwards, the weathermen would have to go on television to apologise, and admit that they had no idea where the storm came from. They insisted that there was nothing on the charts that could have predicted that, on that morning in March, forecast for sun, as much rain would fall as in the whole of the rest of the year so far combined. The leader of the opposition called for an inquiry into Met. Office practices, and a few of the papers followed suit, but the notion was soon forgotten after war broke out unexpectedly between two little-known but oil-rich countries to the south of Russia, and America started making noises about getting involved.

Neil hadn't slept at all that night, just sat in the corridor outside the bedroom where Alice was sleeping. He wanted to go in there and hold her, not sexually, but to wrap himself around her like the shell around a nut.

When she had arrived at his flat, Alice was white-faced and near-catatonic. She had never been to his flat before and it had been one of those moments he'd dreamed about, in which each ordinary room would be gilded by her presence while she glided around them, voicing her approval like a princess inspecting a ship. In that daydream, he had cleaned. In that daydream, she was happy. Instead he had just had time to pick up the worn clothes off his grubby carpet and do the washing up before the doorbell had rung and the wraith had appeared.

Being Alice, she had, of course, apologised profusely – for

what, he wasn't sure – but after that he hadn't been able to get another word out of her. He had sat her in the kitchen and given her tea which she hadn't drunk, and then sat her in the living room and put on the TV which she hadn't watched, and then brought her a bowl of soup which she hadn't eaten but had just looked at in dismay until he realised what pain it caused her to refuse his hospitality and he took it away.

Then he led her to the bedroom – another of those daydream moments, being played out so terribly, terribly wrongly – gave her a T-shirt and a pair of shorts to sleep in, shut the door quietly behind her, and then sat down and waited. He leant back against the cold wall of the corridor and listened to the silence around him. He wanted to protect her, wanted to find the person who had done this to her and to kick the shit out of him (he was sure it was a him, and fairly sure he knew which him it was). But he hadn't been in a fight since school, and even then, what he called a fight had generally involved him cowering in the corner of the playground until a bigger boy picked him up and shoved him inside a locker. The thought of him playing the hero and actually winning – well, it was the kind of fantasy that was like the fantasy of bringing Alice to his home. It was the kind of fantasy that would go wrong.

At nine o'clock in the morning, there had still been no signs of life from the bedroom. He didn't want to wake Alice but he also knew that she wouldn't want to be late for work, so he eased the door open and took a look inside. Alice was lying on her back in the bed, eyes wide open, and the moment Neil opened the door she said, 'I'm not going in.'

'OK,' said Neil.

'Can I stay here today?' said Alice.

'Of course,' said Neil.

'Will you stay with me?'

'Alice, what happened?'

'Please stay home with me today.'

Neil looked at her for a moment. Lying still in the bed, her face so pale, she looked like a corpse.

'Of course,' he said. 'I'll just call the office, let them know I'm not coming in.'

Neil went to leave the room.

'Neil?'

'Yes?'

'Leave the door open.'

Neil went to the kitchen, left a quick message on the answer-phone at work, then made two cups of tea and brought them back to his bedroom. Alice was, finally, sleeping. He left one of the cups on the table by the bedside and crept away.

He sat down at the kitchen table and tried to get on with some work. He opened up some site plans and looked at them. Front elevation. Side elevation. Floor plan.

Maybe it was just about the fight? Thinking about the things he had said to her, he felt ill. It was no wonder she was so upset. But then, if it was the fight, why would she have come to his flat? No, it must have been something else, something that happened afterwards. Something worse.

He looked at the front elevation again. He picked up a pencil to make a note, but it wasn't sharp, so he got up and sharpened it into the kitchen sink.

If only she would tell him what was wrong.

He ran the tap, flushing away the pencil shavings, and went back to the table. Front elevation. What had he been going to write on it? Never mind, it would come back to him. He had another look at the side elevation, and then the floor plans. Something wasn't right. In front of him the familiar combinations of lines and numbers refused to speak to him, withheld their meanings as if written in a foreign alphabet.

The thing was, she had said she was scared. Not hurt or angry: scared. What could possibly have happened to scare her? She would tell him when she was ready. Wouldn't she?

He turned back to the drawings. Now he knew what was wrong: they were from a project that he had completed the previous summer. Idiot, he told himself. Can't you get anything right? Go and get those other ones from your bag. Do something. But he didn't stand up, didn't put the old drawings away. He just sat and looked at them, the pencil in his hand, suspended above the paper, writing nothing.

Around midmorning, he heard Alice get out of bed and go into the shower, and a bit later she came into the kitchen, her hair hanging down wet around her drawn face, wearing her jeans from yesterday and Neil's T-shirt over the top.

'Sorry –' she began.

'Don't,' said Neil. 'You've got nothing to be sorry about.'

'Thanks for the tea,' said Alice, 'and for letting me stay. You're a good friend. I don't deserve you.'

'Please don't say that. You deserve . . . you deserve anything. Everything. Everything good.'

'No, I don't,' said Alice, shaking her head.

'Alice –'

'No. You don't know, so . . .'

'Then tell me,' said Neil.

'I can't. You'd be so ashamed of me.'

'I couldn't possibly be ashamed of you, Alice.'

Alice just shook her head.

'Look,' said Neil. 'It's a lovely day. Why don't we go for a walk? Just as far as the park. It might take your mind off things and it's better than sitting in here all day.'

'With you?' said Alice.

'Of course with me,' said Neil.

'You don't have to. I've disturbed you enough – I can see you're working . . .'

'Don't be silly,' said Neil. 'It's just work. It can wait. Come on, it'll be nice.'

And it was nice, at first. The sun was actually warm, warm

enough that Neil only needed a denim jacket over his shirt, and Alice left her winter coat behind and wore a jumper of his instead. They didn't talk much, but they never talked much, and there was something companionable about the silence. Neil wanted very much to take Alice's arm, but he sensed that she was still too fragile to cope with that, so he didn't. But he enjoyed walking beside her, even though there was nothing special about the walk up to the park: just unremarkable residential terraced streets, the odd ugly lump of a council estate, and then the high street, all kebab shops and pound shops and the kind of estate agencies that made you think twice about wanting to move to the area. There were other people around, other couples, and Neil wondered whether he and Alice were going to be a couple one day, and he felt guilty for wondering at a time like this, but he wondered it all the same. He wanted to take her arm so badly that he had to put his hand in his pocket.

At the gate to the park, Alice stopped and looked him straight in the eye, very serious. He realised that Alice never looked him in the eye; she usually addressed all of her remarks to somewhere in the air just above his shoulder.

'What is it?' said Neil.

'I need to talk to you,' she said. 'I need to tell you about what happened yesterday.'

'OK,' said Neil.

Alice rested her hand on the park railing. She seemed to be holding herself up.

'It's very bad,' she said.

'OK,' said Neil.

'And it was my fault,' said Alice. 'All of it.'

'I'm sure it wasn't –'

'It was my fault,' insisted Alice.

Neil nodded.

'There's two parts to this. The first part . . . the first part is bad. I don't want to tell you about the first part. But I have to.

Because without the first part I can't tell you about the second part, and I have to . . .' Alice choked.

'You don't have to do anything,' said Neil.

'I have to,' said Alice, 'because I have to tell someone and you're the only one I can tell. So OK. The first thing is, I kissed Apollo.'

Neil had been expecting it but anticipating the punch doesn't make it hurt any less. He thought he might be sick, but when he opened his mouth, that wasn't what came out.

'It's OK,' he said, 'it doesn't matter.'

'Yes it does,' said Alice.

And she let go of the railing and reached out, and Neil thought she was going to touch his arm, or even his face, but at that instant the light disappeared and a cold wind blew in from nowhere, as if they had been picked up and dropped into a completely different day.

'What on earth . . . ?' said Alice, looking up.

Neil looked up at the clouds that had materialised, ink-black, seething and swirling, just clouds, yes, but like some kind of angry vortex that could consume them, and then he saw a face in the clouds, of an old man, and the face was distended with fury, and a peal of thunder rang out, louder than anything he had ever heard in his life, and a dagger of lightning hurled down directly towards them, as if guided by some kind of intelligence that was seeking them out.

Twenty-One

When Alice opened her eyes, she was surprised to find herself lying on the ground outside the park, enclosed by a wall of rain. Her ears were filled with the shrill shrieking of car alarms – it seemed that every one within miles had been set off. She couldn't quite figure out what had happened. Something must have happened, or she wouldn't be lying here, but she felt fine. That wasn't entirely accurate: she didn't really feel anything at all. She decided that she must be in shock. In shock from what, she wasn't sure. It occurred to her that maybe the street had been struck by lightning.

She saw feet running towards her, lots of feet. People were panicking. Afraid that she would be trampled, she pushed herself upright. She looked for Neil but she couldn't see him. She felt a pang of terror, that something had happened to him. Then through the crowd she spotted a form lying on the ground, and she ran towards it, wheeling around the people coming in the opposite direction, knowing even before she could see him clearly that it was Neil.

Neil was lying on his back, eyes open, staring upward. Alice dropped to her knees beside him. For one long, grotesque second she thought he was dead. Then he moved. Just his hand, at first, but it was enough.

'Neil, are you all right?' said Alice. 'Say something, please.'

'It's OK,' said Neil, a little too loud. 'I'm fine.'

'Thank goodness,' said Alice. 'I was so worried. Do you know what happened?'

Neil sat up, but he didn't reply. He didn't even look at Alice. He was looking past her, towards the park, at the people who were running away from where they were.

'Oh dear,' said Alice. 'Do you think somebody's been hurt?'

Neil didn't speak. He stood up and looked around. He seemed dazed.

Alice stood up too.

'Neil, what is it? Can't you hear me? Can you see anything?'

She reached out a hand to touch him, but he stepped forward, past her, following the other people who had now clustered together in a group near where Alice had fallen. Alice could hear a woman crying and the sound of an approaching ambulance. Someone must have been badly injured; maybe several people. Of course, it was just like Neil to try to help.

She turned and hurried after him. He was stumbling forward blindly. When the other people saw him coming, they stepped aside to let him through, but they closed together before she could follow him. She stood at the back of the group, seeing nothing. For a few moments nothing happened. Then someone said, 'She's not breathing.'

Alice felt a pang of sorrow, of guilt to have been so relieved that Neil was all right when there were other people suffering.

'I know first aid,' she said. 'Is there anything I can do?'

Everybody ignored her. Nobody even turned around. And then she heard Neil's voice.

'Her name's Alice,' he said. 'She's with me.'

'But I'm here!' shouted Alice, not caring who heard her as long as Neil did. 'Neil! I'm fine!'

'Is she going to be OK?' he said.

'I'm fine!' screamed Alice. 'Neil, I'm back here! I'm fine!'

Nobody turned around.

'I'm doing my best but I don't think it's going to help,' said another voice she didn't know, out of breath.

'Let me through!' said Alice.

Nobody turned around.

So she stepped forward to push her way past, even though she hated pushing, and she grabbed the arm of the man in front of her, even though she hated grabbing, only instead of grabbing his arm, her hand went right though it.

Neil awoke, lying alone on the pavement, dazed. He became aware that it was pouring with rain. Hard. The rain felt oily. People started running, and he said to them, 'It's OK, I'm fine,' but they weren't running towards him. He pushed himself up and looked around for Alice, but he couldn't see her. By the park railings, where he had been standing only a moment ago, was a cluster of people, and he could hear a woman wailing. Then he heard the sound of an ambulance siren, quite a long way away, coming closer. He walked over to the crowd, but he still couldn't see Alice. His wet clothes were sticking to his body, his hair to his forehead. He was cold. Someone was saying, 'She's not breathing.' With eerie calm, he thought to himself, 'That's Alice they're talking about. If I push to the front of this crowd, I'll see her, lying on the ground.' So it seemed quite natural when that was exactly what happened.

'Her name's Alice,' he said.

Somebody put their arm around his shoulders. It seemed odd to him that he could feel his shoulders. Somebody else was squatting over Alice's body, blowing air into her mouth, pumping up and down on her chest with his hands. It looked violent, obscene. He wanted to tear him off her. Underneath this brute, Alice was perfect. There was nothing wrong with her. How could there be anything wrong with her?

'Is she going to be OK?' he said.

Alice walked through the people. She didn't want to walk through the people, but Neil was on the other side of them. So she walked through them. It felt like nothing. They were nothing but air.

She saw Neil before she saw herself. He was standing at the front of the crowd, a little apart from the others, except for a woman who was standing beside him holding his shoulders. He was looking down at a body on the pavement. Her body. Someone was giving her CPR. How could anyone be giving her CPR when she was standing right there? She stared at herself and the man pushing down on her breastbone. It was completely wrong. She should not be looking at her own body. She looked back at Neil. He was shaking.

She walked over to where Neil was standing and finally put her arms around him as she had always wanted to do.

'I'm here,' she said. 'I love you.'

Neil took a step away, out of her arms and towards her prone body. Alice started to cry. Nothing came out of her eyes.

The following minutes – hours? – felt like slow motion and fast forward at the same time. The ambulance came; the crowd stepped back. Paramedics pulled up the jumper and T-shirt that Alice was wearing – Neil's jumper and T-shirt – and used paddles to shock her. It didn't work. More CPR. It didn't work. They talked in low voices; one took Neil aside while another covered Alice's face.

The true meaning of what had happened, that they had watched someone die that day, began to pass through the crowd. As the realisation took, people began to leave, so that they could start the process of forgetting as soon as possible.

'Are you family?' the paramedic asked Neil.

'No,' said Neil.

'Are you her boyfriend?'

'No.'

'Is there anybody that we should call?'

'Me,' said Neil. 'She always called me.'

They were taking her body away. They were putting it into

an ambulance and taking it away. Alice felt panic, horror. She tried to climb into the back of the ambulance but she couldn't get in; she physically couldn't get into the vehicle. She just went straight through it.

And then, still worse, the paramedic guided Neil into the ambulance too.

'There's so much I wanted to tell her,' Neil was saying.

'You still can!' cried Alice. 'I'm still here! Neil, I'm still here.'

But the doors shut behind him and the ambulance drove off, taking with it everything she valued and leaving her completely alone on the pavement.

And then Alice heard a voice say her name.

Twenty-Two

'Alice Joy Mulholland?'

Alice turned.

'Hermes?'

'Yes,' said Hermes. 'How did you know?'

He was leaning against the park railings, wearing his usual smart business suit, and strange matching hat and boots with wings on them. And he was looking right at her, quite surprised, though not nearly as surprised as she was.

'I don't understand,' said Alice. 'What do you mean, how do I know? You know me. You said my name.'

'That doesn't mean anything,' said Hermes. 'I know everybody's name.'

'But you do know me,' said Alice. 'I clean your house.'

Recognition bloomed.

'Of course,' he said. 'Sorry. Out of context.'

He made a goofy little face.

'But . . .' said Alice. 'You can see me.'

'Of course I can see you,' said Hermes. 'You're right in front of me.'

'No, but –' Alice stopped. 'I'm sorry. I don't mean to contradict you. But I . . .'

'What?' said Hermes pleasantly.

'Oh dear,' said Alice. 'I think I must have hit my head. I just had the strangest – vision, I suppose you'd call it. I thought I was . . .' She tailed off. 'Sorry, I'm being ridiculous.'

'You did hit your head,' confirmed Hermes. 'But that's not what killed you.'

'What?' said Alice.

'It was a lightning strike,' said Hermes.

'You mean,' said Alice, 'you mean I am dead.'

Hermes cocked his head.

'Best to make sure,' he said.

He reached inside her chest and pulled out her heart.

'Yup,' he said. 'Definitely not beating.'

He put it back.

Alice screamed. She screamed and screamed and screamed and screamed and screamed. She screamed and screamed and screamed, and as she screamed she became aware that the screaming wasn't exhausting her or relieving her or even making her throat sore. The scream was having no effect on her whatsoever.

Eventually she stopped screaming.

'Are you done?' said Hermes, who had been standing still, watching her, all this time.

'Yes,' said Alice.

'Good,' said Hermes.

He took a pair of plugs out of his ears.

'The screaming is a bit of an occupational hazard,' he explained. 'Come with me. My motorbike is just around the corner.'

Hermes began walking away from her and Alice hurried to follow.

'I don't understand,' said Alice.

'You don't understand much, do you?' said Hermes.

'If I'm dead,' said Alice, 'how come you can still see me?'

'I would have thought that was obvious,' said Hermes.

'Well, no, I'm afraid it isn't really,' said Alice.

'I'm a god,' said Hermes. 'Have you ever been on a motorbike before?'

They had stopped beside a gleaming red motorbike that Alice had often seen parked in the street outside the house.

'I . . .' she said. 'No. You're a – ? I haven't. A god?'

'I wouldn't worry too much about it,' said Hermes. 'If you fall off, you won't get hurt.'

'You're a god?' said Alice.

'That's what I said,' said Hermes. 'Get on the back.'

Hermes swung his leg over the motorbike and looked at Alice.

'Come on,' he said. 'I haven't got all day. Well, technically I have, but it's best not to bother you with the details.'

'Where are we going?' said Alice.

'To the underworld.'

'But I don't want to go to the underworld.'

'If you stay here, you'll be a ghost,' said Hermes. 'The only people you'll be able to talk to are TV mediums. Trust me, the underworld is better.'

Alice didn't move.

'I don't think you understand me. It's either coming with me or staying here by yourself. Think about it.'

Alice thought about it, and got onto the back of the bike.

'Good girl,' said Hermes.

Once he was sure that Alice was securely seated, Hermes pulled away through the car in front, the motorbike drifting silently along. Alice felt no wind resistance against her body; it was as if they weren't moving at all.

'That's one good thing about being in dead time,' said Hermes. 'You don't need any fuel. You don't have to burn anything, because in one sense, you're not actually going anywhere.'

'I don't –' began Alice.

'Don't tell me you don't understand,' said Hermes. 'You've only been dead for five minutes. Of course you don't understand. Once you've had a few centuries to figure it out, then you'll understand. In the meantime, just go with it.'

When Alice didn't reply he looked over his shoulder at her.

'Look,' he said. 'I'm sorry if I seem a little brusque. It's just I have to do this every day, thousands and thousands and thousands of times a day, mostly with people who are just as shocked to be dead as you are. And that's aside from having to keep the entire economy of the globe running smoothly. Which it never bloody does, you mortals are always interfering. So you see, your social niceties do just tend to go after a while. For what it's worth, I thought you did a great job of cleaning our house. You're going to be tough to replace.'

Alice pulled her eyes away from the insides of the cars and the people that they were riding through and fixed them on Hermes, who was still facing her and driving without looking where he was going.

'Oh no,' she said. 'It's sweet of you to apologise, but it isn't that.'

'What is it, then?' said Hermes.

'I was just about to tell Neil – my friend, Neil, he's a lovely man – I was just about to tell him . . .' She broke off, jolted by a sudden wave of shock.

'What?'

'If you're a god . . . Does that mean that the others are too?'

'The others? You mean the rest of the family? Yes, of course. You're pretty slow on the uptake.'

'So Apollo – he's a god too?'

'God of the sun. In practice that means he has absolutely nothing to do. Sun goes up, sun comes down. Child's play. Why?'

'I . . . He . . . I . . .'

'Did you shag him?' said Hermes. 'I wouldn't worry about that. Everybody shags him. Even I've shagged him. That was during a very boring decade. Oops, nearly missed my turn.'

Hermes pulled the motorbike around sharply to the right, cutting a corner though a flock-wallpapered living room where an elderly couple were placidly watching TV.

'I suppose I could go all the way there through houses if I wanted to,' he mused, 'but I've grown quite attached to roads.'

'No,' said Alice. 'No, I didn't shag him. But we did kiss.'

'Kiss?' said Hermes. 'That's nothing. Apollo gets around a lot. Kissing him is like shaking hands with a normal person. So why did you stop at a kiss? Come on, you can tell me. It's not like you've got anybody else to talk to.'

At this thought Alice could feel herself wanting to cry again but, just like before, the tears wouldn't come.

As if he could read her mind, Hermes said, 'You'll find you don't have tears any more. Tears are a mortal thing. There's lots of other things you'll be missing too after a while, all your basic bodily range. You've lost everything corporeal: no eating, no drinking, no sleeping, no sex. No kissing, not even gods. It's definitely the downside of being dead. On the other hand you'll never get hurt or ill or tired or hungry again. I'd focus on that if I were you. So anyway, what happened?'

'Sorry?'

'After the kiss?'

'I can't tell you,' said Alice.

'Why, did he rape you or something? I wouldn't feel too bad about it. He's always raping people.'

'No!' said Alice.

'So what's the matter then?' said Hermes. 'This is your last chance, you know, to discuss it with anyone who knows Apollo. And you're never going to see me again.'

'He tried to rape me,' Alice admitted.

'Only tried?' said Hermes. 'He must have really liked you. Or maybe he didn't like you enough.'

He considered this for a moment or two as the motorcycle ploughed through a crowd of oblivious schoolchildren on a zebra crossing.

'And then Zeus killed you. Interesting.'

'Zeus killed me? Who's Zeus?'

'Our father. Chief god. He lives in the roof. Lightning is a classic Zeus manoeuvre.'

'I never met him,' said Alice.

'Well, he certainly met you,' said Hermes. 'OK, here we are.'

'What?'

Hermes pulled up to the kerb and stopped. A bus pulled up on top of them and began disgorging passengers.

'We're here now.'

'Already?'

'That's what I said.'

'But this isn't the underworld,' said Alice. 'This is Upper Street.'

'Yes, it is,' confirmed Hermes. 'Do you like what I did with that? *Upper* Street. You see?'

'Upper Street is the underworld?'

'No, of course it isn't,' said Hermes. 'Otherwise I wouldn't have called it Upper Street. I don't take you all the way into the underworld, I only take you to the portal. Which is here.'

'I don't under—' Alice broke off.

'Over there,' said Hermes, pointing.

'Angel Tube station?'

'Where else? Yes, just go inside, follow the escalators down to the very bottom. Go through the back wall, and you'll find another platform on the far side where all the other dead will be waiting for the train. You'll know who they are because they'll be able to see you. And some of them have really unpleasant injuries which makes them very easy to spot. There'll be a special train, get on that and it'll take you all the way there.'

'But,' said Alice, 'but I'm not ready.'

'Nobody ever is.'

'I had so much I was going to ask you,' said Alice.

'Well, you should have died a bit further away from Islington then,' said Hermes. 'Look, I'd love to help, but I can't hang around. You mortals just keep dying. I'm sure you can get one of the others to explain it all to you.'

'Please, can you just do something for me?' Alice pleaded. 'Neil – the man I told you about – Aphrodite knows who he is. So does Ares. And, well Apollo, but . . .'

'I can't believe you didn't figure out the god thing for your-self,' said Hermes. 'Weren't the names a dead giveaway? No pun intended.'

'Find him,' said Alice. 'Tell him . . . tell him I love him. Please. And that I'm sorry. And –'

Hermes shook his head.

'I can't do that,' he said. 'Alice, I understand that you're scared and upset and you didn't get a chance to say goodbye. You're not the first, believe me. But I can't treat you any differently from all the mortals I see every day – thousands of them, every single day, Alice. They've all got a message for their loved ones. And a lot of them have died in much worse circumstances than you – wars, plagues, famines, earthquakes, volcanoes, fires, floods, execution, torture, abduction, murder, stabbings, shootings, bombings, ODs . . . I can't help you, Alice. I can't help any of you.'

Alice looked at the ground. 'I'm sorry,' she said.

'Yes, well, I'm sorry too,' said Hermes after a moment. 'Sometimes this job really gets to me. If it makes you feel any better, you were really quite dignified, the way you asked. You should hear the begging that I get sometimes, it's embarrassing. Really, Alice, for a mortal, you're not that bad.'

'Thank you,' said Alice.

'Good luck with the next part of your journey,' said Hermes. 'Don't worry. You'll be OK.'

Alice got off the bike.

'Goodbye, Hermes,' she said.

'Take care,' said Hermes, and he rode away down the street.

Alice looked around her. Upper Street: such a familiar place. She shopped there, she ate there, went to the cinema there. Or at least she used to. The rain was stopping now; half the passers-by had umbrellas up, the others down. They hurried in and out of the Tube station – the portal, thought Alice – read the menus of the restaurants, admired the clothes behind plate-glass windows as they walked around her, sometimes through her, not knowing that the dead were with them, that they were gathering here as if at the departure gate in an enormous airport, headed for . . . where?

'Alice!' said a voice behind her.

She turned. It was Hermes, pulling over again on his motorbike.

'Did you change your mind?' said Alice. 'Will you speak to Neil?'

'No,' said Hermes. 'Sorry. I was just dropping Jean-François off.'

He indicated an elderly man on the back of the bike.

'*Vas-y, c'est là-bas,*' he said to the man. '*Suis cette jeune femme, elle connaît la bonne route.*'

The old man got off the bike and looked at her with shining eyes, full of expectation.

'The old ones are always the happiest,' said Hermes. 'They know it's coming, and they've been scared of it for years. Then when it does come it's a pleasant surprise for them that they're still here, plus they lose all of their aches and pains. Sweet, really. Also, you and I were chatting so much that I forgot to give you your ticket.'

'My ticket?'

Hermes handed over what appeared to be a perfectly ordinary Tube ticket.

'Now, this is very important: don't give it to the Tube driver until you get to the other side,' said Hermes. 'He'll ask you to, but don't give him the ticket. Otherwise he'll just drop you off midway, and you'll end up haunting the Tube tunnels for all eternity. Most haunted place in the world, the Tube. Sometimes you can even see the ghosts, though nobody ever notices them. You have to look pretty close. They're the ones who aren't breathing.'

'Thank you for letting me know,' said Alice.

'It was nice meeting you again,' said Hermes. 'Sorry I couldn't be of more help. Bye! *Au revoir!*'

And he waved to them both as he rode away.

Alice turned to her new dead companion. 'Hello,' she said. '*Bonjour*. It's this way. *Par içi.*'

She beckoned him to follow, and walked away, towards the gaping mouth of Angel Tube station.

Twenty-Three

Apollo was fucking Aphrodite in the bathroom. Again. She was leaning against the wall, one foot up on the toilet cistern, and judging by the look on her face she was thinking about paint samples. Again. This ought to have been a triumphant moment, his victory fuck, when he proved that he had overcome that insignificant little mortal, that he had erased her from this unimportant mortal planet and now he was erasing her from his deeply important body and mind. But he didn't feel particularly triumphant.

How many times, thought Apollo? How many times had he fucked Aphrodite in this precise position in this precise bathroom? How many times would he? The term déjà vu was completely meaningless in his life. He had already done everything, over and over and over again, and he would carry on doing the same things, over and over and over again, for as long as – well, for as long as the earth revolved around the sun. None of it had any meaning any more. Had it ever had any meaning? He trawled through the endless repetitions of his memory, searching for some youthful spark of enthusiasm, some sense of newness. Surely it had been there once. But the only example he could find was how he had felt about Alice.

'What are you looking like that for?' said Aphrodite. 'You're not going to come, are you?'

'Far from it,' said Apollo.

'Good,' said Aphrodite. 'I'm not done yet. Right, I'm turning round.'

His whole life, Apollo thought as Aphrodite shifted position, was some kind of recurring dream. Or maybe a nightmare. But no: it wasn't exciting enough to be a nightmare. Or interesting enough to be a dream. Maybe it was just a persistent hallucination.

How long ago had he killed Alice anyway? Or had been an innocent party to the killing of Alice, he hastily reminded himself, feeling a twinge from the watchful eye of Styx. Was it last week or a month ago? How much time had passed? What year was it? How long had they lived there? Did it even matter if it was all the same?

Well, whether it was a week or a decade, he missed her. He hated to admit it but it was true. He still had her photo on his phone so he could look at her whenever he liked, but it wasn't the same. Because it wasn't just looking at her that he missed – though that was part of it. He gazed over at the bathtub, remembered her thrusting motions as she scrubbed the soap scum off it while he stood in the doorway, pretending to be waiting to use the loo. She would get sweaty under her armpits, sometimes even across her back. The ends of her hair would curl above her sticky pink neck. She was so different from all of the perfect beings who had surrounded him for centuries – who still surrounded him. Her flaws entranced him.

But it wasn't only her flaws. He missed her virtues too. He missed her humility. He missed her kindness. He missed her vulnerability – just thinking about her tears made him shiver. ('Stop shaking,' said Aphrodite, 'you're putting me off.') He missed the way she'd listen to him – nobody in his family listened to him any more. He missed having someone around the place who didn't, deep down, hate him. He missed her cleaning, that was true too – the house was filthy since she'd been gone. He missed her deference to authority, the way she hated breaking those ridiculous Rules. He missed her unassertiveness – it was so exotic, and erotic. And yet in the end she had defied him at the exact moment he'd wanted her to acquiesce.

It was her own fault that she'd died, he could hardly be held responsible for that. But he regretted it all the same. If only she hadn't been so stubborn. If only she'd done what he'd said. Why had they ever decided to give mortals minds of their own?

'I'm thinking of redecorating my bedroom,' said Aphrodite.

He had forgotten she was there.

'Didn't you just redecorate it?' he said.

'No,' said Aphrodite. 'At least I don't think so. Maybe I did.'

They both fucked on, lost in their own confusion.

Returning home from another doomed encounter with the estate agent, Artemis approached the house slowly, wearing her disappointment in the slump of her shoulders. Some rubbish – a couple of sheets of tabloid newspaper, an empty crisp packet, a dripping beer can – had drifted off the street and clustered at the foot of the front steps. She should point it out to Alice, thought Artemis, get it cleaned up. She climbed up to where the brass doorknocker hung, its shine marred by fingerprints. She wondered who had been knocking at the door, and what had happened to them. The family had become even more paranoid about security of late, ever since Zeus's escape attempt. In Hera's absence, it had been Apollo, sulking in his bedroom, who had been first to react when the storm started, had been first to the roof and had coaxed Zeus back into his room and into bed. It was an uncharacteristic show of heroism from Apollo. Artemis was surprised he hadn't taken the opportunity to push Zeus from the roof – she couldn't swear that she wouldn't have. Perhaps her chat with him about the needs of the family earlier that day had had some effect? Artemis shook her head. Her pep talks hadn't got through to him for the last several thousand years so she couldn't see why they would start to work now.

Artemis shut the front door behind her. She flicked the switch of the hall light, but the bulb had gone. The house felt stuffy, what air there was suffused with must and damp. She wasn't in the mood to go out again so she made her way to the back door to get into the garden. Passing through the kitchen, it struck Artemis as unusual that there would be so much wasted food still sitting on the sideboards and the table, and judging by the smell of it, some of it was beginning to go off. On the back doorstep, a parade of ants was marching to and from the garden, carrying minute crumbs to their faraway palaces. Hadn't they dealt with the ant problem? And where the hell was Alice?

'Hey Artemis,' came a voice from behind her. 'Where have you been?'

She turned. It was Hermes, at the bottom of the stairs in his winged boots, swinging his winged helmet by one hand, obviously on his way to start gathering the souls of the dead.

'It's none of your business,' Artemis began, welcoming the argument as an opportunity for her to vent some of her frustration at the lack of viable flats in her price bracket. But then she stopped. She didn't have the energy for it. 'Hermes,' she said instead, 'why is the house so filthy? Have you seen Alice anywhere?'

'Yes, I saw her,' said Hermes, coming to the threshold of the kitchen and leaning against the doorway. 'A couple of weeks ago. I took her down to the underworld.'

'What?' said Artemis. 'Why did you do that?'

'Well, because she's dead,' said Hermes.

'Dead?' said Artemis. 'She can't be dead! Damn it! I've been so preoccupied. I should have known something like this would happen if I didn't supervise her properly. But she seemed so trustworthy! Stupid mortal. What did she go and die for?'

'It's not her fault,' said Hermes. 'Zeus killed her. Lightning bolt. On the day he got out.'

'Zeus!' said Artemis. 'How did he find out about her? I told her not to go up to the top floor.'

'She didn't,' said Hermes. 'If you want my opinion, it's got something to do with Apollo.'

'*What?*'

'Well, she was on that programme he did,' said Hermes.

'She what?'

'– and Aphrodite got me to bring her in –'

'Aphrodite?' said Artemis. 'What's she got to do with anything?'

'– and Apollo was acting all weird around her the whole time she was here, and then they kissed, and then he tried to rape her –'

'Hermes, how do you know all this?'

'It's my business to know. And think about it: Apollo was the first up on the roof when Zeus got out. The day Alice died. Don't you think that's just a little suspicious?'

'There's no way Apollo could have killed her,' said Artemis.

'Well he didn't, did he?' said Hermes. 'He obviously got Zeus to do it. He'll have tricked him into it one way or another, though I don't see why he didn't just do it himself . . . What's the matter, Artemis? You look like someone just tried to pinch your bum.'

'It was a loophole,' said Artemis.

'A what?'

Artemis looked around her. There was too much chance of being overheard.

'I think we'd better continue this conversation outside,' she said.

'Artemis, I'm busy, I've got things to do . . .'

'Outside,' insisted Artemis, in a voice that few, even gods, could argue with.

She took Hermes' arm in a grip that could break a stag's neck, and dragged him out into the garden, shutting the door behind them.

Once they were safely in the garden and out of earshot of the other gods, Artemis explained to him about the oath.

'And then not only does he go and kill a mortal,' said Artemis, 'he kills the cleaner!'

'The sneaky bastard,' said Hermes, a note of admiration creeping into his voice.

'Does anybody else know Alice is dead?' said Artemis.

'Not as far as I know,' said Hermes. 'At least, I haven't talked about it to anybody. Though the others must be starting to notice what a state the house is in. You really should hire another cleaner.'

'Not yet,' said Artemis. 'If anyone asks . . . just tell them that she's on holiday.'

'What's the point?' said Hermes. 'It's not like she's coming back.'

'Just do it,' said Artemis.

'Artemis, I don't see why you're getting so worked up about this. She's just a cleaner. They're two a penny. Get another one.'

'That isn't the point,' said Artemis. 'The point is, Apollo swore on Styx. On Styx! And he broke the vow! And that cleaner was mine – he had no right to touch her! It may have been a loophole, but it was against the spirit of the oath.'

'So let Styx deal with it,' said Hermes.

'She obviously isn't going to,' said Artemis. 'You know Styx. She deals with the letter of the law. Apollo must have found his way around her, or either Alice would still be alive or he'd be in a coma somewhere.'

'So take revenge,' said Hermes.

'That's what I intend to do,' said Artemis. 'But I need your help.'

'But I don't do revenge,' said Hermes. 'Nemesis does revenge. I can call her if you want.'

'No,' said Artemis. 'Nemesis can't do what I want you to do.'

'You mean . . .'

'Exactly.'

Hermes shook his head.

'No way,' he said. 'You know I can't interfere with the dead. Not in my position. If Hades found out . . .'

'Why should he find out?'

'If you start messing around down there he's going to know,' said Hermes. 'Don't be an idiot, Artemis. Can't you just smash up all of Apollo's guitars or something?'

'She's my cleaner,' said Artemis, 'and she should never have died. Don't you care about justice? Do you think she deserved this?'

Hermes sighed. 'She was a nice girl,' he admitted.

'So you agree with me,' said Artemis.

'No,' said Hermes. 'I don't.'

'I don't care,' said Artemis. 'I'm going to do it anyway.'

'You can't,' said Hermes. 'The second you set foot down there you'll be toast. You're a god, Cerberus will sniff you out in seconds.'

'So I'll send a hero,' said Artemis.

'There aren't any heroes any more,' said Hermes.

'I'll make one,' said Artemis. 'I know some mortal men.' She scanned her mind, thinking of the dog owners who employed her. 'Mr Simon? No, he's too wishy-washy. Alex Waters? Too lazy . . .'

'Are those the only mortals you know?' said Hermes. 'The ones whose dogs you walk?'

Artemis thought about the estate agents she had met.

'Pretty much,' she said.

'That's not going to work,' said Hermes. 'Heroes walk their own dogs. You can't use one of them.'

'I'm going to have to.'

Hermes had had many opportunities over the last several thousand years to learn exactly what Artemis's determined expression meant.

'You seem pretty keen to do this,' he said. 'Why?'

'Apollo gets away with far too much,' said Artemis.

'And?' said Hermes.

'And she belonged to me.'

'And?'

'And nothing,' said Artemis.

'Most gods would do anything to avoid going into the under-world.'

'It's a moral issue,' said Artemis.

Hermes was not about to start debating moral issues with Artemis.

'OK,' he said. 'You're right. I liked her. And I'm sick of doing my own ironing. So listen, as long as you promise not to tell anybody – nobody at all, otherwise everyone will want one – I can get you a hero. Someone decent. Someone who is actually going to want to help you. I'll send a message, summon him, disguise it a bit so it's not too obvious. But just this once. And just because she was a nice girl. And to piss Apollo off. And to stop you from getting disembowelled. And because maybe it was slightly my fault she was here in the first place.'

'And you'll show me the way into the underworld?'

'So long as you keep it to yourself.'

'Thanks Hermes,' said Artemis. 'You won't regret it.'

Hermes looked down to the bottom of the garden, where the flowers lay dead in a heap.

'Be careful, Artemis,' he said.

Twenty-Four

Alice wasn't particularly religious, but she counted herself as C. of E., and used to go to church for the usual festivals – Easter, Christmas. She hadn't given much thought to matters of the afterlife, but when she did, her views were quite conventional: heaven above, hell below, angels, clouds, that sort of thing. That was on days when she had believed in an afterlife of any variety. Most of the time she had suspected that it didn't exist at all.

As it turned out, she was completely wrong on all counts.

She had found the train to the underworld exactly as Hermes described – down at the bottom of Angel Tube station and through the back wall. The platform looked like just another Tube platform, only much longer, stretching further than she could see. It was packed, like the busiest of rush hours, and everybody there was – she had expected this, of course, but it still shocked her – dead.

There were those that she thought of as the 'proper' dead – white people, in their sixties, seventies and eighties, or even older, largely in hospital gowns or nightwear, and relatively unmarked. They looked the way dead people were supposed to look. But then there were those who, it was graphically clear, had died mid-surgery, or from accidents. Almost all of these seemed too young to die. And worst of all, everywhere she looked there were black and brown faces, far, far younger than any dead person should be. The majority of the adults were emaciated, from AIDS, Alice supposed, or malnutrition, and among them thronged thousands upon thousands of babies and small children, some wailing tear-lessly, others seemingly stoic about their fate, probably failing to understand what had befallen them, and no longer subject to the relentless stimuli of hunger and disease. Many of the adults were trying to lift and comfort the children, but their arms swept uselessly through them. Watching them, Alice realised that she would never again experience the sensation of holding someone, or being held.

Just as she was working up the courage to go and talk to some of the children, a train pulled in – a totally ordinary Tube train – and they piled inside it, at first allowing each other their personal space, then squeezing up closer, and finally overlapping completely. Closing her eyes, it was as if nobody else was there. Closing her eyes, it was as if she wasn't anywhere at all. When she opened her eyes, they had left the station – she hadn't even felt them go. In the darkness of the tunnel it was impossible to tell whether the train was moving, though the sound of the rattling carriage suggested that it was.

Some time after they had left Angel Tube station, Alice heard a voice calling, 'Tickets please!' and she looked up as a man pushed his way through the passengers, wearing blue overalls and a cap, skin a clammy, maggoty white, untouched by the sun. Although it went against her nature, Alice remembered what Hermes had said and kept her ticket out of sight. Next to her, though, Jean-François, the old French man, held his ticket out.

'Don't –' cried Alice.

But it was too late. Charon took the ticket and the moment that it left Jean-François's hand a gust of wind blew through the carriage, taking hold of him and sucking him out through the wall. Alice shrieked and tried to grab hold of his flailing arms, but her hands went right through him, as he was engulfed in the blackness beyond. Within a second there was no sight of him.

Nobody else in their carriage gave up their ticket.

★   ★   ★

Alice was still feeling shaken as the train pulled in at its destination. It was with scant relief that she got off; who knew what awaited her here? The platform was entirely unremarkable, just another Tube station. They could have been in some suburb of London that Alice had simply never visited before, if there was a suburb of London called 'Underworld'. The only difference was a conspicuous absence of maps or of passengers waiting to get on. Apart from that, from the cement floor to the tiled, sloping walls, it was all completely familiar.

She followed the directions to the exit. The station was completely deserted and, except for the low conversational murmur of a few braver members of the dead, completely silent. The escalators were working, though – upwards only – and she stepped onto one and was carried, soundlessly, to the top. There was no sensation of movement, just the walls passing behind her, the light outside getting closer. She hadn't realised how much her body had felt until she stopped feeling anything at all.

She abandoned her ticket to an automated machine and stepped out into the underworld. Nobody here either, aside from a few of the newly dead who had also found their way out. Alice wondered what would become of all the babies who couldn't be carried out, but there was nobody around to ask.

Outside the sky was dull and the land was flat. The light gave no indication of the time of day. In every direction, as far as the eye could see, stretched featureless streets of unvarying mock-Tudor semi-detached houses. In any case she assumed they were mock-Tudor: who knew how long they had been there? The only variation that she could see was the concrete block housing the Tube station that she had just left, a No Entry sign above the door. There was no buzz of traffic, no birdsong. Nothing natural at all. Not a tree to be seen, no insects in the air, not even a blade of grass poking its way up through the gaps between the paving stones.

As she tried to figure out what to do next, Alice felt something cold and wet touch her ankle. There was no mistaking it:

she actually felt something real against her, touching her, as if her body truly existed. She spun round. Beside her was a monstrous creature: some immense kind of dog, taller than she was, with three slathering heads – one of which was currently sniffing at her feet as if considering having her for lunch – and a writhing snake for a tail. Something in its solidity, contrasting with her unpresent presence, and in the cool damp trail it was transmitting across her not-real calves, made her understand that although she was made of little more than air, this dog-thing was real, it was corporeal, and, moreover, that she was real to it – solid, with a form and a smell. It could consume her if it wanted to – the look on each of its faces told her that. She felt terrified, or her brain told her that she was terrified, and the small part of her that was touching the dog-head experienced the sting of adrenaline. The rest of her was – well, dead. In the face of the monster, she realised that this wasn't heaven: of course not. It must be hell. Why would she, of all people, have been sent to heaven? She tried to resign herself to her fate, and waited for the dog to eat her soul.

But behind her, the other members of the dead were spilling out of the station, spreading slowly outwards like a slick of oil. The creature lost interest in her and took off in their direction, its three heads reaching out and sniffing each of them in turn. Alice felt little relief. The dog had spared her. But she was still dead. And she was, in all probability, in hell. She would have to make the best of it.

She picked a street at random and began to walk.

Twenty-Five

Neil was aware that time was passing, but it didn't feel like time as he was used to it. Time had split in two. There was time before: time that seemed so real and sharp, and short and over. And then there was time after: there was now. And this time had no features, and no end. A slow, lugubrious present without future, without hope. A hideous now that he would be stuck in for ever, always on the wrong side of the cruel, finished, intransigent past. A past that he could look at whenever he liked, and often when he didn't want to, but that he could never touch again.

He didn't have the energy to be angry, and yet he was angry, without the strength to support it. He sat in strange places in the flat, in the hallway, on the stairs, because he didn't want to be in any of the rooms, and he looked at the floor because he didn't want to look forwards. Sometimes he stared at small spaces, the bottom shelf of the cupboard under the stairs, or the gap between the loo and the bathtub, and he imagined crawling into them and tucking his limbs in, like a tiny animal, hiding. He would never come out.

Most of the time he lived in silence. At other times he would try out words. 'Dead,' he might say, to see how it sounded. 'Dead.' Or 'Alice'.

Or he tortured himself. He tortured himself by thinking of all of the missed opportunities, all the things she didn't have a chance to do, the things they never had a chance to do together. He had never even told her how he felt.

And he tortured himself by thinking about how it was all his fault that she'd died. He had been the one who suggested going on the walk; she had wanted to stay in the flat. Further back, he had been the one who had told her to go freelance; if it wasn't for that, she would never have got the job in the house, and she wouldn't have been so upset that night, would not have come round to his flat. And it was his fault that she'd needed the job in the first place – if it wasn't for him, she wouldn't have been sacked for being in the audience for that damn television programme with Apollo.

Apollo. That was a source of torture too. Apollo and Alice, kissing. And who knew what else? He tortured himself thinking about what that second thing was, the thing she never told him. He wanted to know, he didn't want to know. He would never know. But if he could have just brought her back, if she could just be alive, it didn't matter. Apollo could have her. As long as she was happy. As long as she was here.

When he was done torturing himself with all of the bad things he could think of, he tortured himself with the good times, just thinking about her, how wonderful she was, and of all the fun things they'd done, all of the good times they'd had. And if, at any moment, a part of him started to feel better, he would torture himself all the harder, because he didn't want to feel better, because that would mean letting go.

Sometimes, he lay on the bed, just for the smell of her that lingered on the sheets. Or he took her coat into his arms and buried his face in it, as he had once wanted to do with that cardigan he would never see again. He could barely pick up the trace of her, she wore no perfume, used no particular soap. But just knowing these things had touched her skin was enough.

It seemed strange to him that he still had to do normal, everyday things. Eat and sleep, use the loo. He did them when he had to. There was no routine. Sometimes he might sleep for an afternoon on the sofa, then sit up all night leaning against a kitchen counter. At some point he must have called work to tell them he wasn't coming in, but he couldn't remember having done it.

There must have been a funeral but nobody knew to invite him. So he didn't go.

There had been phone calls, from friends, concerned that they hadn't heard from him. He answered in monosyllables, got rid of them as quickly as possible. From journalists, too, interested in what they called the 'lightning angle'; he had hung up on them. Now when the phone rang, he ignored it.

He wasn't eating much, never sitting down to a meal, but picking at things from the fridge or tins from the cupboard when his hunger threatened to distract him from thinking of Alice. He didn't run out of plates, because he was eating straight out of the packets. He did, however, eventually run out of food. This made him violently furious. He opened up all the cupboards, searching for some last thing, slamming the doors again when there was nothing but salt and Marmite. He kicked the fridge. He went back to the cupboard with the Marmite in it and took it out and threw it at the wall. The jar bounced off the wall, leaving a mark, and landed on the floor. It didn't break. He picked it up and threw it again, harder, but with the same result. Then he kicked the jar across the room. This time it finally broke. Neil watched it, and then he sat down at the table, heart pounding.

He found a calm voice with which to reason with himself.

Come on. It's not a problem. You'll just go and get something. There's nothing to be angry about. It doesn't matter. You have to eat.

He thought he was going to cry. Over having no food. He kept thinking about Old Mother Hubbard. He kept repeating in his head, the cupboard was bare. The cupboard was bare. The cupboard was bare.

Come on, said the calm voice again. You're being silly now.

What's the problem? Just go and get yourself something to eat. You can do that. If you make yourself ill, you won't be able to think about her any more.

He decided to go and get a takeaway. He had absolutely no idea what the time was or even what the day was, but it didn't occur to him to wonder whether anywhere would be open. Mechanically he went to the front door, took a jacket off its hook and pulled it over the clothes that he had been wearing since he last changed them, which was something he couldn't remember having done. He picked up his keys and wallet from the table by the door and let himself out.

It was cold. The light was grey. It might be early morning or late evening. The light seemed bright to him though; he hadn't had the lights on in the flat for a while now. He started walking in the direction of the high street. The wind pinched at his cheeks, and he rubbed them, noticing for the first time that he had a beard. He kept his head down, looking only at the pavement in front of him. He didn't want to see any people. Most of all, he was terrified he might see someone that he knew. Or someone that he didn't know, looking happy.

He wasn't hungry for anything in particular so he stopped at the first place on the high street that was open and walked inside. There was a strong, hot smell of fat in the air, but even so the young Asian man behind the counter flinched when he walked in. Neil realised that he must look and smell terrible. Like death, he might once have said. There was nobody else in the shop. It was probably a strange time of day to buy food.

'Hello,' said the man behind the counter. 'What can I get you?'

'Um,' said Neil. 'I don't know.' His voice sounded odd to him. 'What have you got?'

'Cod, haddock, plaice . . .'

'Yes,' said Neil. 'Whatever. Cod.'

'Chips with that?'

'Um,' said Neil. 'Yes. I suppose so.' That meant longer before he had to eat again.

A silence as the man got his order together.

'Ketchup? Vinegar? Mayo?'

'No,' said Neil.

The man shook salt onto the chips.

'Open or closed?'

'I'm sorry?'

'Open or closed?'

Neil felt a wave of panic. He had to make a decision and he didn't know how to. He didn't want to eat here and he didn't want to go home. He didn't want to do anything at all.

'I don't know,' said Neil. 'I don't know.'

'I'll give it to you closed,' said the man. 'Then you can always open it when you like.'

Carefully, the man wrapped Neil's fish and chips in white paper, and then wrapped the packet again in a sheet from the local newspaper. He put the package in a white plastic bag with a little wooden chip fork.

'Three fifty, please,' said the man.

Neil paid him, took his change, and went out into the icy street. He thought maybe it had got darker. He turned back the way he had come and, without lifting his eyes from the pavement, walked home.

Returning to the kitchen, he realised how disgusting it was. Alice would not be impressed by all the detritus littering the surfaces: apple cores, banana peel, biscuit wrappers, soup cartons, abandoned mugs with the remains of milky tea beginning to solidify in them, empty tuna tins with bits of old tuna stuck and hardening on their edges. He was suddenly repulsed by himself. The bin bag that was in the bin was already overflowing, so, putting his fish and chips to one side, he pulled it out and tied it shut, then put in a new one and filled it with all the rubbish that was lying around. The broken jar of Marmite was still where he had left it on the floor, so he unwrapped the top layer off the fish and chips, and started gingerly putting the pieces of broken glass into the newspaper.

That's when he saw the picture. He froze. A cold hand squeezed at his guts.

It wasn't from the front page. There was a caption – LOCAL LUNATIC IN SUICIDE BID – below a photograph, apparently taken with a long lens, of an old man standing on the roof of a house. He was completely naked and had long hair and a beard. He had one arm raised as if throwing something. The picture wasn't too clear, as it had been taken in the pouring rain, but the expression on the man's face was unmistakably livid. It was – and Neil was absolutely certain of this – the face that Neil had seen in the sky, just before he and Alice had been struck by lightning. It wasn't possible. Surely that had just been a trick of the light? But when he looked again at the picture, there was absolutely no way it could be anybody else. Neil knew it was him. And even more so, Neil knew without a doubt that the decrepit roof he was standing on was that of the house which Alice used to clean.

Twenty-Six

'You're late. Don't you read the papers?'

The man who had come to the door was young and handsome, dressed in a close-fitting pinstriped suit that flattered his elegant physique. Neil had never seen him before in his life.

'I think you've got me mixed up with someone else,' he said. 'I'm here to see . . .' The naked old man on your roof?

'Are you Neil?' said the young man.

'Yes.'

'Then I'm Hermes. And you're late. Wait here.'

Hermes shut the door firmly in Neil's face.

It was cold. Neil shoved his hands into the pockets of his coat and shifted from foot to foot. He had had a shower and a shave, washed his hair and combed it back, and dressed in clean clothes. And as he washed and dressed, and all the way on the bus and the Tube that had brought him here, he had puzzled over the image from the newspaper, and the face he had seen the day that Alice died. It just didn't make any sense, and now more than ever Neil needed things to make sense. Was it some kind of trick, he thought, was that why this man knew who he was? But he couldn't see how the trick had been done. Or perhaps it was an hallucination – but then what about the newspaper article? That was real – he had it in his pocket. There must be some kind of rational explanation. Even though nothing that had happened to him recently seemed all that rational.

The door opened again to reveal Hermes and a woman whom Neil had also never met, dressed in a blue tracksuit with her hair tied carelessly back. This woman looked a lot like Apollo, except with dark hair, and she was looking at Neil with a mixture of shock and contempt.

'Is this him?' she said to Hermes.

'I think so,' said Hermes.

'You mean you hadn't met him before?'

'No,' said Hermes.

'He can't be right. Look at him. What am I supposed to do with that? He's so scrawny and mousy and short.'

'Odysseus was scrawny,' said Hermes. 'And he was one of the best.'

'He didn't look like a mouse,' said the woman.

'He was pretty short.'

'Yes, but he didn't have such rodenty features.'

'Well, it was the best I could do at such short notice.'

'Short being the operative word.'

'Excuse me,' interrupted Neil, 'enjoyable as this is, I really think you've got me mixed up with someone else.'

'No,' said Artemis, 'we were definitely talking about you.'

'I'm here about Alice,' said Neil.

'We know,' said Hermes.

'Look,' said the woman to Hermes, 'why don't you go back in and I'll see what I can do with him. You're right, appearances can be deceptive. Occasionally.'

'OK,' said Hermes. 'Call me if you need anything.'

And he went back inside, slamming the door behind him once again.

'Right,' said the woman, 'we'd better go.'

'Go where?' said Neil. 'Who are you? What's this got to do with Alice?'

'I'm Artemis, Alice was my cleaner, and we need to get away from the house before anybody sees you.'

'But I want to go in,' said Neil. 'There's someone I need to see.'

'You can't go in,' said Artemis. 'Nobody goes in.'

'I've been in before,' said Neil.

'You have?' said Artemis. 'When?'

'The day before Alice . . . died.'

Artemis eyed him with new appreciation.

'And you're still alive?' she said. 'Impressive. Maybe I'll be able to use you after all.'

'Use me?' said Neil.

'Come on,' said Artemis, 'let's go.'

'But –'

'Now.'

Suddenly feeling as powerless to resist as an iron filing confronted with a magnet, Neil nodded.

They walked to the Heath in silence. Artemis wasn't running, but she walked so briskly that Neil had trouble keeping up. He noticed that every time they passed a dog, she would look at it in hopeful anticipation, before invariably turning away in disappointment and carrying on marching even more quickly than before.

'Did you lose your dog?' Neil asked her.

'They died,' said Artemis.

Because of the cold, Parliament Hill wasn't busy, just a couple of people flying large, complicated kites, and a small yellow dog barking first at one, then the other. Artemis glanced at the dog with what seemed to be pity. She selected a bench from where they could see the view across the city but which also looked over the path.

'You never know who could have followed us,' she said, sitting down.

Neil didn't reply as he sat down beside her. The hugeness of London, spread out in ashen miniature before him, filled him with such terrible sadness that he thought he might weep. What was the point of living here without Alice? There wasn't a single building or street out there that he wanted to visit without her. He thought that maybe he would move away, start a new life somewhere else. A new life. The thought didn't give him any hope. He pulled his coat tightly around himself against the bitter air.

'We can talk relatively freely here,' said Artemis. 'The trees won't tell. They're on our side.'

'The trees?'

'Apollo's taken terrible liberties with them over the years.'

'That I can believe,' said Neil.

'You know him?'

'We've met.'

'And still you live,' said Artemis, shaking her head. 'You are tenacious.'

'Look, I have some questions,' said Neil, reaching for the square of newspaper in his pocket.

'Of course,' said Artemis. 'We should get down to business. Tell me, Neil. Have you ever done anything that might be described as heroic?'

'What?' said Neil.

'Please,' said Artemis. 'It is important.'

'I thought we were here to talk about Alice.'

'We are,' said Artemis.

'I don't see the connection,' said Neil.

'I do,' said Artemis.

Neil sighed. 'Well, as it happens,' he said, 'I did once try to do something heroic, and you're right, it was about Alice. She asked for my help and I tried to give it. And now she's dead. So, that went well. Aside from that, no, I have never done anything in my life that could ever even remotely be described as heroic. It's not really the kind of thing you're called upon to do, when you're an engineer. I always try to make the buildings I work on as safe as I possibly can. I suppose some people might think that was heroic, in the very loosest sense. I've given blood a few times; they say that's heroic, but I don't think it counts as real heroism if they give you a cup of tea and a digestive biscuit afterwards. But if you're asking if I'm the kind of person who would risk their life rescuing strangers from a burning building . . . Well, I don't know. I'd like to think I was. But I'm not sure. I don't think you can ever be sure until you're tested.'

On the grassy slope beneath them, a toddler ran away from his mother, fell, and began to wail. The mother scooped him up in her arms and held him as he screamed. Alice would have been a good mum, Neil thought.

'Do you think Alice saw you as heroic?'

'What's this all about, anyway?' said Neil.

'I was the one who hired her, you know,' said Artemis. 'I liked her. She was a lot stronger than she looked.'

Neil glanced at her. She was looking straight ahead, at the view in front of them. He couldn't read the expression on her face. He realised that she was beautiful, something that he hadn't noticed before. She seemed to be the kind of woman who didn't want people to notice that she was beautiful. Like Alice.

'I liked her too,' he said. 'More than she knew.'

'Did you love her?' said Artemis.

'Yes.'

'Good. That'll help.'

'Help what?' said Neil. 'It doesn't seem to be helping much at the moment.'

'You're having trouble getting over her.'

'Yes.'

'Do you think you could replace her with someone else?'

'You can be pretty blunt, you know that?'

'Well, do you?'

Neil looked away.

'You know,' he said, 'that's the thought that frightens me most of all.'

'Why?' said Artemis.

'Because how I feel about her is all I've got left.' Neil looked down at his hands. 'I don't know how to think about it,' he said. 'I know how I feel about it – shocked, angry, devastated – but I don't know how to think about it. I didn't want it to happen and it happened. I don't know why it happened. There is no reason.'

'Sometimes,' suggested Artemis, 'there is a reason, but you just don't know it.'

Neil shook his head. 'I don't believe in that kind of thing,' he said. 'I'm here, and she's gone. And I'm stuck. There's no direction I can go in. If I met someone else, what meaning would there be left? If the pain goes, does that mean I never loved her? How can I get over it? I can't, I mustn't. But what else am I going to do?'

They sat in silence for a few moments. Neil noticed that his breath steamed in the cold air, but that Artemis's didn't. Somewhere, he could hear the thin song of a bird.

'I've never had sex,' said Artemis suddenly.

'I'm sorry?' said Neil. He really hoped that she wasn't going to proposition him.

'I've never had sex,' repeated Artemis. 'Never wanted to.' It was her turn not to look at him as she spoke. 'Not with a man or with a woman, or with an animal, though my family joke about it. And I never will. The thought of it disgusts me. But the others – my family – they think that means I haven't got any feelings. That I could never care about anyone, that I don't know what love is, just because I don't –' she shuddered. 'But you know what?' she said, turning to him now. 'I really loved my dogs. Everyone laughs at me for it, but it's true. The time I spent with them, running, hunting, those were the happiest times of my life. They understood me. They were animals but they understood me far better than anyone in my family ever will. We shared something, we were the same. And they made me kill them.'

'What?' said Neil.

Artemis turned away again. 'We couldn't afford to look after them any more.'

'That's terrible,' said Neil.

'I do understand loss,' said Artemis.

Neil didn't know what to say but he didn't feel as if he could just say nothing. He shifted uncomfortably.

'I've never had sex either,' he said eventually. 'I wanted to with Alice but I was too scared to touch her.'

Artemis beamed. 'I like you,' she said. 'This could work.'

'What could work?' said Neil.

'Do you want to be a hero?' said Artemis.

Neil rubbed his forehead. 'It's too late,' he said. 'I failed Alice. The night before she – she died, and all of that day up until it happened, Alice was really scared. As if she knew what was coming. And then, just before . . . She was about to tell me what was going on. But then it happened. Before she could. I couldn't save her from dying.'

'It isn't too late,' said Artemis.

'Yes it is,' said Neil.

They both watched as a pair of red-faced joggers went by.

'Did she tell you she kissed Apollo?' said Artemis.

Neil's head snapped round to look at her.

'How did you know?'

'She told Hermes.'

'Hermes?'

'Don't worry. It was all Apollo's fault. He's very persuasive. She was never interested in him. If that's what's been bothering you. It was Apollo's fault she died as well, that's why we have to do something about it.'

It was as if all of the emotion had been sucked out of him, leaving only emptiness. There was something about her; he'd actually started to believe she could help him. But Artemis's claim was insane. She didn't know what she was talking about after all.

'But it wasn't Apollo's fault,' he said. 'She was struck by lightning. If anything, it was my fault. If it wasn't for me, she would never have been there.'

'Why did you come to the house?'

'It doesn't matter now.'

'What was it you wanted to show me?'

'Now you want to talk about that?'

'Just show me.'

Neil put his hand in his pocket and pulled out the small square of newspaper. He unfolded it and looked again at the picture: the face he had seen in the sky. He handed it to Artemis who looked at it for several seconds in silence, her jaw tight.

'Not everything is as it seems,' she said eventually.

'I disagree. I think everything is always exactly as it seems,' said Neil.

'Then why did you keep that piece of paper?' said Artemis.

'I don't know,' said Neil. 'It was just a stupid thought. It doesn't mean anything. Who is it, anyway?'

'That's my father,' said Artemis. 'I haven't seen him in a very long time.'

Neil folded the paper up and put it back in his pocket.

'When you came to the house,' said Artemis, 'you were looking for him, weren't you? Because of what happened.'

'OK. Yes, I thought that he might have had something to do with what happened to Alice,' he said. 'But he couldn't possibly have. It was just an accident, that was all it was. One of those cruel meaningless things that happen to people all the time and this time it happened to Alice. It happened to me. And at times like that you clutch at straws. And this was my straw. My last straw.'

'But why did you think he had something to do with it?' persisted Artemis.

Neil didn't reply.

'You saw him, didn't you?' said Artemis. 'In the sky.'

'I don't know what I saw,' said Neil.

'Do you know the story of Orpheus and Eurydice?' Artemis asked.

'What's that got to do with anything?'

'Well, do you?'

'I'm not a big fan of religious stories,' said Neil. 'Even old ones.'

'Orpheus was a young musician,' said Artemis anyway. 'Long hair, a bit of what you might call a hippie. Eurydice was his wife, a very nice girl, very pretty. They were terribly in love. But she didn't live long after the wedding. She was bitten by a snake and died.'

Artemis shot a glance at him. Neil gave her a quick, tight smile to show that he was following the parallels.

'Orpheus, as I'm sure you can understand, was devastated. So devastated in fact that he went into the underworld to get Eurydice back. He went to the palace where Hades and Persephone live – well, I haven't been there, it's described as a palace but it's not like anyone can check – and he sang to them so movingly about his loss that they let him have Eurydice back. Can you sing, Neil?'

'Not at all.'

'Never mind. The tragic thing was that they allowed Orpheus to take his wife back with him to the upperworld – to this world, the world of the living – on the condition that he didn't turn around and look at her as they were returning. But of course he loved her so much that he did, just to make sure that she was following. And so Eurydice was snatched away from him and sent back to live for ever amongst the dead.'

'What happened to Orpheus?' said Neil.

'Oh, he was torn limb from limb and his head was thrown into the river Hebrus. But that's not the point of the story.'

'What is the point of the story?' said Neil.

'The point is,' said Artemis, 'that it establishes a precedent.'

'What are you talking about, a precedent?'

'Precedents are very important,' said Artemis. 'It means if you've done it before you can do it again. You can do it, Neil.'

'What?'

'You could go down there and get her back. They'd have to let you! It's been done before! All you'd have to do is prove that you love her, and it's obvious to me that you do.'

Neil felt disgusted. With Artemis and, even more than that, with himself, for having got into this situation.

'You're mad,' he said.

'No, I'm not,' said Artemis. 'I'm trying to help you. Let me just explain.'

'You told me,' he said, 'we were here to talk about Alice. I listened to you. I talked to you. I told you things that nobody else knows . . .'

'You don't understand!' said Artemis. 'I can make it happen! I can get you down there!'

She reached out to put her hand on his arm.

'Don't touch me!' Neil jumped up, started backing away from her. 'I should have known it would be something like this. I should have left when you started talking about seeing faces in the sky. You live in that house with Apollo and obviously you're just like him.'

'But I'm not!' cried Artemis, jumping up to face him. 'We're total opposites! Trust me, Neil.'

'Trust is not the issue,' said Neil. 'You seem like a nice woman, a well-meaning woman, and I'm sure you believe what you're saying. But I don't believe you. I don't believe any of it. When you die, you die. It's over. Don't try to give me false hope. You think you're helping, but you're not helping at all. You're just hurting me.'

'But Neil –'

'No. If you really care about my well-being you'll leave me alone. I used to think this kind of thing was funny but it's not.

You're all the same, you just hurt people when they're too weak to resist.'

'But you're wrong,' pleaded Artemis. 'I can help you. I know what you mean, I understand you more than you can imagine, I know about all those so-called religious people who are just peddling lies and false comfort, believe me I know. But I'm different. I promise. Everything I've told you, it's all true.'

'They all say that.'

'But I'm different! I'm a goddess, Neil.'

'*What?*'

'Let me show you.'

Seeing the earnestness on her face as she reached out to him, Neil was filled with such revulsion that all he wanted to do was to punch her in the jaw. The only way he could avoid hitting her was to do what he actually did, which was to turn round and to run as fast as he could down the hill and away from where she was standing. When he was at a safe distance from her, he was filled with sudden embarrassment, and looked over his shoulder, half expecting to see her running after him. But she was still standing at the top of the hill, watching him go.

He didn't slow his pace, but ran on, following the path into a copse of trees. Then suddenly he felt what seemed to be a gust of wind blowing past him, and there was Artemis, standing in front of him. He stumbled and half fell at her feet, gasping for breath.

'How . . . how did you . . .' he stuttered.

'I ran,' said Artemis.

'But . . .'

'I am a goddess,' she said.

'There's no such thing,' said Neil.

'How else could I get down here so fast?' said Artemis.

'I don't know. Roller skates? A tunnel?' said Neil. 'It'll take more than some trick to convince me.'

'I know deep down you believe me. I know this is what you want to do.'

'You're wrong,' said Neil.

'You will change your mind,' said Artemis.

Neil shook his head. Artemis took a small white card out of the pocket of her tracksuit.

'You know as well as I do that we can't let Apollo win,' she said. 'Don't come back to the house, it isn't safe. This is Hermes' number. You can call it any time of the day or night, he'll always answer, and he can get a message to me.'

She handed him the card. He looked at it. There were only three digits on it.

'This can't be his number,' he said.

'It is,' said Artemis. 'Call him when you're ready.'

'I'll never be ready,' said Neil.

'Yes you will,' said Artemis.

Without saying another word, she turned from him and began to run, and in what seemed only to be a split second, she was gone.

Twenty-Seven

Alice had no idea how long she had been in the underworld. All of the things she was accustomed to using to measure time had been lost the moment she had stepped down the escalators at Angel Tube station and Upper Street had disappeared behind her, taking the real world with it. There was no sense of the time of day here; the light never changed. There was no sense of time of year either. There was nothing that she could class as weather, no sun or rain or snow, and she didn't have a body with which to feel the temperature. Having no body meant that she felt no sensations that marked the passing of time, like needing to eat or to sleep, and she had no menstrual cycle to help her keep track of the days. Had she been here weeks, months or years, or merely hours? And did it matter? In the scheme of things, it wasn't very long, considering that she still had all of eternity left to go.

She had walked for what seemed like a very long way before finally getting out of the suburbs of hell. She didn't see any more monsters. She did, though, pass other people. Veteran dead, they glanced at her without curiosity. There were white people, black people, oriental people, Indians, Arabs, Aborigines, Pygmies, Maoris, Inuit, and people the like of whom she had never seen before, people who looked completely different from anyone that she was familiar with, from populations that had become extinct centuries before she was born. As with her own consignment, there were people of every possible age, including the tiniest of babies, who seemed to propel themselves along the pavement with no effort or movement of their bodies at all.

After some time – hours? days? – some tall buildings began to emerge from the dim light ahead of her, so she headed towards them. As she approached, the skyline looked almost, but not quite, familiar: like Manhattan, but drawn from memory, by a committee. This was, she discovered later, pretty much exactly what it was. The Tudors ran straight up to the skyscraper district. The last houses on the row looked like tiny pieces of striped liquorice, dwarfed by their gleaming steel and glass neighbours.

Despite a higher density of people, the streets of the city centre were no less silent than the suburbs. And the cleanliness was almost eerie – no litter, no graffiti, no pollution, no grime of any kind. Even Alice, who hated dirt, felt uncomfortable, as if she was tarnishing the place just by being there. The buildings were stunning, massive and glorious, seeming to shine with the reflected light of a sun that didn't exist here. She couldn't believe that such beauty could exist in hell, and she wondered what the buildings were for. There didn't seem to be any doormen or restrictions on entry, and streams of the dead passed constantly in and out. Alice waited for a small group to go inside one of the buildings, and followed them in through the automatic doors, hoping she wouldn't be noticed.

The building had an immense marble and gilt lobby which had been modified for practical purposes. Carpeting had been laid down in orange-brown felt, and the room was divided into more manageable spaces by enormous filing cabinets. Some of these makeshift rooms had desks inside them, where dead people were engaged in a series of earnest-looking interviews. Alice, who didn't like being interviewed, started to back away, but she caught the eye of a beautiful, fine-boned black woman in her forties, wearing a hospital gown, who was seated behind one of the desks. The woman beckoned to her. Not wishing to be rude,

Alice went over and sat down. The woman had no hair, and only one breast. A small sign on her desk revealed her name as Mary.

'Do you speak English?' said Alice.

Mary replied something that Alice couldn't understand.

'I'm so sorry, I speak many languages but I don't understand what you just said,' said Alice. '*Je ne comprend pas. Ich verstehe nicht?*'

'I said "Newbie?" My meaning was "Are you a newbie"?' said Mary in a lilting African accent. 'Of course, you are. Otherwise you would know that we all understand each other here. There is no real language. We are not really speaking you see. We cannot move the air with our lungs. It is metaphysical communication that we are sharing. It sounds like words, but it is not really.'

Alice tried to understand, but there was too much to take in.

'What is this place?' she asked, trying to start with something simple.

Mary's eyes widened with concern. She reached out and patted Alice on the hand. Alice could see the patting, but she felt nothing.

'It is the underworld, darling,' Mary said. 'Do not worry, many people suffer from such confusion. You are dead, my dear.'

'Oh, I'm sorry,' said Alice. 'That's not what I meant. I know that I'm dead. What I meant was, where am I now? Is this hell?'

'No my dear, this is not hell,' said Mary. 'All of the dead are here. Do not worry. You are not being punished.'

'What is this building?' said Alice.

'Ah,' said Mary. 'This is building F of the administrative centre for Sector A. Sector A is the arrivals district.'

'I thought this was the centre of the underworld,' said Alice. 'It's just one small sector?'

'Do you know how many billions of people have died?' said Mary. 'Do you think that they all fit into one city?' Seeing Alice's stricken face, her tone softened. 'It takes a long time to get used to it,' she said. 'But you will get used to it, slowly by slowly. Do not worry. I am still uncertain about many things myself.'

'How long have you been dead?' said Alice.

'I do not know,' said Mary. 'Not so long, I think. I died in Kampala, Uganda, in 1956.'

'That's about fifty years,' said Alice.

'A very short time,' said Mary. 'But already I have learnt much. Soon I will move out of the arrivals sector myself. Now, what can I help you with today?'

'I'm not sure,' said Alice. 'I've only just got here.'

'If you are here, it is because you are ready to be here,' said Mary with a smile, clear and warm like tropical water. 'There are many, many thousands of dead, arriving every day. They move in their own time. Those who can already walk find their way here. Those who cannot walk find their way here too, but it takes longer.'

'But from the station you could go in any direction,' said Alice. 'How do you know people won't get lost?'

'All directions lead here,' said Mary. 'And when you are ready, you arrive.'

'So now what do I do?' said Alice.

'It is up to you,' said Mary. 'There is no need for you to do anything at all. You have no body. You have no needs. You require no food, no shelter. There is no money. Many people choose not to have a home. Others have homes that they never leave. If you wish to have a home, I can find one for you.'

Alice thought of the endless rows of houses outside and tried to imagine living in one, all alone.

'Equally, if you wish, I can help you to find a job. Many people when they arrive, they do not wish to be in employment. They feel they have worked hard enough already. But I would not advise this. It is good to work. You have purpose. You meet people. You do not get depressed. Depression is a very bad thing in the underworld. Many people are depressed here. It is a terrible thing. People become motionless. You will see them. They stand by the sides of roads or they lie in their beds in their houses, and they do not move. They may not move for many centuries, many thousands of years. They cannot see the point of moving. Because there is no point.'

'Oh dear,' said Alice. 'Poor things.'

'So, I ask you again. What can I help you with today?'

'I think I would like a job, please,' said Alice.

'Very good, very good!' said Mary, clapping her hands silently. 'That is what I had hoped that you would say. You are a very intelligent girl. I will send you up to our careers department immediately.'

The careers adviser was a nude Aboriginal boy aged around four who introduced himself as Mr Kunmanara. He took her through her options, explaining to her that the employment market amongst the dead was both highly competitive and exceptionally fluid.

'People only work because they want to,' he said, 'so the waiting list for the most popular jobs is, shall we say, a little daunting. You'll find you can only become a movie star or a pop singer if you have a lengthy CV showing your commitment to post-life employment by having taken on some of the less prestigious, but perhaps more necessary, positions. Working as a careers adviser, for example.'

He waited for the laughter, but Alice forgot to laugh.

'Having said that,' he continued, in a slightly piqued tone, 'if you are prepared to wait for long enough, an opening will always arise, and of course waiting is a luxury that you most certainly can afford.'

Alice smiled weakly and nodded.

'Now, tell me,' said Mr Kunmanara, 'what is your pre-death work experience?'

'I am – I mean, I was – a cleaner.'

The boy shook his head and tutted. 'I'll put it down,' he

said, 'but we don't really need cleaners here. No dirt. Anything else?'

'Not really,' said Alice. 'After I left university I temped for a while, but I wasn't very good at it. I'm not very comfortable in an office environment. I don't like talking.'

'That will be a hindrance,' said Mr Kunmanara, 'but we'll put it down all the same, just in case. What did you study at university?'

'Linguistics,' said Alice.

The child sighed. 'I'm afraid there's very little use for that here either.'

'Yes, the woman downstairs explained,' said Alice. 'No languages.'

'I fear I'm going to find you very hard to place,' said the boy, leaning back in his specially-designed high chair. 'There are certain fields here that are endlessly in demand. Architecture for example. Engineering.'

Alice, who had been trying hard all of this time not to think of Neil, flinched. The boy misunderstood her.

'You may well think these professions beneath your contempt, Miss Mulholland, but you will find that the whole fabric of the underworld is held together by such people. Without them, there would be nothing here. What do you think holds these buildings together? None of it is "real". It's all done with the power of the mind. And that takes skill and training. If you were to try to hold up this building, Miss Mulholland, with the power of your mind, I have no doubt that we would be conducting this interview waist-deep in rubble. You need proper structural knowledge.'

'Yes,' said Alice. 'Of course.'

'It is a shame,' mused the boy, 'that no kind of pre-death training programme can be established, to make sure that we have enough of these useful skills to keep us going here, and to dissuade people from pursuing the areas that have no function here at all. Such as cleaning. And linguistics.'

'I'm sorry,' said Alice.

'To resume,' said Mr Kunmanara. 'Do you have any other abilities at all? Any hobbies? Interests? Anything?'

'I collect porcelain miniatures,' said Alice.

The boy yawned.

'And I like playing Scrabble.'

The boy snapped to attention.

'Scrabble? Why didn't you say that in the first instance?' He sat forward eagerly. 'Are you gifted?'

'Not really,' said Alice. 'I did come third in the British national under-16 championship.'

'You are too modest,' said Mr Kunmanara. 'At last this is something which can be of some use! Leisure, entertainment, these are the lifeblood of the dead community. You cannot yet imagine, Miss Mulholland, how very boring it is to exist here. A person of advanced skill at board games – this is a rare find indeed! Believe me, you will find yourself endlessly in demand.'

'But –' said Alice.

'Of course, we will have to train you up first, in the precision movements you will require to pick up the Scrabble pieces. Then we can put you to work in one of our highest class gaming establishments.'

'I'm not really sure that I –'

'Congratulations, Miss Mulholland!' The boy leant back in his chair and smiled. 'I believe we have found your vocation.'

Twenty-Eight

Apollo was depressed. At first he thought he was just bored, which was a sensation he was familiar with, having suffered from boredom for the best part of several thousand years. But none of his usual distractions seemed to work this time: getting drunk and watching near-impossible acts of lewdness at *Bacchanalia*; recreating those lewd acts with Aphrodite back at home; writing songs about himself on his guitar and performing them to whichever members of the household he could bribe to listen, then basking in their efforts to conceal their enjoyment; taking long walks through London and attempting to seduce whichever mortals caught his eye – this last failing, even when he did manage to persuade them to have sex with him, because no mortal could live up to his memories of Alice. He thought losing himself in work might help, but when he phoned them, both his agent and the production company that made the pilot of *Apollo's Oracle* told him they were busy and promised to call him back, but neither of them ever did. Subsequent calls were diverted to voice-mail. After the first few attempts, he took to picking up his guitar and singing his messages to them down the phone, but it did no good.

What he really wanted to do was lie in bed and not move for a few years, but sharing a bedroom with Ares made that impossible. The war between Athena and Hera was reaching a critical stage, and Ares was using his half of the room as a centre of operations, with Athena constantly dropping by and requesting updates and changes in that way that she had – 'What would be the plausibility of countermanding the redeployment of rear-most forces in consideration of the UN amendment?' – while Hera sent down peacocks with notes tied around their necks who inevitably took the opportunity to shit on the floor as they passed. That the shit was never cleaned up was yet another reminder of Alice's absence from the house, an absence which he felt more keenly than the presence of any of the members of his family, infuriating as they were.

So he did get up, though he rarely bothered to dress, prefer-ring to wrap himself in the comforting folds of a sheet or blanket, which reminded him of the robes they used to wear long ago in better days, back when the mortals cared. He would drift down to the rooms on the ground floor of the house, like a ghost, he hoped, varying the rooms he brought his dark mood to, though not varying the actual mood. He was deeply, desper-ately unhappy, and torn between inviting the sympathy he craved from the rest of his family by showing them how he felt, and the certain knowledge that all he would get from them was contempt and mockery.

One afternoon as he sat, alone, on a listing chair in the corner of the living room, plucking sporadically at a single note on his least favourite guitar, the door to the room opened and Eros came in. He was dressed very sensibly, in pressed khaki trousers, a navy round-necked sweater and a green and white striped shirt, and his hair was carefully combed as always. He didn't appear to notice Apollo as he sat down on the sofa with a pad and a pen, so Apollo twanged particularly aggressively at his solitary note.

'Oh,' said Eros, looking up. 'Hello, Apollo. I didn't see you there.'

'What are you up to?' said Apollo. He didn't really care. He just wanted Eros to tell him quickly and then ask him what he was up to, so that he could say 'Nothing,' in a mournful voice.

'I just got back from a rehearsal for the youth club Easter show,' said Eros.

'Easter? Already?' Apollo was genuinely surprised.

'I know,' said Eros. 'Persephone will be back soon. Actually she should probably be here already. Anyway, the show's only next week, I hope she's back by then. The kids are really looking forward to it. They've persuaded me to do a rap.'

'You? A rap?'

'I know,' said Eros. 'It'll be completely humiliating, I'm sure that's why they asked me to do it. I'll live it down eventually, but by then they'll probably all be dead.'

'Doesn't it bother you?' said Apollo. 'Looking stupid in front of mortals?'

'No,' said Eros. 'Why should it? They're just children, Apollo, even the adults. Do you worry about looking stupid in front of babies?'

Apollo did. 'No,' he said.

'You could help me write it if you like,' said Eros. He waved the pen and paper at Apollo. 'I'm going to do a terrible job of it. You could come and perform it with me.'

'I'd rather not,' said Apollo.

'Of course not,' said Eros. 'I know how much you hate being the centre of attention.'

Apollo wondered whether Eros was being sarcastic. 'Yeah,' he said.

'I'm sure I'll come up with something,' said Eros. 'Though this is hardly the most conducive place to write.'

Apollo looked around the room. The walls were covered with scorch marks from Hera's temper tantrum. Only the very tops of the curtains remained where the rest had burned away, and what furniture was left was even more dilapidated than it had been, upholstery singed, arms and legs broken or missing.

'Hephaestus should really do something about it,' Eros continued, 'or that cleaner, when she gets back from holiday –'

He broke off. He looked at Apollo with what appeared to be genuine concern.

'What's wrong?' he said.

This was Apollo's chance. 'Nothing,' he said, in the most grief-stricken tones he could muster.

'Really?' said Eros. 'Are you sure?' When Apollo didn't say anything more, he went on, 'I tell you what, I can't wait for Persephone to get back. At least the weather will start to pick up properly then.'

'It's a while since I've been out,' Apollo said.

'Why not?' said Eros.

'No reason,' said Apollo, and sighed.

'Apollo, if you're upset about something, instead of dropping hints, why don't you just tell me what the matter is?'

'Why would I want to talk to you?' said Apollo. 'I don't even like you.'

'Well I do agree it seems strange,' said Eros, and waited.

'Alice is dead,' Apollo blurted out suddenly.

'The cleaner?' Eros said.

He looked genuinely shocked, Apollo thought. The colour had bleached out of his face leaving an ungodlike pallor.

'I thought she was just away,' said Eros. 'What happened?'

'Zeus,' said Apollo. 'He found out we'd had a mortal in the house.'

Eros looked relieved for a moment, but only for a moment.

'How did Zeus find out we'd had a mortal in the house?'

'Well, you know,' said Apollo, waving one hand vaguely in the air. 'Omnipotent. Omniscient. That sort of thing.'

'We both know Zeus is a long way from omnipotent or omniscient,' said Eros. 'Somebody must have told him. Apollo? Did you tell him about the cleaner?'

'Why would I have done that?' said Apollo.

Eros rubbed his face with his hands. 'I really wish I didn't know the answer to that,' he said.

'I don't know what you mean,' said Apollo, 'seeing as I didn't do it.'

Eros was looking fidgety now, squirming in his chair.

'Why?' said Apollo. 'What is the answer?'

Eros didn't reply for a few seconds, and when he did, he just said, 'Did you want Alice to die?'

'Yes,' admitted Apollo. 'That doesn't mean I did anything.'

'Why did you want her to die?' said Eros.

'Because I loved her and she didn't love me,' said Apollo.

'I was afraid that was the reason.' Eros put his pad and paper down on the floor beside him. 'And now you feel – nauseous?'

'Yes.'

Eros swallowed. 'Restless.'

'Yes.'

'Clammy palms.'

'Yes.'

Eros wiped his hands on his trousers. 'A strange gnawing at your insides that you can't ignore.'

'Yes.'

'A persistent wish that you had done things differently.'

'I did do things differently. But, theoretically, yes.'

'Half of you wants to make amends but the other wants to bury yourself away somewhere and to deny that it ever happened at all.'

'Eros, do you have the power to read minds? You've never done it before.'

'No,' said Eros. 'It's just that, unlike you, I am familiar with feeling guilty. It's one of the things you have to learn, if you're going to be a Christian.'

'Guilty. Right.' Apollo nodded slowly. 'You think that's what it is?'

'Almost certainly, if you feel in any way responsible for Alice's death.'

'Why would I feel that?' said Apollo. 'Zeus killed her.'

'There are a lot of ways of being responsible,' said Eros.

He seemed to forget that Apollo was in the room, his attention drifting over to the charcoal-stained window.

'So if that is what it is,' said Apollo, loath to lose the sympathy, 'If I am feeling guilty. Whether I am actually guilty or not. How can I make it go away?'

Eros turned back to him. 'That's a good question,' he said. 'If you were a good Christian you would atone for your sins and pray for forgiveness.'

'And that would work?'

'Apparently.'

'Forgiveness from a god that doesn't exist gets rid of guilt?'

'Only if you believe in him,' said Eros. 'That's what I've been trying to explain to all of you for decades. Belief is a powerful thing. For mortals, belief changes everything, what they do, how they feel . . .'

Apollo could sense that Eros was about to go off on one, so he leapt in.

'So it doesn't work if you don't believe in that god, then.'

'Unfortunately, no,' said Eros.

'So then what are you supposed to do?'

'Well, you have the choice,' said Eros. 'Either you can let the guilt burn inside you like the fiery torments of hell until it destroys you utterly. That's where the idea of hell comes from, I've always thought. Or you can apologise to the person that you've wronged, and see if they will forgive you.'

'But Alice's dead. I can't apologise to her.'

'But she isn't the only person affected by her death,' said Eros. 'There are many people you could apologise to. Her friends, her family . . .'

'Right. And then this feeling will go away,' said Apollo.

'That's the idea,' said Eros.

'So why doesn't everyone apologise all the time?' said Apollo.

Eros crossed his legs and uncrossed them again.

'I suppose apologising takes a certain amount of courage,' he said. 'You have to face up to what you've done, be ready to take the consequences, whatever they are. Sometimes it's easier just to live with the guilt. And . . .'

Apollo waited. 'And what?' he said eventually.

'What do you mean?'

'I don't know, I thought you were going to say something else.'

'No, no,' said Eros. He picked up his pad and his pen and stood up. 'Was that all you wanted to talk to me about?'

'I suppose so,' said Apollo.

'Well, I hope you feel better,' said Eros. 'Anyway, I'd better go. There's something I forgot to do, back at the church.'

And as Eros left the room, Apollo could see the wings under his sweater twitching and jumping in their haste to get him out of there.

Twenty-Nine

Every time Neil thought about his encounter with Artemis, he got upset. It wasn't the thought that she didn't believe what she had said to him; it was the thought that she did. There was something about her utter certainty that Alice still existed in another form and another place, and that somehow he could reach her there, which made him doubt. It made him doubt that she had really gone. And he didn't want to doubt, because doubt made him hope, and the hope was more painful than the despair: it gave him more to lose.

So he decided that his meeting with Artemis would be the spur for him to Get Over It, Let Go and Move On – the words were fixed in his head like a caption on a daytime talk show. He went to the supermarket. He called work and told them that he would be in at the beginning of the following week. And he forced himself to clean the entire flat the way Alice would have done it, even though every act of cleaning reminded him agonisingly of her. The only thing he couldn't bring himself to do was to change the sheets that she had slept in. He knew he would have to do it eventually. Just not yet.

He was putting his laundry in the machine when the doorbell rang. His first instinct was to ignore it. There wasn't anybody that he wanted to see. But that wasn't in the spirit of Getting Over It, Letting Go and Moving On. So he dropped the rest of the dirty clothes on the floor and was just straightening up when the doorbell rang a second time, its intrusive shriek holding on for just a second longer than was necessary.

'I'm coming!' yelled Neil.

He took the keys off their hook by the flat door, and went out into the chilly communal entrance hall, immediately regretting not having put a jumper on. Through the distorting glass of the front door he could see the silhouette of the caller raise its arm to ring the bell a third time. He leapt forward and pulled the door open before it had a chance. The caller dropped his arm in a gesture that was uncharacteristically sheepish.

'What the hell are you doing here?' said Neil.

'Hello,' said Apollo.

'How did you find out where I live?' said Neil.

'Hermes told me,' said Apollo.

'Hermes? But he's supposed to be –' on my side, was the end of that thought, but it was swiftly overtaken by a new one: 'How does Hermes know where I live?'

'It's his job.'

'His job?'

Apollo didn't elaborate. An arctic wind blew in off the street, lifting the hair on Neil's arms and bringing him out in goose bumps the size of peas. He ignored it, crossed his arms, tried to look like the master of the house.

'What do you want?' he said.

'I, ah,' said Apollo. He shifted on his feet a bit, hands in his pockets. 'I'm . . . Forget it. Nothing.'

'Nothing?' Neil repeated.

'Nothing,' Apollo confirmed.

'You found out my address and came all the way to Hackney for nothing?'

'That's right,' said Apollo.

'Goodbye, then,' said Neil, going to close the door.

'Wait!' said Apollo. He locked his eyes on Neil's in a way that reminded him of Artemis. 'I do need to talk to you. Can I come in?'

Neil hesitated. He tried to look away but he couldn't.

'Sure,' he found himself saying, apparently in direct contradiction of his will.

He pulled the door further open rather than shutting it, and Apollo followed him down the corridor and through into the flat. Neil shut the door behind them.

'Come through to the kitchen,' he said. 'I for one could certainly do with a beer.'

Neil went to the kitchen, wondering what the hell he was doing. Behind him, Apollo was chattering nervously but politely about the flat. 'Very cosy,' he heard him saying, 'I like your carpet.' Neil couldn't get the image of Alice kissing Apollo out of his head. Why had she done it? Of course, Apollo was far more handsome than Neil could ever hope to be. But Artemis had said that Alice wasn't interested, that Apollo was very 'persuasive'. Though why he should believe a thing that insane woman said was another matter. Still, Apollo did seem quite persuasive, Neil had to admit, as he opened the fridge and offered his arch-enemy a beer.

'No, thank you,' said Apollo.

Neil took a bottle out of the fridge for himself and they both sat down at the kitchen table.

'So,' said Neil. 'What was it you wanted to talk to me about?'

Apollo didn't reply. Instead he started scanning the room as if searching for an escape hatch.

'If you'd rather not be here,' said Neil, 'feel free to leave.'

'No, I'm fine,' said Apollo. 'Thank you.'

'You're welcome,' said Neil.

Apollo, who had eyeballed him so intensely on the doorstep, was now looking anywhere but at him. He had crossed his legs and was violently jiggling his hanging foot.

'It's a nice flat,' said Apollo.

'Yes, you said that,' said Neil.

'Nice kitchen, very clean. Oh. Except for the dirty clothes.'

'Thanks,' said Neil.

Neil had thought that if he was ever in a room with Apollo again, he would be filled with a searing rage that could only end in bloodshed. Instead he sat calmly as waves of anxiety flowed off his visitor.

'Well,' he said eventually, 'it was lovely to see you again, but I have some things to do, so –'

'I'mverysorry,' said Apollo.

'Excuse me?' said Neil.

Apollo took a huge breath as if about to blow out the candles on a birthday cake for a relative of extremely advanced years.

'I'm. Very. Sorry.'

'You're sorry,' said Neil.

Apollo smiled weakly. 'Yes?' he ventured.

'What exactly are you sorry for?'

'Oh,' said Apollo. 'Do I need a reason?'

'In general,' said Neil.

Neil watched as Apollo squirmed in his chair.

'I'm sorry that Alice is dead. There.'

'You're sorry that Alice is dead?' said Neil. 'Well, so am I. I'm very sorry that Alice is dead.'

Apollo nodded. 'I forgive you,' he said.

'You –' said Neil. 'You what?'

'I forgive you,' said Apollo. 'I forgive you for Alice's death.'

'You forgive me? That's very good of you,' said Neil. 'But I don't need your forgiveness. I didn't kill her. And even if I did you wouldn't be the right person to forgive me.'

'But you said you were sorry,' said Apollo.

'Not that kind of sorry,' said Neil.

'There's more than one kind?' said Apollo.

'I'm not going to give you a class,' said Neil. 'Apollo, what are you doing here?'

'I came to say sorry,' said Apollo.

'Well you said it,' said Neil.

'But I think I might have said the wrong kind of sorry,' said Apollo.

'Well then try again,' said Neil, 'and then please go home.'

Neil watched as Apollo visibly collected his thoughts. In all of the angry fantasies he had had about Apollo, in all of the jealous hours that he had spent imagining Apollo and Alice in congress, and feeling inadequate as he compared his unimpressive form with Apollo's glorious beauty, it had never once occurred to him that Apollo might be stupid.

'I kissed Alice,' said Apollo eventually.

'I know,' said Neil.

'You know?' said Apollo. 'Really? Well, I'm sorry for that. No I'm not. I'm not sorry for that at all. It was one of the finest moments of my life, and I have a lot to choose from. So I'm not sorry I kissed her. I loved her. And I know you loved her too, but – and I hope you don't mind me pointing this out to you – I'm twice the man you are. More than twice. I am an infinite number of times the man you are.'

'Why on earth would I mind you pointing that out?'

'Exactly. It's obvious to us both. So it was entirely reasonable for me to stake my claim.'

'Stick your flag into her, so to speak.'

'You shouldn't feel bad about it,' said Apollo.

'Tell me something, Apollo,' said Neil. 'Did Alice like you kissing her?'

Apollo bit his lip, considering.

'She liked it,' he said. 'She just didn't know that she liked it.'

'Then I think you should be sorry,' said Neil. 'But you're apologising to the wrong person.'

'Who should I be apologising to?'

'Alice.'

'But Alice is dead,' said Apollo.

'Yes,' said Neil. 'I know.'

'And I already apologised for that,' said Apollo, 'so I don't know what else you want from me.'

'I don't want anything from you,' said Neil. 'I want you to leave.'

Apollo made no move to go.

'The thing is,' he said, 'I don't like being rejected.'

'I'm not rejecting you,' said Neil. 'Please go home.'

'I'm not talking about you,' said Apollo. 'I'm talking about Alice. And usually, if someone like that turned me down, I'd just take it out on them there and then, and if I could have hurt her, that would have been fine –'

'No it wouldn't,' said Neil.

' – but I couldn't,' said Apollo, 'because of Artemis –'

'What's Artemis got to do with this?'

'She made me swear not to harm any mor—' He broke off.

'Any more what?'

'Any more. Anybody, any more.'

'You've harmed a lot of people in the past then?' said Neil.

'Oh yes,' said Apollo. 'But mostly they deserved it.'

'Oh well, that's all right then,' said Neil.

'But because I couldn't punish Alice there and then,' said Apollo, 'it all got a bit out of hand. I didn't really want her to die. Well I did, but only because I was hung-over and angry. If I could have done it straight away, I wouldn't have got drunk. And I wouldn't have been so angry. And she wouldn't have died. This is all Artemis's fault.'

Neil suddenly realised that he had to get Apollo out of his flat as fast as possible because he was going to cry and there was no way he was going to cry in front of Apollo.

'Look,' he said. 'It's nice of you to come round. But you didn't kill Alice. She was struck by lightning. It was a horrible accident. And I don't want to sit around talking about it to you. So if you don't mind, I'm going to ask you again. Please leave.'

'No, you don't get it,' said Apollo. 'I know she was struck by lightning. It was my idea.'

'It couldn't possibly have been your idea,' said Neil. 'Lightning isn't an idea. And you didn't make us go out when we did. You didn't make her stand . . . there . . .'

'He would have found her anywhere,' said Apollo. 'He would have found her inside a lead-lined tennis ball. She didn't have a hope.'

'He?' said Neil, despite himself.

'Zeus. I'm really sorry, Neil.'

Zeus. That's what Artemis had said too. He thought of the photograph in the newspaper and the face of the man in the sky. But it couldn't be true. It couldn't possibly be true. If it was true, he would have to rethink everything in his life and he wasn't going to rethink everything in his life because he'd already had to do that when Alice died, and he wasn't ready to do it again, especially not at the behest of – of all people – Apollo. Apollo! And suddenly all of the anger that he had been holding back broke through the dams and flooded into him.

'You're sorry,' he said. 'You're *sorry*?'

He felt as if he had been electrified, as if every atom in his being had unexpectedly been awakened. He jumped to his feet. Apollo was cowering, wearing the face Red Riding Hood must have worn when the wolf pulled off its grandmother costume. Neil felt something completely unfamiliar: he felt powerful. It rushed into him like a drug.

'You didn't kill Alice,' he said. 'You did not kill Alice! You're delusional! You think you've got power over lightning, you should be in an institution! And then you come over here, to my home, where I'm grieving, and you tell me you're sorry, like I give a fuck whether you're sorry or not, like that's going to make it better, like that's going to bring her back!'

'But,' stammered Apollo, 'I thought you would forgive me. I thought I would feel better. That's what Eros said. I thought that was the deal.'

'That is not the deal!'

Apollo was almost shrinking, his proud warrior's body hunched up and whimpering like a timid schoolboy in front of the head-master.

'You do not apologise because you feel guilty and you want the feeling to go away,' said Neil.

'You don't?' said Apollo.

'No. You apologise because you feel guilty and that guilt is how you know that you've done something wrong. And then you want to make amends. You don't apologise because you want to make yourself feel better. You apologise because you want to make the other person feel better.'

'But why should I want to make you feel better?' said Apollo. He was beginning to uncurl. 'I couldn't care less how you feel.'

'Yes, I think I gathered that.'

'But I do care about how I feel . . .'

Now Apollo got to his feet, but Neil wasn't scared. He'd tasted power and he wasn't going to let go of it that easily.

'I need you to forgive me,' said Apollo.

'Forgive you? As if.'

'I don't think you understand. I demand that you forgive me.'

'No.'

Apollo swung his arm round as if to hit Neil, but staggered back, as if he himself had been hit.

'Forgive me now! I command you!' he shouted as he regained his balance.

'You can't command me to do anything!' Neil shouted back. 'Who the fuck do you think you are?'

'I think I am your Lord Apollo, god of the sun,' Apollo spat.

'God of my arse,' said Neil.

'Oh really?' said Apollo. 'Watch this.'

Apollo strode over to the window and, his eyes fixed on Neil's face, pointed into the sky with a flourish, like an impresario about to reveal an exciting new act.

A split second later, two things happened at once. Apollo collapsed to the ground. And the sun went out.

Thirty

Artemis was on the Heath when it happened. Even though she felt every movement of the moon as if they were umbilically linked, she hoped for one wild second that it was a total eclipse of the sun, but she already knew, with a fist of horror gripping her stomach, that something terrible must have happened to Apollo. Day had turned into night. She knew, without having to see them, that birds would be returning to their nests and nocturnal creatures emerging from their lairs. Across the park, she could hear the screams of mortals. Someone would have to return them to their homes as, inferior even to birds, they couldn't make their way back by themselves. But she didn't have time to help them herself. Undaunted by the darkness, Artemis turned and ran home as swiftly and precisely as if the sun had been blazing high at the peak of its arc.

On the doorstep she met Aphrodite, who spoke to her for the first time in decades in tones untainted by superciliousness.

'Are you OK? What's going on? What's happened to Apollo?'

Artemis shook her head. 'I don't know,' she said.

They went inside. Upstairs they could hear feet running and doors slamming – no doubt someone checking for Apollo from room to room. Hermes was standing in the hallway, his mobile phone in his hand.

'I can't find him,' he said. 'I can't feel where he is.'

This was a painful admission for Hermes who could usually locate any god, anywhere in the earth and heavens, in a matter of seconds.

'We have to do something,' said Aphrodite.

Artemis was too worried even to point out that she was stating the obvious.

'This planet won't last long without the sun,' she said, 'but with all the other powers that we've got we should be able to keep it going for a short while, at least long enough to find out what's happened to him. And if there's any way we can help him.'

They all considered the dark implications of that 'if'.

'But it's going to take all our power,' said Artemis. 'And once that's gone . . .'

Ares came thundering down the stairs. 'Have you seen him?' he said. The two goddesses shook their heads. 'What about the others?'

'They're all on their way,' said Hermes, 'aside from Hades and Persephone.'

'Persephone should already be here,' muttered Aphrodite.

'Maybe we should leave them where they are,' said Hermes. 'Who knows how long we've got before the mortals start to die.'

'How are the tides?' said Artemis.

'Unaffected so far, according to Poseidon,' said Hermes.

'The moon will do her best,' said Artemis, 'but she can't give out heat, or any light, without the sun.'

'Can we bring one of the stars nearer?' suggested Ares.

'Do we have enough power?' said Aphrodite. 'Even between us. What if we try and we run out of steam? And then all of us will be –'

'Hesperus and Phosphorus will be here soon,' interjected Hermes. 'We can talk to them about it then, see what they can do.'

'What about Zeus?' said Artemis.

The question did not need elaborating.

'Eros is upstairs now, talking to Hera,' said Ares. 'Seeing if she thinks it's worth the risk of letting him out.'

Aphrodite's mobile phone rang, its music piercing the collective anxiety with its cheerful tinny tones. She yanked it out of her handbag.

'Apollo?' She listened for a couple of seconds. 'Use your imagination, limp prick, I'm busy,' she snapped and returned the phone to her bag.

'I take it that wasn't him,' said Artemis.

'Mortals!' said Aphrodite. 'Even I wouldn't think of sex at a time like this.'

'So should we all go and look for him, or is it better to stay here?' said Ares.

'I don't know,' said Hermes. 'I don't know where to send you. I've no idea where he is.' Hermes sounded almost tearful in his admission of failure. 'I've spoken to Dionysus, and Apollo isn't there. Of course he had no idea what was going on. That club of his hasn't got any windows.'

'Where's Dion now?' said Artemis.

'He's just locking up the club and he'll be on his way,' said Hermes. 'Even he sounded pretty worried when I told him what was going on. Apollo might be in Hackney. He was asking me about a mortal's address –'

'Maybe we shouldn't worry so much,' said Aphrodite. 'Maybe we should just let it happen.'

They all turned to her. Her perfect face was cold.

'Give up,' she said, 'let the planet die. Conserve our strength 'til we can create something new, somewhere else. Somewhere better than this. Aren't you sick of it? I'm sick of it.'

They all stood in silence for a few moments, absorbing this suggestion. Only a goddess as selfish as Aphrodite could have thought of a plan like that, reflected Artemis, and yet she couldn't deny that it had a certain logic to it.

'It might happen anyway,' said Ares eventually. 'Even if we manage to keep the mortals alive without the sun, they'll probably just go and kill each other anyway. They don't like change, it makes them skittish.'

'This is a pretty big change,' said Artemis.

'But we don't know if we would get stronger, waiting without doing anything,' said Hermes, 'or if without the world we would weaken completely and . . .' Die, he didn't say, but they all thought it.

'We should discuss it with Athena,' said Artemis. 'Where is she?'

'Upstairs with Demeter, trying to get her out of bed,' said Hermes. 'If we are going to keep the mortals going, Demeter's going to have a lot of work to do. The plants won't survive without her. Then what are they going to eat?'

Another mobile phone interrupted them, this time Hermes'.

'Is it him?' said Ares.

Hermes shook his head and handed the phone to Artemis.

'It's for you,' he said.

Artemis put the phone to her ear. 'Hello?' she said.

'OK, I believe you,' said a voice at the other end of the line.

Hearing it, Artemis felt an odd sensation, like a surge of strength coursing through her body.

'Is that Neil?' said Artemis.

'Yes it is,' said Neil, 'and you'd better come quick. I've got a god passed out on my kitchen floor and I think the world's about to end.'

Thirty-One

Artemis ran all the way to Hackney. The temperature was dropping fast and the pavement was beginning to ice over. Traffic blocked the streets as mortals rushed to get to their homes, or perhaps some were already trying to flee – though where they were fleeing to, Artemis could not fathom. Shopkeepers were closing up their stores, slamming doors and yanking down shutters, those without grilles boarding up their windows for fear of looting. Artemis thought about what Ares had said, how disaster brought out the worst in mortals, how they would start killing one another if the gods did not act soon. But she could understand it: they had so few options. She thought of how a cornered animal on a hunt will turn and fight, no matter how little hope they have. Survival at all cost.

With her innate sense of direction, it didn't take long for her to find the address that Neil had given her. It was a small terraced house down a curving side street that looked grimy and abandoned in the darkness. At the far end of the road she saw a fox sniffing at some dustbins, confused into thinking it was night. For once she felt no urge to chase after it. Instead she rang, as instructed, the middle of the three doorbells. Before long, the door opened, revealing Neil, looking rumpled and dishevelled, fully clothed with a dressing gown over the top to protect against the growing cold. Seeing him, Artemis burned with unexpected energy.

'I don't know what's going on,' said Neil without greeting her, 'but I know you were telling me the truth.'

'Where is he?' she said.

'In the kitchen,' said Neil. 'All things considered, I thought it best to keep him away from the hospital.'

'Is he still alive?'

'Gods can die?'

'Sometimes,' admitted Artemis.

'I didn't check. I thought he must be. I hope he is.'

Artemis followed Neil down the corridor and into his flat.

'What happened?' she said.

Neil explained how Apollo had come over to apologise, how they had argued and how Apollo seemed to have switched off the sun in revenge for Neil's doubt in him. He couldn't offer any explanation as to why Apollo had collapsed.

'It could be that switching off the sun used up too much of his power,' said Artemis, as they approached the prone figure of Apollo, stretched out across the floor tiles in a strange posture.

'Gods don't have unlimited power?'

Artemis didn't really want to answer that one. 'Unfortunately not,' she confessed eventually. 'But don't tell anyone. I'm only trusting you with this knowledge because it's an emergency.'

Neil glanced out of the window to the darkness outside. 'I won't tell anyone,' he said.

'The other explanation could be that Styx punished him for turning off the sun, because of the immense harm it would do mortals. He swore a vow on her not to hurt any mortals, and she doesn't take kindly to her vows being broken. If it is Styx, he'll be out for nine years, that's her standard rate. And we can't keep the world going for nine years without the sun.'

'Who's Styx?'

'She's a river in the underworld.'

'A river could do this?'

'She's not any old river.'

Standing over Apollo now, Artemis tried to think of what she could do to revive him.

'Did he fall like that?' she said.

'No, I put him in the recovery position,' said Neil. 'I wasn't sure if it would help, but I didn't think it could do any harm.'

Artemis knelt down beside her brother. He was lying turned half onto his side, his arrogant face drained of colour and lifeless. She felt her throat constrict like a fist holding onto a sob. He looked so vulnerable. There was no worse way for a god to look. She called into his ear, felt for a pulse, lifted and dropped his arm, and slapped him, which was fun at least.

'Well?' said Neil.

'He's definitely still alive,' sighed Artemis.

'Isn't that good?' said Neil.

'I'm not sure,' said Artemis. 'If he were dead, we could go down to the underworld and bring his spirit back to the upperworld, which might be easier than waking him out of a coma. But I don't know if that would do any good anyway, if he'd have any power left or would be able to use it. I don't know what happens to a god's power when he dies, and I'm not prepared to kill him just to find out. As he's alive, I suggest we keep him that way. So we need to find a way to wake him up.'

'So you can't wake him up, then,' said Neil.

'It takes a lot of power,' said Artemis. 'It would be easier if we had the god of healing to help us.'

'Who's that?'

'Apollo.'

'Oh.'

Artemis sat back on her heels.

'Let's at least make him comfortable,' she said. 'I don't think this recovery position of yours is going to help him to recover. Why do they call it that?'

She picked Apollo up in her arms like a baby.

'Do you have a bed, or a sofa I can put him on?'

'This way,' said Neil, leading her into the living room. 'So,' he said as they walked, 'how many of you gods are there?'

'Far more than you'd expect,' said Artemis. 'The most important gods are based here in London, but there are many others,
scattered across the globe, all incognito. There's a god for everything. God of time, god of sleep, god of revenge . . .'

'If you group together, surely you'd be able to bring him back,'
said Neil.

Artemis shook her head.

'Unfortunately it's not that easy,' she said. 'The life-force of a
god is the strongest force that there is. So it will take a huge
amount of our power to revive Apollo. And we've been . . .'

She hesitated, but the utter blackness outside the window
spurred her on. If necessary she could always wipe his memory
later.

'We've been terribly weakened over time,' she made herself
say. 'Most of the gods only have the bare minimum of power
left – enough to fulfil their own function, but no more. Some
gods don't even have that any more. So if Poseidon, for
example, were to put his power into reviving Apollo, he might
be able to help, but the seas could dry up. So yes, if we work
together, we could probably wake him up again, but, in our
current state, we could do ourselves so much harm that we
wouldn't have the collective force left to keep the rest of the
world going. You might get the sun back, but lose everything
else.'

'That doesn't sound like a great option,' said Neil.

'And then on top of that, if it's Styx who put him in this state,
we wouldn't be able to undo it anyway, no matter how much
force we used. A god can't undo what another god has done.
That's why we can't restore the sun ourselves, even if we were
strong enough to, which I doubt.'

'So what are we going to do?' said Neil.

'We?' said Artemis.

Neil nodded. Artemis looked at her twin, silent and still, impo-
tent in sleep. Now that it seemed that she might lose him, she

felt more love and protectiveness towards him than she could remember ever having felt in their long, long past.

'I think the first thing to do is to go to the underworld and find Styx, see if she has anything to do with this, and if she can reverse it,' she said. 'And if it's nothing to do with her, maybe while we're there I can persuade Hades and Persephone to use their power to help us keep the world turning until we can figure out what else to do.'

'Won't that take too long?' said Neil, shivering inside his dressing gown.

Artemis shook her head. 'Not in dead time,' she said.

Thirty-Two

It wasn't the notion of going down into the underworld that bothered Neil so much as having to leave his body behind at the flat. He could take it with him, Artemis explained, but then he would stay in live time, and they couldn't afford that luxury. Apollo was still on the sofa, with a blanket over him to protect against the growing cold, so Neil got into bed and then, with Artemis's help, his spirit got out again.

'That was easier than I expected,' said Artemis. 'It's strange, usually I feel drained after using so much power, but actually I feel quite energised.'

'It was easier than *I* expected,' said Neil, but then he caught sight of his own body lying between the sheets. 'I wish I'd thought to close my eyes,' he said.

'Nobody will see you, unless Apollo wakes up, and I doubt he'll care,' said Artemis.

'All the same,' said Neil.

'Come on, we'd better go,' said Artemis.

Neil took a last look at his body, lying still as tarmac, as they left the room.

'I hope no looters set fire to my flat while we're gone,' he said.

'You wouldn't feel a thing,' said Artemis. 'And you'd already be in the underworld, which would save you the trouble of getting there.'

'Thanks,' said Neil. 'That's very comforting.'

'You're welcome,' said Artemis.

Walking out of the flat through the closed front door was easy but felt wrong. At least that way the flat stayed locked. Though any looter, Neil reflected, was likely to get the shock of his life when he found the two comatose men inside. Or the second biggest shock of his life, after the sun going out, anyway.

'So how do we get to the underworld?' asked Neil.

'There's a portal in Islington,' said Artemis.

'Islington?'

'Yes.'

'*Islington?*'

Artemis did not elaborate, but led the way along the pavement.

Outside, the streets had started to ice over. Neil negotiated the slippery surface without difficulty, oblivious to the cold. As he craned his neck to catch a last glimpse of the house with his body in it disappearing behind them, he wondered whether this was how a mother might feel if her baby was taken away from her. One part of his awareness was desperately trying to reach out to his body, but the bond between them was completely severed. It was funny, while he was still corporeal he had thought his body and his mind were quite separate, but now that he was leaving his body behind he realised quite how attached to it, so to speak, he was. Out of his body he didn't feel quite real – in fact he didn't feel anything at all. There was a shallowness to his experience now, with only his intellectual responses to rely on. And he hadn't realised to what extent it was his body that was missing Alice. Of course, his mind missed her too. But it was his body that felt it. His grief was like an illness, had caused him actual pain in his heart, his stomach, his limbs. Fever, dizziness, weakness: all of this had been part of the intricate patchwork of misery he had been carrying around with him ever since Alice had died; and now it, too, was gone. He missed her; and now he missed missing her, as well.

Neil was going down into the underworld in order to save the planet. This was ridiculous enough; it was like something out of the books he read and the films that he loved, all that science fiction – with the emphasis on fiction. But deep down, he knew that he was also going there in order to save Alice, and this seemed even more absurd. How many times had he already failed her? What made him think that this time would be different? But he knew he had to try again. He had known it ever since the moment that he had exploded into belief and picked up the phone to call Hermes: that if only he could bring Apollo and the sun back for humanity, he would take as reward Artemis's offer to help him bring back Alice. If he couldn't find Alice in the underworld, he would do his best to save the world anyway – he was nice like that – but it would be more like a cub scout good deed, a virtuous chore. Without Alice, his world had already ended.

Looking up, he noticed that, deep in thought, he had started lagging behind Artemis, and trotted faster to keep up with her, the increase in speed coming to him effortlessly. The streets were still gridlocked with cars escaping to who knew where, but the freezing pavements were deserted, except for around a church up ahead of them, which appeared to be full, with more people on the porch outside clamouring for admittance. As Neil and Artemis got closer they heard the sound of sobbing, singing and amplified prayers coming from within.

'That's not going to do any of them much good,' commented Artemis. 'They'd be better off staying at home and deciding which item of furniture they want to burn first.'

'They don't know that,' said Neil, surprised to find himself defending organised religion. 'They don't know which god they're supposed to believe in. And I suppose it provides comfort.'

'A big duvet would provide more comfort,' said Artemis.

'Was that a joke?' said Neil.

Artemis smiled quickly at him. 'It might have been,' she said.

'You know,' said Neil, 'until today, I was an atheist. I wasn't even C. of E. I thought I was so superior to anyone who believed any of that crap. Not just religion but psychics and ghosts and everything. I went out of my way to laugh at it. I enjoyed laughing at it.'

'So?' said Artemis.

'I'm starting to feel a bit guilty about it now.'

'Why should you have believed in any of it?' retorted Artemis. 'I'm just as contemptuous of those other religions as you are. More so, if anything. After all, if it wasn't for Jesus, I'd probably still be living on Olympus, running on the hillsides with my beautiful dogs. Frankly I respect you more for not having bought into any of these modern superstitions.'

'Thanks,' said Neil.

'Although of course some of it is true.'

'It is?' said Neil. 'Like what?'

'There are a lot of ghosts about,' said Artemis. 'Not that most mortals can see them, and even if you could, I doubt very much that you'd notice them. But that means most of the television mediums you see are in fact really talking to the dead. They're about the only people who will listen to them. Ghosts never stop complaining. Personally I'm not impressed. There's no real difference between talking to a dead mortal and talking to a live one.'

Neil took a moment to absorb this new, somewhat disappointing, knowledge.

'So can cats really see ghosts?' he asked.

'Oh no,' said Artemis. 'They're very inferior creatures, cats.'

Then Neil had a thought that almost made him stop walking.

'And Apollo, could he really tell the future then?'

'He used to be able to,' said Artemis. 'I'm not sure how much he can now.'

'In that case I owe him an apology,' said Neil.

'I don't see why,' said Artemis. 'He still tried to seduce the woman you love. And killed her. That god has got all the morality of a rabbit.'

The reminder hurt, but Neil couldn't help but smile at the primness of Artemis's tone. He was beginning to grow quite fond of her.

When they got to Upper Street, the road was deserted except for a few gangs of young men, hoodies pulled up less to hide their faces and more against the cold, looking for shops to loot. Angel Tube station was closed, grilles pulled forbiddingly across its entrance like teeth clenched shut.

'This way,' said Artemis, leading the way inside.

'Into the station?'

'Hermes says that there's a secret platform on the other side of the wall at the bottom that leads to a train to the underworld.'

'What do you mean, "Hermes says"? Haven't you ever been there before?'

'Of course not.'

Neil stopped, halfway through the grille.

'If you don't know the way, why are you the one taking me? Why isn't Hermes going?'

'Hermes has never been either. He just brings the dead this far. None of us are supposed to go down there otherwise it would interfere with the boundary between the living and the dead, and apparently we'd spend our whole time bringing back mortals that we liked. It would be chaos. Hades and Persephone say we can't be trusted.'

'Can you?'

'Of course not. So aside from the two of them, the only other god who's ever been to the underworld is Dionysus, and I wouldn't recommend going on any kind of a journey with him – he'd just get drunk and forget what he was doing there in the first place. That's probably OK for what you mortals call a stag weekend, but not so good when you're trying to save the planet. Now are you coming?'

Neil sighed. 'Yes, of course I am.'

They crept into the entrance hall of the Tube station. It was pitch black and completely silent. Neil walked close behind Artemis, afraid to lose her in the darkness. Everything was wrong: he associated the station with noise, people, bustle, life, and the absence of all these things made him feel as if he had actually died, as if this trip to the underworld was one that he would never return from. With each step that he took into the blackness he wanted to turn back, to run to his familiar flat and crawl back inside his body and hide, but what good would that do? If the world ended he'd only be straight back here again, following another god down these stalled metal steps.

Finally the ground flattened out and Neil understood that they had reached the bottom of the stairs.

'Wait,' whispered Artemis before they crossed through the back wall. 'This is very important. I don't know if the train is going to be there when we get through the wall, but if it is, don't get on it.'

'Why not?' said Neil. 'I thought we were going to the underworld?'

'We are,' said Artemis. 'But we're sneaking in. If Charon – the train driver – finds us on the train, he'll throw us out and feed us to Cerberus.'

'Cerberus?'

'The triple-headed hound of death who guards the gates of hell. He eats the souls of those who try to escape from Hades. And those who try to break in.'

'Why didn't you mention any of this before?'

'It's all right, we'll creep down the tunnel and with any luck they won't see us.'

'With any luck? What if they do see us?'

'For a hero you ask a lot of questions.'

On the far side of the wall there was light, although it was dim and came from no discernible source. There were a lot of dead people on the Tube platform. In fact there were more dead people gathered here than Neil could ever remember having seen live people gathered anywhere, and most of them were standing completely quiet and utterly still, as if they were observing a two-minute silence marking their own demise. He tried not to look too closely at some of the individuals who had died in ways that he was pretty sure he'd prefer to avoid trying himself.

'Is this how many people normally die every day?' whispered Neil to Artemis. 'Or is it because of the sun thing?'

Artemis gave the dead multitudes an appraising look. 'No, I'd say this was pretty standard,' she said.

'This many people die every day?'

'More or less.'

'I'm never going to find her,' said Neil.

'Styx? She's easy to spot. She's a river.'

'I meant Alice,' said Neil.

'Oh,' said Artemis. 'Of course. I'd forgotten about her.'

She looked again at all of the gathered dead and turned back to him.

'Do you know much about Heracles? It is relevant.'

'No,' said Neil.

'I'll tell you on the way. Jump down onto the tracks.'

'We can't just jump down in front of them all, what's everyone going to think?'

'It doesn't matter,' said Artemis. 'They're just mortals, and dead ones at that. Don't worry about what they think. They probably won't even notice. Everything's strange to them, they won't know what's supposed to happen and what isn't. The only ones we need to worry about are Charon and Cerberus. And Hades and Persephone, but that's not until later.'

'Hades and Persephone? Is there anybody else who wants to eat our souls that you care to mention?'

'As long as the mortals don't guess that we're trying to sneak into the underworld we'll be fine,' insisted Artemis. 'And right now I don't think any of them are expecting that the underworld will be somewhere worth sneaking into. And even if they do guess, we're fine as long as they don't tell anyone. And who exactly are they going to tell? So go on, jump.'

Neil looked at the group of dead people nearest him: a cluster of bewildered old Japanese men in hospital pyjamas, who, almost in sync, would look down at themselves, and then over at the crowds of variously mutilated people disappearing off to their right, and then down at themselves again, but never at each other.

'I take your point,' he said, and jumped down onto the tracks, a long drop, but of course he felt nothing as he landed.

As Artemis landed lightly beside him, a confused and apparently completely normal mouse ran through their feet and then disappeared under a rail.

'So,' said Artemis, walking off in the direction of the tunnel, 'Heracles. One of our better heroes, aside from that unfortunate incident when he went mad and killed his wife and children, but that was really Hera's fault. Anyway, amongst his many other endeavours, he successfully performed twelve near-impossible labours. Twelve! And you only have to do two! The first one was to kill the Nemean lion, a truly ferocious beast that even I would have found difficult, though of course not impossible, to defeat . . .'

Oddly comforted by the sound of her voice, Neil followed Artemis into the tunnel that snaked off ahead of them in an absolute darkness that would only be relieved once they reached the world of the dead.

Thirty-Three

It was easy enough to avoid Charon. He had got lazy, Artemis remembered; both Hermes and Persephone had mentioned it. Thousands of years of driving his train back and forth between the worlds of the dead and the living, and even more thousands before that taking them over by ferry. It was a task of Sisyphian monotony and these days Charon did the bare minimum, barely aware of the passengers whom he transported, his only pleasure being to throw the occasional soul overboard; he had more than once mooted replacing the whole set-up with a conveyor belt, which, after all, would only have to run one way. So when they heard the train rattling down the track towards them to pick up its consignment of dead, and again back underworld-wards packed tight full of freshly-culled souls, all they had to do was throw themselves to the ground and lie flat as the carriages rattled harmlessly over their heads. Of course the train could have rattled equally harmlessly through their heads, but even Charon might have noticed two skulls poking up through the floor.

Cerberus was going to be more of a problem. If Charon had become lazy, Cerberus was still hungry, starving for the souls of incursers or escapees. As they neared the end of the tunnel, a thin tendril of deathly light clawing its way back to them, Artemis made Neil stop as they considered their strategy.

'Orpheus,' said Artemis, 'sang Cerberus to sleep. But we've already established that you can't sing.'

'My singing,' said Neil, 'would only incite him to eat me all the faster.'

'Heracles tempted him out of the underworld by being nice to him.'

'I can be nice,' said Neil. 'I'm actually very nice. It's one of my best qualities.'

'But it won't work again,' said Artemis. 'He doesn't trust nice any more. He'll know what we're up to.'

'That's a shame,' said Neil, 'because I think it's the only thing I'm good at. What else do you suggest?'

'Aeneas and Psyche both used drugged honeycakes. Cerberus likes a honeycake.'

'Do we have any drugged honeycakes with us?'

'No.'

'That's handy. What else?'

'There's a golden bough which guarantees entry . . .'

'Which we haven't got?'

'Correct.'

'Any other suggestions?'

'That's it as far as I know,' said Artemis. 'People don't make it down here very often. They make it past Cerberus even less often.'

'So what are we going to do?' said Neil.

Artemis sighed and tried to make it sound like the worst-case scenario. 'I suppose I'll just have to fight him while you make a run for it and look for Styx,' she said, and was grateful that the darkness hid the excitement twitching around her mouth. 'The river Styx circles the underworld nine times. It doesn't matter which direction you head in; you'll reach her.'

'But what about you? What if you get hurt? What if Cerberus kills you?'

'Well then the world will just have to live without hunting, and chastity, and the moon. Come on, let's go. Try to look dead.'

Neil and Artemis crept down the last part of the tunnel and

stepped into the thin light, which after all that time in the dark would have made them blink, had they had real eyes to be dazzled. In anticipation of the fight to come, Artemis wordlessly regained corporeal form as they walked, feeling the ground becoming solid beneath her feet. Maybe it was knowing what was to come, but she didn't feel the moment of exhaustion that she generally experienced after using her power. Instead she felt strong as a flexed muscle. Beside her, Neil was doing his best not to stare at the hordes of assembled dead who had been ejected from the train and now mingled on the platform, in disoriented solitude or comparing injuries in low voices.

Artemis scanned the crowded station but Cerberus was nowhere to be seen. She pulled herself up onto the platform and Neil followed her, attracting some confused glances from the mortals nearby.

'We missed the train,' explained Artemis. 'Come on,' she said to Neil. 'There's no point hanging around here. He must be outside.'

'He?'

'Cerberus.'

'You sound like you're actually looking forward to this,' said Neil.

'Don't be ridiculous,' said Artemis, looking away from him.

They made their way quite literally through the crowd and to the exit, comprising the most pointless ticket barrier ever created, which they also both walked straight through. A few of the dead had already made their way out and were standing around in visible confusion, staring off down the identical unmarked streets.

'Is this really the underworld?' said Neil. 'It's very different from how it's described.'

'This is probably just the suburbs,' said Artemis. 'I'm sure the centre is more distinctive.'

'Alice could live in any one of these houses,' said Neil. 'If this is dead time, can I knock on all of the doors and still be back in time to save the world?'

Artemis shook her head. 'Time here passes in a completely different way,' she said, 'but it does pass. Sorry. If we didn't have anything else to do here, then maybe. But . . .'

'I will find her,' said Neil.

'I'm sure you will,' said Artemis. 'Now listen. You remember the plan don't you? When Cerberus makes his appearance, I fight . . .'

'And I run. Yes I know,' said Neil. 'It doesn't feel very heroic being the one doing the running.'

'Just make sure that you run fast,' said Artemis. 'The last thing we want is him getting both of us.'

'Do you think he's going to get you?'

'When I win,' said Artemis, 'I'll take his body with me to the palace so you'd better meet me there. Somebody has to tell Hades and Persephone what's going on.'

'And if you lose?'

'I'm not going to lose.'

'Where's the palace?' said Neil.

'I have no idea,' said Artemis.

'Artemis, is this actually going to work?'

'Look, I'm doing my best,' said Artemis. 'Ares and Athena are the ones for strategy, but I wouldn't fancy either of their chances fighting a triple-headed . . .' She tailed off.

'What is it?' said Neil.

'Run.'

Neil didn't wait to be asked twice.

She had never seen Cerberus before. Watching his wild silhouette stalking towards her against the neat black-and-white stripes of the mock-Tudor buildings, she felt a constriction in her chest and a buzz racing through her limbs which might just have been the presence of another immortal – she could always sense when there was one near – but seemed to be more than that. It gripped her, nailing her to her place on the dismal pavement yet also pulling her towards him. Her mouth was dry. She hadn't met anything like her match in so long.

He was huge. She could see the hard muscles almost bursting out as they pushed with every step against his gleaming black hide. His body was a compressed ball of power ready to explode. Each leg was like a tree, rooted in the iron curve of his claws. In place of his tail writhed a snake as thick as her torso, whipping back and forth with vicious hisses that sliced through the air like hail. And his heads: all three identical in size and might, glowing red eyes rolling as large as her fist, leathery lips pulled back revealing teeth as big as her palm and sharp as honed blades, dripping in thick, foaming drool. Two of the heads were sniffing to either side but the one in the middle was staring straight at her, unblinking.

'Now that's what I call a dog,' Artemis breathed. Without waiting another moment, she launched herself at Cerberus, picking up speed in the few steps that separated them before flying off the ground, both feet forward, stamping into the eyes of the central head to blind it as the two outer heads turned inwards, snarling, fangs ready to rip.

Thirty-Four

Neil was running. He could hear the sounds of a dreadful fight taking place behind him, growls that shook the ground like an earthquake, and the wordless battle cries of Artemis. He didn't turn around. If Artemis lost, he knew that he'd be pudding to her main course, and he didn't think he'd be able to put up quite as much of a fight as she clearly was. The only thing he could do was to put as much distance as possible between himself and Cerberus. And anyway, he didn't need to know what Cerberus looked like, as he was fairly certain it wouldn't make his vision of being eaten any more pleasant.

Not knowing where he was or where he was going, he decided as far as possible to keep heading straight. He ran easily, without tiring. When he passed the dead, they invariably looked at him strangely, as if they couldn't understand why he was there or what he was doing. At first he thought it was because he was still wearing his dressing gown, until he realised that, of course, many or even most of the dead were walking around in variations on nightwear. It was only when he had been running for a while that he noticed the disjunction between his velocity and the pace at which the dead moved: strolling, loitering, dawdling. Nobody here was in a hurry; they had no time to run out of. He, on the other hand, had to keep moving as fast as he possibly could. The only times that he slowed were whenever he saw a petite blonde woman on the pavement, and thought that it might be Alice. But it never was.

The streets went on and on. They never varied and he never tired. He felt as if he was floating through a strange, repetitive dream where nothing was real, not even himself. Maybe he was dreaming. But when had the dream started? When he had left his body behind in his icy bed and his spirit had followed Artemis out into the cold, black day? When Apollo had come around to his flat and then collapsed, taking the sun and Neil's sceptic soul with him? When he had seen that old man's face in the sky and the lightning had come down and murdered Alice? When had his life last seemed real? Ultimately the unreality of everything that was happening now just seemed to underscore how false his sense of security had been before, when he thought that everything was clear and obvious and easy to understand, and that people who thought differently were gullible fools. And all along it had been he, thinking that everything could be so easily explained, who was the gullible one.

As these thoughts propelled him onwards, he realised that something had changed. For all the time that he had been running – impossible to say how long that was – the two rows of fake Tudor houses had stretched endlessly out ahead of him, breaking only from time to time to branch off into equally endless, identical fake Tudor streets. But now, for the first time, the street seemed to have an end. He couldn't see what lay at that end, only that where the houses had once extended as far as his eyes could see, they now were finite, stopping at some future point that his running feet drew him closer and closer to with every step. This world, apparently, did have an edge, and he had finally found it.

He didn't know how fast he had been running or for how long, but as he reached the final few blocks, he slowed, and eventually stopped. The river was here, as Artemis had said that it would be, cutting off this freakish suburb as cleanly as a scalpel. The river was wide and the water was black. He could see the far shore, but the light was hazy and the shore indistinct, hidden behind a wall of fog. Where the asphalt of the street ended, the riverbank beneath his feet sucked away the light like the water before it, and lay flat, colourless, devoid of life. There was nobody within sight, and the river moved swift but silent.

There was something else, but it took him a moment or two to figure out what it was. Then he realised that he could feel the river. The touch of icy damp in the air, the cold smell of the water, the sharp sour taste in his mouth. This river, somehow, was a real, physical thing. Even if he was not.

Neil cleared his already clear throat, feeling foolish, and the sound echoed out over the water.

Nothing happened.

'Hello!' he called out, feeling more foolish still.

Nothing happened. What had he expected? He was talking to a river.

'Hello!' he called out again. He thought of Artemis, locked in mortal combat with some hideous monster that he had been too afraid to even look at. The least he could do was speak to the river. 'Are you Styx?' he said.

A woman appeared. Neil could not say where she had come from, or even exactly where she was. She seemed to be in the river, or above it, or in some way part of it. She had long, straight black hair that flowed like the water, was wearing some sinewy black garment that twisted into the river, and her slender arms and face had skin so white it seemed to be tinged with green. Her eyes and lips were black.

'I am Styx,' she said.

'You're the river?' said Neil.

'I am the river,' said Styx. Her voice came from her mouth, but it also seemed to come from the river itself.

'I'm Neil,' said Neil. 'From, ah, Earth. Unless we're still on Earth. In which case I'm from Essex but I live in London now.'

'You live?' said Styx, or the river. 'Are you therefore not yet dead?'

Neil hesitated. He had quite clearly said the wrong thing – that hadn't taken long. From everything Artemis said, it was obvious that the living were far from welcome in the under-world, with all kinds of dire repercussions for those who broke this rule, notably having their souls eaten. He wasn't sure what the river could do to him, but were she to drag him inside her, he didn't much fancy his chances against that fast-flowing current of ink. On the other hand, he didn't feel that lying was going to be the best way to start a relationship with a body of water whose principal function, from what he understood, was to keep people from breaking oaths.

'I am a hero,' he said eventually, hoping that this was a cate-gory that transcended notions of dead or alive.

The river raised an eyebrow. 'You are most unlike any hero who has visited me before,' she said.

'It was an emergency,' said Neil.

'It always is,' said Styx.

'The world is ending,' said Neil. 'The world above. Or possibly on the far side. I'm not too sure of how the geography works . . . Anyway we were hoping you could help us.'

'We?'

'I'm here with Artemis. Or I was . . . The thing is, earlier on today – I think it's still today –'

'Days mean little here.'

'Apollo came to my flat. Apollo, the god of the sun?'

'I know him.' Styx quoted, Apollo's sulky voice suddenly filling the dank air around them: '"I swear, *on Styx*, that I won't cause any unnecessary harm to mortals for the next ten years or until I get stronger again, whichever comes first. Satisfied?"'

'We argued and he put out the sun. The next thing I knew he was unconscious on the kitchen floor and there was nothing I could do to wake him up. Until then I didn't even know who he was.'

Neil paused, remembering the sick thud in his gut followed

by the stinging thrill of icy hysteria that had accompanied the realisation that all the spiritual superstitious bullshit that he had been so dismissive of all his life was actually true. He swallowed by instinct although he had no saliva in his mouth to swallow.

'I called Artemis,' he continued, 'and she thought that maybe . . . maybe . . .'

'Maybe I was punishing him for breaking his oath by putting him to sleep for nine years?'

'Exactly.'

'And you hoped that by coming here, I would relent and revoke his punishment, so that the sun would be restored and your world would be saved?'

'That was the idea,' said Neil.

Styx shook her head and the waves in the river rippled.

'You won't do it?' said Neil.

'Why should I do it?' said Styx. 'We are immortals, all of us, and we have power, but we live by rules. There are rules that I must obey. I must stay in this lifeless place, surrounded by the souls of the dead, drowning all those who would attempt to cross me. In either direction.' Styx held his gaze for a moment. 'And there are rules that I enforce,' she continued, 'and one of those is that no god who swears an oath bound on me shall break that oath without losing nine years of his or her existence. I cannot change that even for the pleas of a brave, if minor, hero such as yourself.'

'But without the sun everyone on my planet will die,' said Neil. 'Or on this planet. I'm not entirely sure where we are.'

'I have explained to you,' said Styx, 'why I should not help you. But I did not say that I would not help you.'

'You mean you will?' Neil took an eager step forward, danger-ously close to the brink.

'No,' said Styx. 'Unfortunately I cannot. Because I did not do this.' She sighed and the river shivered. 'Apollo did not break his oath to me. It would seem that his intention in eliminating the sun was not to harm mortals. I cannot think why else he did it though. Perhaps he wished to harm himself?'

'I don't think so,' said Neil. 'Actually I think he might just have been showing off. I didn't believe in him then, you see. I think he was proving a point.'

'In that case, it is possible that he only meant to take away the light of the sun for a few seconds, causing no harm, but the effort he expended made him collapse before he was able to restore it. That would not fall under my jurisdiction, so it is not something that I can reverse.'

'So there's nothing you can do to help me?' said Neil.

'I would like to,' said Styx. 'But I am just a river.'

'You're hardly just a river,' said Neil. 'I've seen a lot of rivers, and they don't look like you. They don't have bodies for a start.'

Styx shrugged, and a spattering of foam broke the river's surface.

'All rivers have a spirit,' she said. 'To see it, all you need is to know their name.'

'What, like, even the Clyde?' said Neil.

'If that is a river,' said Styx. 'Though I doubt very much that her real name is Clyde.'

Neil stood for a few moments watching the black water pass. He could sense Styx's eyes on him, pitying but cool with distance.

'Do you know a girl called Alice?' he said eventually.

'Many of the dead are called Alice,' said Styx.

'This one only died very recently,' said Neil, 'on March 21st. She's thirty-two, very petite, blonde hair. She's beautiful.'

'That could be many women,' said Styx.

'No, this one's unique,' said Neil. 'Pale skin. Blue eyes. A little beauty spot just above her right cheekbone that she used to call a mole.'

'She has not been to the river,' said Styx.

'I need to find her,' said Neil. 'I desperately need to find her.'

'I cannot help you,' said Styx. 'I do not find things. I stay in this place. Things find me. All I can do is bind a god to his oath. That is all I can do.'

Neil half turned to go, but then he turned back.

'What about mortals?' he said. 'Does it work on them? Can you bind a mortal to his oath?'

'It is a long time since any mortal knew of me to swear on,' said Styx.

'But I know you,' said Neil.

Styx didn't reply but Neil thought he saw encouragement in her face.

'And if I did swear something on you, and it was completely binding, then you might be able to help me keep that oath?'

'I might,' said Styx. 'I am not entirely without powers.'

'I swear,' Neil said, 'on you, on Styx, that I will find Alice. I swear it.'

Styx smiled, and for a moment, the surface of the river danced with light.

'Then you must,' she said.

Thirty-Five

Alice was playing Scrabble against a Victorian scientist who had drowned when he fell off a boat whilst trying to collect algae samples off the side. She was beating him quite comfortably, though she could see that, with more practice, he had the makings of a very good player.

'Such a marvellous game,' he kept saying. 'Such a sadness that we didn't have it in my day.'

Their table was in the twentieth-century gaming zone of a huge entertainment complex in downtown A sector. The twentieth-century gaming zone consisted of a chain of pubs – an actual chain: a series of individual pubs from different eras which interconnected, each room providing games from an appropriate era. The Scrabble area was modelled after a spit-and-sawdust boozer from the 1940s, with grimy tiles, sticky-look carpet, authentically-yellowed paintwork and fake cigarette smoke hanging in the air, which Alice didn't mind too much as it smelt of nothing and didn't irritate her eyes or throat. They were lucky enough to have a piano player – the coordination necessary to play an imaginary piano was one of the toughest skills to acquire – which was far better than what the Boggle professionals had to cope with, housed as they were in a 1970s underground bar with a series of punk bands, who had certainly not learnt much by way of coordination. The twentieth century gaming zone was just one of the gaming zones that formed one of the districts in the entertainment complex which was the size of a small town, and featured every kind of entertainment that could possibly be imagined – every kind, that is, aside from sex shows. For the decorporealised, even thinking about sex was too frustrating without having to look at it too.

The game would soon be over and the sands in the huge egg timer that marked out the shifts had nearly run out. Alice had agreed, after much persuasion, to meet one of her new friends, A sector's Risk champion, for a drink after work in one of the musical revue bars. She wasn't particularly looking forward to it. Alice had never drunk much when she was alive, and she didn't drink much now. And aside from that, in the underworld, it wasn't alcohol that they drank, but the waters of the river Lethe, which helped you to forget your life before. Everybody in the underworld wanted to forget. Everybody except Alice. She wasn't ready to forget yet.

Her afterlife wasn't so bad, Alice often reminded herself. Although it was a little too sociable for her taste, Alice enjoyed her job, and was grateful to have a challenge and a distraction. The other members of the Scrabble team were friendly, and at least their work gave them something in common aside from being dead. But Alice missed her friends and family from the upperworld, and most of all she missed Neil. When he died, she told herself, maybe he would come looking for her, or even find her by mistake – he had always liked playing board games. But by then he would, if he was lucky, be an old man, who would have moved on since her death, and probably found love with someone else. Hopefully found love with someone else, she had to force herself to think. Hopefully.

She never mentioned Neil to any of her colleagues, but listening to them tell her about their former lives, it soon became clear that all members of the dead had had to undergo similar losses. Some had only died a matter of months apart from their partners and had still been unable to find them in the vastness of the underworld; others had devoted eternities to rediscovering long lost friends and relations, even their own babies who had died, only to find that they had been irrevocably changed by the passing of time. Everyone agreed that it was best to forget, not to go looking for the past in this endless sea of present. And Alice nodded and pretended that she agreed, but the moment that she had any time off from work, she would go walking the streets of A sector, looking for Neil's face in all of the men that passed, both young and old: she didn't know what he would look like when he got here, she didn't know how old he would be, but he had to arrive here eventually.

The Victorian scientist had just put the Z down on a double letter score – quite good, but Alice could see a triple that would have been better – when suddenly she experienced a powerful pull to go outside, as if she had got caught up in the current of a river dragging her in that direction.

She leant over to the man at the next table, a friendly Norwegian with a bullet through his head who was right now between clients.

'Lars, can you cover for me?'

'Of course,' said Lars.

Alice apologised to the scientist and hurried to the door as Lars took her seat and resumed the game.

'I'm so sorry,' she said to her supervisor. 'I have to go.'

'Have to?' repeated the supervisor, more confused than annoyed. The dead never had to do anything.

'I have to go,' said Alice again, and, under the amazed eyes of her colleagues, she ran out of the bar and down the street, not knowing where she was headed.

She knew better than to question the direction of her feet, as soon enough she'd arrive where she needed to go. But she was astonished when she found herself at the gates to Hades and Persephone's palace. What possible reason could they have for summoning her? Had they somehow found out about her connection to the gods in the upperworld?

She had never been to the palace compound before, but it was legendary amongst the dead. When Persephone had first been kidnapped by Hades to be his bride, the underworld had been a bleak and featureless wasteland, more haunted than inhabited by the souls of the dead, and the palace itself a twisted and grim and darkly foreboding tower, the kind of place that would make you long for a brief sojourn in a nice prison. But once Persephone had finally accepted that this really was going to be her home, she had taken it upon herself to brighten up the place. She had started with the palace. Cherry-picking the best of the world's dead architects and engineers, Persephone had exploited their talents to indulge her every whim. The palace was bathed at all times – unless she was in a very bad mood – in the glow of imagined sunshine. The building's exact appearance changed constantly, depending on her preference at that exact moment. It took on the form of the past and present upperworld's most glorious buildings, from the Taj Mahal to the Pyramids, as well as some that were completely original designs of her architectural team. Only once Persephone had improved her living conditions to meet her exacting standards did she allow the less experienced members of her team to work on the outside, bringing the rest of the underworld up to scratch so that she would have a nice place around her to go on walks.

The palace compound spread over hundreds of acres and was entirely surrounded by high stone walls. The entry was through ornately fashioned golden gates, leading into an exquisitely manicured park dotted with groves of pomegranate trees. The palace compound was the only place in the whole of the underworld, aside from the Elysian Fields, which had vegetation of any sort. An enormous team of landscape gardeners and horticulturists worked exclusively on the plant life there, but the mental power it took to imagine each individual leaf and blade of grass meant that it was considered a nonessential service and therefore not extended to the rest of the underworld. To Alice, the presence of nature had become an unimaginable dream, and even if she hadn't felt the calling from inside, she would have found it hard to resist slipping through the gates and into the park beyond.

The driveway was made of gravel – an astonishing luxury, as each individual pebble had to be imagined by someone – and it actually crunched under her feet. It was just a trick of the design, but even so, the feeling that her body was having an impact on something was a bliss so intense as to be almost frightening. Alice's feet led her all the way up the main drive to the palace. She could see it through the trees in the distance, gleaming under the false sunshine. It was Versailles today.

There were a couple of bored guards lolling at the entrance to the palace, members of the squadron recruited by Persephone from the hordes of soldiers who had died in battle. She picked them based not on ability but on whose bodies and uniforms had remained the most intact in the process of dying. In practice, this meant that most of the men in question had been killed by poison gas. Their distinctive sallow skin tone made the rest of the dead refer to them by the nickname the Yellow Pages, a handle that had started amongst some of the most recently deceased, and subsequently spread, even to those who had been born long before the invention of the telephone. Alice eyed the guards warily. Her one meeting with Cerberus had been enough to convince her that there were ways in which the dead could yet die.

Seeing her coming, the guards shuffled into a position that might approximate standing to attention.

'Halt, who goes there?' said one of them, just as the other said, 'What are you doing here?'

The look they then exchanged was suffused with mutual irritation. Alice wondered how long they had been stationed together at these gates.

'Hello,' she said. 'My name's Alice Mulholland.'

The less formal of the two guards looked at her with some recognition.

'Alice Mulholland?' he said. 'Aren't you a Premiership Scrabble player?'

'Oh no,' said Alice. 'I'm just First Division.'

'I'm sure we had a game once,' said the guard. 'You won.'

'I probably just had better letters,' said Alice.

'What's your business here?' said the other guard.

'I don't know,' replied Alice.

'What do you mean, you don't know?'

'I felt a . . .'

The rules of existence in the underworld were different from those in the upperworld, in any number of ways that she hadn't got the hang of yet, so Alice didn't know whether what she was about to say would sound ridiculous to the guards or not.

'A force.'

'A force?'

'Drawing me here. I thought maybe it was Persephone. Or Hades.'

'You'd better hope it wasn't Hades,' said the guard.

'Or Persephone,' said the other guard.

'Oh dear,' said Alice.

'Tell you what,' said the Scrabble-playing guard, 'why doesn't Dieter go inside to find out what's going on, and you and I can have a nice game of I Spy while we wait.'

'Why do I always have to go inside?' said the guard called Dieter. 'I'll wait here, you go in.'

'I said so first.'

'But I went last time.'

'Maybe I could just go in by myself,' said Alice.

'No,' said both guards at the same time.

'OK,' said the game-loving guard. 'Paper Scissors Stone.'

'No,' said Dieter. 'You always win.'

'It's random,' said the other guard.

'Fine,' said Dieter.

Dieter chose Scissors and the other guard chose Stone.

'Off you go, then,' said the other guard cheerfully.

'Best of three?' said Dieter.

'OK,' said the other guard.

They played twice more with exactly the same result.

'See you later,' said the winner, waving.

'But –' said Dieter.

'It was a fair contest,' said Alice.

'Fine,' said Dieter eventually. 'I'll go. But next time, Eddie, it's your turn.'

He stomped off to the huge doors that formed the main entrance to the palace and disappeared inside.

'He always chooses Scissors,' said Eddie once he'd gone. 'And he never remembers. I think the gas went to his head.'

'It must have been very hard, being a soldier,' said Alice.

'Actually, I think Dieter misses it,' said Eddie. 'He was a career soldier, you see, skilled with a bayonet. Very efficient, good at his job. Every so often we meet someone that he killed, and that's a bit embarrassing. We were on different sides, you know. But no hard feelings, all's fair in love and war, et cetera, et cetera. You can't hold a grudge for a thing like that.'

'What about you?' said Alice. 'Have you ever run into anyone you killed?'

Eddie looked around before replying. 'Don't tell anyone,' he said, when he was sure that there was no other guard creeping up behind him, 'but I never killed a single person. Not one.'

'Did you die before you got the chance?' said Alice.

'No,' said Eddie. 'I was a big fat coward. I was in loads of battles, never once shot my gun. But please don't tell. If it got out I'd be a laughing stock with the lads.'

Alice smiled. 'Don't worry,' she said. 'I won't tell anyone. Cross my heart and hope to . . . Well, cross my heart, anyway.'

'You can still die, dear,' said Eddie. 'And maybe sooner rather than later by the looks of things.'

'What do you mean?' said Alice.

'It's Cerberus.'

'Cerberus? Here?'

Eddie pointed down the drive behind her, and Alice turned to look. He was still a long way off but even at a distance Alice could tell that Cerberus was a changed animal from the last time she had seen him. He walked slowly, his six huge shoulders stooped as he advanced with his magnificent heads bowed. As he shuffled closer, she could see the places where his hide was ripped open, glistening patches red with blood. His serpent tail hung motionless, dragging in the gravel behind him. And pulling him forward by his leftmost ear was a woman, a woman whom Alice initially thought was just another of the dead, but as the unlikely pair approached she suddenly recognised her.

'Artemis!' she couldn't help but cry out, waving.

'You know that lady?' said Eddie.

'Oh no,' said Alice. 'That isn't a lady. That's a goddess.'

It had been a tough fight. Satisfyingly so. She couldn't remember the last time she had met a real physical challenge, couldn't remember the last time she had had a fight that she might lose. In Cerberus, at last, she had found a worthy adversary. She'd had the advantage at the start, the element of surprise: Cerberus was not used to coming under attack, was not expecting her assault, and had stumbled back for a few precious seconds, away from her two-footed onslaught. Then he had gathered himself and fought back, giant paws beating her away, all three heads and that vicious snake of a tail tearing at her flesh with their terrible, hungry jaws. It was fantastic. Here in the land of the dead, facing the possibility of her own demise, Artemis had never felt so alive. She fought back, kicking, biting, snarling, scratching, as much of a monstrous beast as her opponent. She felt his skin and muscle tearing under the force of her fingers, tasted the steel of his blood in her mouth. They rolled together on the ground, their deadly fight making them one, a single, writhing mass with the solitary intent of destruction, impossible to separate. Artemis felt pain and the pain felt good. She knew she was inflicting as much on her partner. She felt stronger and stronger the more Cerberus hurt her. Sounds emanated from her throat, growls and shrieks, as she fought harder and harder, every ounce of herself determined that she would defeat this beast, knowing that he was fighting back with equal determination, and that only one of them would prevail. But as they tumbled and tore at each other, she felt her exhaustion growing even as she found more strength to fight. This had to end soon. She gathered together her power, drawing it from every last part of her aching body and hurled everything into a final assault. She was hardly aware of the last moments of the fight, her body taking over entirely, acting with some instinct that was beyond conscious thought. And then she came back to herself, and she realised, panting, that it was over, that she had the monster down, motionless on the ground, utterly vanquished. She had won.

Leading her conquest up the long drive to the palace of Hades and Persephone, she walked with pride, though her body throbbed with pain, knowing that she had defeated their champion. Not through trickery like the others, but in an honest battle of equals – or near-equals, she thought, watching the beast following at her command. In the upperworld she had grown accustomed to thinking of herself as weakening, deteriorating. Here she was no such thing. She wondered what special power this place had that made her feel so mighty.

As she and her conquest approached the palace, she heard, much to her surprise, a voice calling her name, and she looked up to see a small blonde mortal waving at her with huge enthusiasm. A fan? Had word of her victory spread so soon? As she got closer, though, she recognised her: it was her cleaner, the mortal who had started off all of this fuss! It was astonishing, thought Artemis, that such a small girl could cause so much trouble. In a fight with a large rat, she looked as if she would lose. Still, she did recall that before all this business with the impending apocalypse she had had every intention of bringing the girl back up into the upperworld, so it was a happy coincidence that the mortal was standing there now.

Artemis swept up to the girl and spoke to the pasty-faced guard who was apparently holding her prisoner.

'I am the goddess Artemis,' she announced, 'and this is my slave Cerberus.'

'Your slave?' said both the guard and the girl at the same time.

'That's right,' said Artemis. 'I fought him and I won, and now he belongs to me. Thank you very much for looking after my mortal for me, and now I am taking her in to see Hades and Persephone.'

'Your mortal?' said the guard and the girl.

'Strange,' said Artemis, peering at them. 'You look like two separate individuals.'

'Sorry, Eddie,' said the cleaner to the guard. 'I think I'd better go with her. I'm sorry we didn't get to have our game of I Spy.'

'That's OK,' said the guard. 'I would have let you in anyway. I was just enjoying the conversation.'

The cleaner carefully positioned herself on the far side of Artemis from Cerberus' three heads, and they proceeded towards the palace entrance.

'Artemis, it's lovely to see you,' said Alice when they were a safe distance from the guard. 'I do hope you're not dead, though.'

'No,' said Artemis. 'I'm alive. For the time being.'

Thirty-Six

After leaving Styx, Neil hurried as fast as he could to Hades and Persephone's palace. He had asked Styx for directions, but she told him that there was no need; if he wanted to get there, eventually he would. And eventually, just as she'd said, he had indeed arrived at a long stone wall, on the far side of which he could just see the tops of some trees. He went to walk through the wall, but to his surprise it was solid. He could actually feel it when he touched it with his hands, and where his palms met the wall he could feel them too. For a moment, he pressed himself up against it, just to enjoy the sensation of having a body again. But he didn't have time to waste. With some difficulty, he hauled himself up to the top of the wall, gripping at cracks between the stones with his fingers and toes. He paused at the top for a moment, scanning the parkland in front of him for any sign of dead people. But there was nobody to be seen. The bright grass extended in front of him, sloping gently upwards, and in the far distance he could just see the palace, looking like a Lego brick on the horizon.

He jumped down onto the grass, feeling nothing again, and headed up the hill. As he got closer, he could see that he was approaching the palace from the back. He still couldn't see any guards. This had to be the worst-defended palace he had ever heard of. He wasn't even sure whether he needed to be sneaking in anyway. Artemis had been vague on the subject of Hades and Persephone. On the one hand, she'd implied that if they caught him in the underworld, they'd destroy his soul, which he definitely didn't want. But on the other hand, Artemis was planning to ask them for help saving the upperworld, so they couldn't be entirely bad. Not to mention that they were the only ones that could give him Alice back.

This helpful recap did nothing to suggest a best course of action for Neil, so in the absence of anybody actually challenging him, he decided that he may as well just walk straight in. It was reasonably hard to sneak anyway, if there was nobody trying to stop you.

He chose the most humble-looking door at the back of the building, and found himself in an enormous kitchen, with flagstone floors, whitewashed walls and a huge fireplace. There wasn't a trace of food to be seen, nor a single kitchen implement anywhere. In the middle of the room was a large wooden table, and around it sat a group of the dead, both men and women, of varying ages and states of disrepair. They were all facing inwards with looks of deep concentration on their faces. He tried to slip past, but one of them, an old man in a surgical gown with a huge open wound down the front of his chest, noticed him and spoke.

'What are you doing here?' he said.

'Are you a guard?' said Neil.

'Don't be absurd,' said the man. 'Do I look yellow to you?'

'Um, not particularly,' said Neil.

'I'm an architect,' said the man. 'Are you an architect?'

'No,' said Neil. 'I'm an engineer.'

'Then you're in the wrong room,' said the architect. 'Kitchen wing is architects only, engineers are in the ballroom. Though why the engineers get to be in the ballroom I have no idea. They're just structure, we're design.'

'I'll make my way through,' said Neil. 'Thank you.'

'Pay close attention to the main hall carpet,' said an old woman at the end of the table, as Neil went to leave. 'It's one of mine. Each tuft is individually imagined.'

Neil left the kitchen and made his way deeper into the palace, picking his way along panelled corridors until he came out to a huge open hallway – with, to his eye, an entirely unremarkable carpet – where an imposing flight of steps swept up to an enormous pair of heavily-gilded doors, guarded by two uniformed men, both (and he now realised the meaning of the architect's words) with queasy yellow faces. He guessed that this was probably where he wanted to head.

The two men watched with curiosity but no aggression as he climbed up the stairs towards them.

'Hello,' said Neil.

'Hello,' said one of the guards.

'I'm looking for Hades and Persephone,' said Neil.

'I think they're in here,' said the guard. 'But they keep moving the rooms around. Are you an architect?'

'No,' said Neil.

'Shame,' said the guard. 'I was going to ask you to keep everything where you put it. It would make our afterlives much easier.'

'So can I go in?' said Neil.

'You want to go inside?' said the guard.

'Are you sure?' said the other guard.

'I don't want to go in,' said Neil, 'but it's what I'm here for.'

'Well, that makes more sense,' said the second guard.

'What are we supposed to do when people ask to go in?' said the first guard.

'Search me,' said the second guard.

'Give us a moment,' said the first guard. 'Usually we're here to stop people coming out.'

The guards put their heads together and conferred in whispers. After a while, they appeared to reach some agreement, and turned back to face Neil.

'We've decided,' said the first guard. 'We'll let you in, because stopping you is not within our remit. But we might not let you out again. Depends on commands from them inside.'

'That sounds reasonable,' said Neil.

'Good luck,' said the second guard. 'And be careful. You're only small.'

The two guards stepped aside, and Neil stepped forward, putting his hands up to push the doors open. Instead he went straight through them, arms in front of his face, like a sleep-walker. He heard the guards chuckling on the other side of the doors.

The throne room looked familiar, and it took only a few moments for him to recognise it as the Hall of Mirrors from Versailles, which he'd visited the previous summer. It was an enormous, arched chamber, spanning dozens of metres, brightly illuminated by crystal chandeliers whose light was reflected in the row of huge mirrors that extended along one of the ornately gilded walls. Closer examination proved that it wasn't an exact copy of the original Hall of Mirrors. When Louis XIV had his built, he had commanded it to be decorated with images and statues of himself in various heroic guises. Hades and Persephone had had these replaced with representations of themselves.

At the far end of the room was a dais with two ebony thrones on which the two gods were seated. Hades was gigantic, his swarthy bulk filling every inch of his huge, ornate throne and spilling out over the sides, his vast head reaching up to the ceiling. His skin was waxy and black, like something burnt, his body bursting with muscle, with great twisted cables of sinew pushing their way through. His eyes glittered hard and unwelcoming, like rain on the road on a cold winter's night. At the sight of him, everything in Neil wanted to turn away and run. He looked like the devil – he looked like death itself. Next to him, pretty, incon-sequential Persephone seemed tiny, like a doll.

'Is there a mortal in here?' said Persephone to her husband. 'What a cheek!'

'And he isn't even dead,' said Hades. 'Come on then,' he called to Neil. 'Approach! Let's see what you're made of.'

Neil crept across the enormous chamber towards the dais.

'Why are you here, live thing?' said Hades.

'Um. Is Artemis not here yet?' said Neil.

'Artemis is in the underworld?' said Hades, his giant eyebrow raising like a flexing bow. 'Why didn't Cerberus inform me?'

'Oh bother,' said Persephone. 'Don't tell me she's poking around down here. Once she starts they'll all be at it. They don't care two hoots for my privacy.'

'Did Artemis tell you to come here?' said Hades to Neil.

The closer Neil got, the more he, too, felt like a toy in the presence of Hades. A very fragile toy that would rather be back in its box.

'Yes she did,' said Neil.

'Why?'

'Well,' said Neil, 'mainly because the world is ending.'

'Mainly?' said Hades. 'There is another reason, then?'

'Ah, yes,' said Neil. 'It's . . . kind of personal.'

'More personal than the world ending?' said Hades.

'Yes,' said Neil. 'It's a woman.'

'It always is.'

'Her name is Alice.'

'Alice?' Hades' gigantic muscles rippled as he turned to his wife. 'Darling, do you know an Alice?'

'I know millions of Alices,' said Persephone. 'Everybody's called Alice these days. It's such a bore.'

'I can't give you millions of Alices,' said Hades to Neil.

'I don't want millions of Alices,' said Neil. 'I want my Alice. Alice Joy Mulholland. She's thirty-two. She died on March 21st of this year.'

'Oh poo,' said Persephone. 'Is it spring already? I'm supposed to be back on the surface now. How tiresome.'

'Darling, I'm sure you don't need to go back up there if the world is coming to an end,' said Hades. 'The weather's bound to be ghastly.'

'So can I have her?' said Neil.

'My wife?' said Hades.

'Alice,' said Neil.

'Of course not,' said Hades. 'Now leave before I have you destroyed.'

'But there's a precedent,' said Neil.

Hades growled. The walls of the throne room shook. Neil wanted to take a step back – a mile-long step – but he didn't. He clenched his fists by his sides, chose one of Hades' enormous eyes, and looked him in that eye.

'You're just a mortal,' said Hades. 'Not even a dead one at that. How dare you come here into my palace and start talking about precedents?'

'Precedents are very important,' said Neil. 'It means you can do it again.'

'I ought to eat your soul right now,' said Hades, 'only I just had my lunch.'

'Artemis says all I have to do is prove to you that I love her and you have to let her go.'

'Artemis is wrong,' said Hades. 'There's always a sacrifice involved. A sacrifice, a test –'

'Or maybe a dance, darling,' said Persephone. 'We could make him do a dance.'

'Persephone, darling, please,' said Hades. 'No, we'll have to cut off some limbs at least.'

'Done,' said Neil.

'Done?' said Hades.

'I don't need my legs, I don't need my arms. Take them. I need Alice.'

'Well that's no fun at all,' said Hades. 'You gave in far too easily.'

'I still think a dance would be better,' said Persephone.

'I'm quite happy to dance,' said Neil.

'No, no,' said Hades. 'Something else. Do stop talking about dances, darling. The thing is,' he explained to Neil, 'the more souls I get, the more powerful I am. If you want to take just one away, that hurts me. I wouldn't expect a mortal like you to understand.'

'I understand perfectly,' said Neil. 'It hurt me when you took Alice away.'

'Oh, isn't he sweet,' said Persephone. 'Why don't you ever talk about me like that?'

'So if you hurt me,' said Hades, ignoring his wife, 'I need to hurt you.'

Hades reached over and picked Neil up with one hand. Neil could feel the realness of Hades, and his body against his palm. Neil's real body was very, very frightened. But he refused to struggle. Hades closed his other hand around Neil's head.

'Hurt me,' said Neil into Hades' fingers.

'You're taking all the joy out of it,' said Hades.

'For her, hurt me,' said Neil. 'Do whatever you like.'

Hades' hands began to grip him more tightly. But then they stopped. Hades put him back down in front of the dais.

'No,' he said. 'It's not worth it. You can't have her. Sorry, goodbye.'

'Wait,' said Neil.

'I said goodbye,' said Hades, waving towards the door.

'If you don't want to let me have her, then let me stay in her place.'

'Oh, bless him,' said Persephone.

'The same number of souls. You don't get hurt. You lose nothing. Just let her go and I'll stay.'

'It's really adorable that he's trying so hard,' said Persephone. 'I don't mind keeping him instead. I don't even know this Alice. Let's swap them.'

Hades looked at his wife and then down at Neil.

'I've got a better idea,' said Hades. 'Why don't you choose?'

'Choose?' said Neil.

'Yes. You can save the world or you can have your Alice. We'll put you up somewhere nice in the Elysian Fields – it's the underworld's most exclusive neighbourhood. You can have all of eternity together, I'll guarantee not to eat either of your souls. You'll have pure, uninterrupted bliss until the end of time itself. You and Alice. Together. For ever. What do you say?'

'And the world?'

'Ends. Everybody dies. Or otherwise, you can save the world but I'm keeping the girl.'

'What do you mean, you're keeping her?'

'She stays here, you go back, and you never see her again. It's up to you.'

'Oh Hades, you are nasty sometimes,' said Persephone.

'Be quiet for once, Persephone,' said Hades. 'So, mortal, what do you say? World? Alice? World? Alice? World? Alice?'

'I have to decide right now?'

'Right now,' said Hades.

Neil nodded.

'OK,' he said.

'What's your choice?' said Hades.

'World,' said Neil.

'World?' said Hades. 'You choose the world? You came all the way down here, to the underworld, to my palace, for this woman, you offer your limbs, you offer your soul, and yet you choose to save the world?'

'Yes,' said Neil.

'But why?' said Hades.

'Everybody loves somebody,' said Neil. 'So I lose her. But everybody else gets to keep theirs. It's what she'd do. And she's probably better off without me anyway.'

Hades laughed. It wasn't a pleasant sound. Like crows celebrating after picking out some nice, juicy eyes. Neil shut his eyes. He didn't know what he'd just done, but his life, either way, was over.

'Well, as it happens,' said Hades, 'I don't have the power to save or end the world, so it's kind of irrelevant. Still, it was a nice answer. So anyway, did you say that Artemis was on her way here? I do wonder what she's done with our dog.'

Thirty-Seven

It was a nice palace, Artemis had to admit. Irritatingly so, when she considered the squalor that she had to put up with in the upperworld. No wonder Persephone was always in such a mood when she came up; no wonder she always acted so superior. Even being a god felt different down here, like the clear, clean water of a shower after swimming in a murky stream. It wasn't at all fair. She would have to have a word with Hephaestus about some urgent refurbishments.

It was easy enough to find Hades and Persephone as she could simply follow the draw of their godly presence through the (well, perhaps rather gaudy, now she really considered it) palace, to the (tastelessly ostentatious, some might say) doors where two decidedly surprised-looking guards eyed her, her mortal and her dog.

'Stand aside,' commanded Artemis. 'I am the goddess Artemis, niece of Hades, sister of Persephone, and these are my chattels. I demand admittance into the presence of my fellow gods without whom you would be nothing but dust and air.'

The guards looked at one another.

'Again?' said one of them.

'Do you have an appointment?' said the other.

'Oh, just let them in,' called a voice from inside the room, dark and booming, like tombstones being knocked over: Hades.

The guards stepped away and the doors to the chamber swung silently inwards. Artemis, Cerberus and Alice stepped across the threshold and the doors swung shut equally silently behind them.

'Greetings, fellow Olympians,' Artemis began.

'Leave out the formalities,' said Hades. 'Come over here where we can see you.'

The three of them approached the dais. Alice walked bravely, Artemis noted, with barely a hint of a tremor.

'Uncle,' said Artemis. 'You've grown.'

'With every soul, dear niece. With every soul.'

Hades grinned, showing off long, sharp teeth. Beside his obscene bulk, little Persephone eyed Artemis with a smirk.

'Isn't this just like the *Wizard of Oz*,' said Persephone. 'You're the Wicked Witch of the West, that mortal child is Dorothy, and Cerberus is the Cowardly Lion.'

Cerberus growled.

'Or maybe Toto.'

Cerberus growled louder.

'That would make the pair of you the Wizard,' said Artemis. 'A fraud with a hand crank and some whistles and bells.'

'That's enough,' said Hades. 'What are you doing here?'

'The upperworld is in danger,' said Artemis. 'Apollo, for reasons best known to himself – you know how hot-headed he can be – put the sun out, and now he's in a coma and we can't wake him up. We haven't got the sun, we haven't got Apollo, and if we don't work together to keep the earth going, the world is going to end.'

'And then all of the mortals will die?' said Hades.

'Yes.'

'And this is a bad thing?'

'Well . . . yes . . .' began Artemis.

'The way I see it,' said Hades, 'once the upperworld ends, all of the mortals there will become my subjects.'

'Our subjects,' interjected Persephone.

'We'll own them. We'll have all of the power, and you'll have nothing. Why should we help you?'

'Because . . .' said Artemis. 'Because . . .'

'Because if everybody dies,' said Alice, stepping forward, 'nobody will be born. Sorry to interrupt.'

'Please,' said Hades, gesturing for her to continue.

'And so,' said Alice, 'it seems to me, that although you will rule over all the mortals who live in the upperworld right now, you'll never gain any more souls after that. Not a single one. Everyone who is alive at the moment is going to be dead in a hundred years anyway, so it's only for the next hundred years that you'll be disproportionately powerful. After that, effectively you'll start losing power.'

'Feisty little thing, aren't you?' said Hades.

'Not on the whole,' said Alice.

'Give us back Cerberus,' said Hades, 'and maybe we'll think about helping you.'

'Cerberus is mine,' said Artemis. 'I defeated him in combat, and now he belongs to me. I will not part with him merely in order to win your consideration.'

'OK, if that's how you feel,' said Hades, surprisingly lightly. 'But maybe in that case you'll swap him for this.'

Hades reached behind his throne and pulled out a small, metal cage. And inside that cage, crouched down on all fours, was Neil. Alice's eyes widened, and she was about to speak, but Neil shook his head, and she stayed silent.

'Now tell me,' said Hades, 'what exactly were you thinking bringing a live mortal into my kingdom?'

'He's alive?' said Alice.

Neil nodded. Alice smiled.

'So far,' said Hades.

Alice stopped smiling.

'Give us the dog and you can have your mortal back,' said Hades.

'No,' said Artemis.

'That's right!' said Neil. 'Well said, Artemis!'

'We will eat his soul,' said Hades.

'No!' cried Alice.

She made a move towards the cage, but Artemis held her arm out, signalling her to stop.

'Don't worry about it, Artemis, stick to your guns,' said Neil. 'It's worth it for a few more seconds with her.'

'I'm really going to start sulking now,' said Persephone. 'You could do with being a bit more romantic, Hades. You really take me for granted.'

'Neil, forget about me, just get out of the cage and run,' said Alice.

'I can't,' said Neil. 'It's solid. I can't get past the bars.'

'Are you Alice Mulholland?' said Persephone.

'Yes,' said Alice, wondering how she knew.

'They're such a sweet couple,' said Persephone to Hades. 'You can't possibly separate them. You really should eat them both.'

Alice thought fast. 'You can eat me, but you should spare Neil,' she said. 'He's an engineer. Very skilled. One of the best in the country.'

'What kind of engineer?' said Persephone.

'Structural,' said Alice.

Persephone turned to her husband.

'Darling,' she said, 'do you have to eat his soul? Can't I keep him? I'll look after him, I promise. You know how much I love engineers. And structural is my favourite kind.'

'I will give you Cerberus,' said Artemis, 'in exchange for the mortal in the cage, and the girl, and your help.'

'Me?' said Alice.

'But I want to keep him,' whined Persephone.

Hades drummed his fingers against the arm of his throne.

'Just what exactly would this help entail?' he said.

'Well,' said Artemis, 'it's hard to say. I don't know what's been going on on the surface since I left. But if you come back up there with me –'

'No,' said Hades. 'Never.'

'But –' said Artemis.

'Not even for Cerberus,' said Hades.

'But that's where we need you.'

'It's out of the question. I do not go to the upperworld. That is final. And I see the little girl's point about more people being born in the future, but actually I think we'll just take the souls of all of the mortals that are on the surface now and be done with it. At least that way we'll have dominion over you. You've been lording it up on that upperworld for far too long.'

'Hades is right,' said Persephone. 'The surface is horrible and I don't see why it's worth saving.'

'But Persephone,' said Artemis, 'I thought you liked the upper-world. You always used to complain about having to come back down here.'

'That was before,' said Persephone. 'Back when we were young and powerful and we lived on our lovely mountain in our beau-tiful palace, and people used to bring us sacrifices and pretty things. But it's horrid now. We're getting old and we have to live in that disgusting tiny house and I have to sleep on the floor, and I can't do anything up there. I like it much better down here where everybody knows who I am and I can do whatever I like.'

'From what Persephone tells me you've really let standards slip up on the surface,' said Hades.

'It's not their fault,' said Neil. 'Nobody believes in them there. Of course they're not powerful any more.'

Artemis looked at Neil. Her mouth opened, then shut again. Then it opened again.

'What did you just say?'

'Sorry, but it's true,' said Neil.

For a couple of seconds Artemis stood absolutely still. Then she turned to Hades.

'Forget it,' she said. 'I've changed my mind, I don't need your help. Just give me the mortal in the cage and this girl, and you can have your dog back.'

'Why do you want the girl so much?' said Hades.

'Do you know how hard it is to get a decent cleaner in central London?' said Artemis.

'But I thought you said without our help the world will end?' said Persephone.

'Maybe it will,' said Artemis, 'but until then I'm still going to need someone to do the vacuuming. Do we have a deal?'

Hades' eyes narrowed as he stared at Artemis, trying to work out what the trick was. But he couldn't spot it. Then he looked across to his cowering hell-hound, who gazed back imploringly. He turned back to Artemis.

'We have a deal,' he said.

Alice ran over to the cage and threw herself down next to Neil, half laughing, half weeping dry tears, kissing the air that housed his image through the bars. Neil reached out and stroked the place where he could see her hair.

'But –' said Persephone.

'Persephone darling, engineers die all the time. Even this one, eventually. Sooner rather than later, probably, given the situation. There's only one Cerberus.'

'You never let me have anything I want,' whined Persephone, but she knew from the look on Hades' face that the door had slammed shut and no amount of banging and hollering would get it open again.

'Great,' said Artemis. 'So that's settled. Listen, while you let the mortal out of his box, would you mind if I used your telephone? I need to put in a quick call to Hermes.'

'Why?' said Hades, eyes narrowing again.

'Oh, just to let him know we're on our way back.'

And Artemis smiled in a way that Hades knew meant that she'd got away with something, but he had no idea what.

Thirty-Eight

Aphrodite was packing. She didn't know where for. All she knew was that if the world was ending she wasn't planning to stick around. It wasn't going to be pretty and Aphrodite liked everything to be pretty. It wasn't a weakness of hers: it was what she was for.

She was going to miss her bedroom, with its roses and filigrees and the swan-shaped bed and all the lovely mirrors. She would probably miss this planet too. It was such a sensual place: there was so much to enjoy. Wherever they were going next was unlikely to be so pleasant, as they were going to have to create it without a sun. Mortals had a saying that she adored: 'All you need is love'. But the thing was – though she would never admit this out loud – it wasn't true. If she had to set up a world by herself, the sex there would be phenomenal, and if you could see anything it would be beautiful too, but you wouldn't be able to see anything because you needed light to see, and light was not her department. She needed Apollo for light, for light and for warmth, otherwise any creatures that she created would spend eternity having cold dark sex and there was nothing beautiful about that and – she stifled a sob. Where was he?

She redoubled her efforts at packing. Any mawkish dwelling on Apollo might lead to feeling bad about how she had treated him and Aphrodite didn't do feeling bad. It was not what she was for. And the packing, she thought to herself, was going very well, mainly because most of her clothes folded up extremely small so she could fit them into compact luggage with ease. The shoes, though, they were going to be a problem. Wherever she was going next, Aphrodite was going to need lots of pairs of shoes. Aphrodite refused to go anywhere where you didn't need lots of pairs of shoes.

The door opened. Aphrodite looked up, hoping for one stupid moment that it might be Apollo, but it was only Eros.

'Oh,' she said, 'it's you.'

'Are you OK, Mum?' said Eros.

'Of course I'm OK,' said Aphrodite, folding clothes at double speed.

Eros sat down at the tail end of the swan bed. His shirt was untucked and he hadn't brushed his hair.

'You mustn't give up hope, Mum,' he said.

'I'm not giving up hope,' said Aphrodite. 'Who's giving up hope? I'm just being prepared.'

She stuffed some handfuls of lingerie inside a pair of thigh-high boots and put them in the bottom of a new suitcase.

'Apollo's going to be fine,' said Eros. 'Artemis will find him.'

'Of course she'll find him,' said Aphrodite. 'Artemis is a great huntress. She can find anything.'

'I wish she'd told us where she was going,' said Eros, 'instead of just running out of the house like that.'

'I'm sure she had her reasons,' said Aphrodite. 'Can you hand me one of the boxes of sex toys from under the bed?'

Eros reached down and passed his mother one of the matching translucent pink crates.

'So you're definitely fine,' said Eros.

'Definitely.' Aphrodite tipped the contents of the box into a rattling heap in her bag.

'Full of hope?'

'Overflowing.'

A switch on one of the vibrators must have flicked on as they fell, because Aphrodite's suitcase was now buzzing and jiggling. She started digging though it, searching for the culprit.

'The thing is,' said Eros. 'The thing is . . .'

'What is the thing? – Ah, here it is.' She switched the errant item off.

'The thing is . . .' said Eros again, 'is that I'm kind of, you know, giving up hope, you know.'

'Oh,' said Aphrodite. She put the vibrator down. 'Oh, Eros. Why didn't you say?'

She pushed her suitcases to one side and sat down on the bed next to her son, putting her arms around him and holding his head against her shoulder.

'Darling,' she said, 'it's going to be fine, you know. Everything's going to be fine.'

'But you're packing,' said Eros.

'Darling, remember, this is me,' said Aphrodite. 'Everybody else might be happy to flee with only the clothes they have on their backs, but some of these things are designer. Look, just because I'm packing doesn't mean we have to go, I just like to be ready, that's all. I don't like surprises. And I'm a materialistic bitch. Everybody knows it. You can't take me as an example. Don't tell anyone about the hugging thing, by the way.'

'I won't,' promised Eros into her collarbone. 'But Mum, I don't think it's going to work out this time. Nothing like this has ever happened before. We need Apollo. We just can't do without him.'

'We need all of us,' said Aphrodite. 'We need me to keep looking good, it gives the mortals something to aspire to. We need Artemis to zoom off to who knows where so it looks like something is being done. And we need you to have faith.'

'But I don't have faith,' said Eros.

'Well if you don't, nobody else is going to,' said Aphrodite. 'There haven't been this many gods in the house since Zeus's last big birthday and they're running around like headless chickens. Dear me, what a hideous thought. They're running around like sperm looking for an egg, and the fact of the matter is that you're the only person who has any experience in this area, you're the only one who knows how to believe in things that aren't true. So you'd better get out there and start persuading everybody that we're going to find Apollo and things are going to be all right, and that'll keep everyone busy until . . .'

'Until what, Mum?'

'Until either it does work out fine or I can get us all packed and ready to go. We're gods, Eros. We'll find a way around this, even if it isn't a way we like the look of much. We always do.'

Eros sat up straight and nodded.

'OK,' he said. 'You're right.'

'I always am,' said Aphrodite.

Just then the door opened again and Hermes came in.

'Doesn't anybody knock any more?' said Aphrodite.

'I think you'd better come downstairs,' said Hermes. 'I've just had a call from Artemis.'

Thirty-Nine

It was a tense walk back to the surface. Having got everything she could have wanted, Alice was now terrified that it would all be taken away from her. Following the precedent established by Orpheus, Neil was made to walk in front of her and told that if he turned around to look at her before they got out, she would be sent back down to the underworld forever. So for the first part of the journey, from Hades and Persephone's palace to the underworld Tube station, she didn't say a thing aside from, periodically, 'I'm still here,' afraid that were she to begin a conversation, Neil would forget himself and look back to reply. Instead she focused on the back of his beloved head, his brown hair rising above the scrubbed pink neck speckled with freckles, and then, beneath that, the soft blue of his dressing gown, and, oddly, poking out beneath that, jean cuffs and trainers.

As the black of the tunnel closed around them, though, Alice felt herself starting to panic, and she could no longer wait.

'Don't turn around,' she started. 'Artemis, I don't mean to be at all ungrateful, I'm just a bit worried. I don't have a body any more. Am I going to be a ghost now?'

'Don't worry,' said Artemis. 'Aphrodite can take care of that.'

'Aphrodite?'

'Yes. She'll probably make you a bit prettier than you are now but she's very good at making bodies on the whole. She was the one who made Helen beautiful, and people are still talking about her.'

'That's very nice,' said Alice, 'but I'm not sure Aphrodite likes me very much.'

'She will once we've finished,' said Artemis.

'But are you sure she'll agree to do it?' said Neil, his voice as anxious as Alice felt. 'I thought you were all supposed to be conserving your power, especially now that the sun's gone out.'

'That's all going to be fine now,' said Artemis.

'But how? The world's about to end, we still haven't woken Apollo up . . .'

'Trust me.'

They walked on a little further in silence.

'Don't turn around,' said Alice. 'But I can't just turn up alive again. Everybody knows I died. I had a funeral. Didn't I have a funeral?'

'Well, I wasn't exactly invited,' said Neil to Artemis, 'but I'm sure that she did, and not only that, her death was in all of the papers and on the news because of her being struck by lightning. There was a photograph. Everybody knows who she is. Everybody knows she's dead.'

'Good,' said Artemis.

'So we can't just bring her back.'

'Yes we can,' said Artemis, 'and we will.'

'But –'

'Didn't I just say to trust me?' said Artemis.

By the time they reached the end of the tunnel, Alice was so nervous that she could no longer speak at all, just cough out the occasional 'Still here' in her terror that Neil would turn around to reassure himself. The three of them scrambled up onto the platform, Neil holding his head perfectly still to prevent himself from turning back even accidentally, and then stepped through the wall into the mortal station. The lights were still out but after the total darkness of the tunnel, there was a certain shape to the shadows that was just enough to tell Alice that she was in a place that she knew, and the banal familiarity of it closed around her like a soft glove.

'Are we here now, can I look at her yet?' said Neil, and the pain and longing in his tones struck Alice so deep that it was as if she was experiencing them herself.

'I'm not sure,' said Artemis. 'I don't know exactly where the portal is. I think you'd better wait until we're out of the Tube station completely, just to be certain.'

And so they faced the long, long climb up the stairs to the exit, together yet still alone.

It was only when they finally stepped through the ticket barriers and half ran, half fell through the grille into the street outside, that Alice finally believed that this was really happening, that she was being given a second chance at life, and Neil finally turned round and looked at her, his face transformed by joy, and they threw themselves into each other's arms, and went right through each other and ended up falling onto the frozen pavement on either side, and then picked themselves up and laughed, and turned to each other and looked at each other, and looked, and looked, and looked.

'You look exactly the same,' whispered Alice, shaking her head. 'You haven't changed a bit.'

'Right then,' said Artemis, 'when you're done. We don't have a lot of time. We need to go back to Neil's flat and pick up the bodies.'

'Bodies?' said Alice.

'I'll explain on the way,' said Neil.

As Neil told her what had happened with Apollo and the sun, Alice was trying to listen – it was obviously very important – but she couldn't focus on his words. Like parched earth in the rain, she drank in the wonderful contours of his face, the lively expression of his eyes – lively! Was anything lively in the underworld? – the tightening and slackening of his skin as he spoke, every hair, every pore, everything she had tried to conjure up for herself – and tried not to conjure up for herself – throughout that long lonely time without him. And she could see Neil staring back at her, and she wondered if her own face was reflecting back that same dazed, amazed look.

'I love you,' she interrupted him. 'Neil. I can't wait another second to tell you. I love you.'

'I love you too,' said Neil.

'That's lovely,' said Artemis. 'Keep walking.'

Artemis led the way back to Neil's flat through the scummy back roads and miserable cheap shopping streets that constitute the crumbling edifice holding up the shining façade of London. The orange neon of streetlights bounced off the metal shutters of shops and takeaway restaurants boarded up against looters, illuminated scraps of litter blowing along the pavements like tumbleweed. To Alice's eyes it was one of the most beautiful sights she had ever seen.

'I'd forgotten,' she told Neil, 'just how many places there are here just for selling food. All these restaurants and supermarkets and corner shops. Nobody eats in the underworld. There are a few bars, like the one I worked in, but they're just places for people to go and socialise. But there's no food, aside from the pomegranates in the palace, and there aren't any drinks aside from Lethe. Here there's food all over the place. I wish I could eat some. Or even just smell it. You don't know how much I've missed it, I can hardly remember what it's like to eat.'

'It's so nice to hear you speak,' said Neil.

'I feel like I haven't spoken in years,' said Alice. 'Of course I have, but not to people who know me. Not to you.'

'But you haven't been gone all that long,' said Neil.

'Dead time,' interjected Artemis, without turning around.

'What does that mean?' said Alice. 'Hermes said something about it too but I couldn't understand what he meant.'

'Time down there passes more quickly than time up here,' said Artemis.

'So how long exactly have I been dead?' said Alice.

'Twenty-six days,' said Neil.

'Twenty-six days?' said Alice. '*Days*?'

'How long did you think you'd been gone?' said Neil.

When Alice replied it was in a very quiet voice. 'I thought it had been years,' she said.

'So you've been there all that time on your own?' said Neil, just as Alice said, 'You poor thing, you must still be in shock.'

'Well, she's back now,' said Artemis. 'Look, there's the house. Let's hope neither you nor Apollo have frozen to death.'

Forty

It was only when Neil got back inside his body that he realised how cold it had got. And yet, looking at the clock, he saw that only a few minutes had passed since they had left.

'How long have we got?' he asked Artemis.

'Now we're back in live time, not long,' she replied, and turned and hurried out of the room.

Alice, meanwhile, was looking around the bedroom as if she had never seen it before.

'I really feel like it's been years,' she said. 'I'd forgotten what your bedroom looks like. And I was only here a few weeks ago. How can it only be a few weeks?'

Artemis came back into the room, the immobile bulk of Apollo slung over her shoulder like a heavy fur wrap.

'Come on,' she said. 'We have to hurry.'

'Where are we going?' said Alice.

'Trafalgar Square.'

'Why Trafalgar Square?' said Neil.

'That's where everybody is.'

'Who's everybody?' said Neil.

'Everybody,' said Artemis. 'Get a move on.'

Neil pulled on his warmest jumpers and coat over the clothes he was wearing, and stuffed a few more woollens into a bag.

'What's that for?' said Alice.

'For you,' said Neil. 'For when you get your body back.'

They both smiled.

'Would the two of you stop swooning over each other and please hurry up?' said Artemis. 'We all know you're in love, but in case you hadn't noticed, the world is ending. The love will keep.'

She swept out of the room in a manner that was supposed to be imperious, but spoilt it somewhat by smacking Apollo's lolling head into the doorframe.

'Well, come on!' she called from outside.

Now that Neil had his body back the going was much slower. Alice still skimmed over the pavement feeling nothing, and Artemis, as befitted a goddess and a huntress, marched with a steady foot even with her improbable burden, but Neil was slipping and sliding all over the ice, and struggling to stay warm. On top of that, with the panic and the gridlock, there was no public transport and not a taxi to be had. They had little choice but to walk from Hackney all the way to the centre of London, and it was getting colder by the minute. Neil and Alice didn't mind too much, though, as it gave them the chance to catch up on the past four weeks / several years, before the serious business of world-saving kicked in. Even so, Neil couldn't help but ask whether it might not have been a better idea to do this part of the journey whilst they were still in dead time.

'I know it's frustrating,' said Artemis, 'and I know you're cold, but I needed your bodies, yours and Apollo's. I wish I could have woken up Apollo in the flat, but I'm not strong enough yet.'

'What do you mean, "yet"? I thought you were getting weaker,' said Neil.

'Not any more,' said Artemis.

They heard Trafalgar Square before they got there, the noise of mass conversation that was more of an angry buzz than a hum, as well as the inevitable sound – could Londoners ever gather without it? – of white people with dreadlocks drumming. Neil was exhausted: he had been walking for over two hours and the temperature had plunged far below zero. Just staying warm was taking up all the energy he had.

'Apollo is going to be insufferable when he wakes up and sees what happens to the world without him,' said Artemis, shifting the body from one shoulder to the other. 'Typical of him that it would all be so dramatic. If I was the one in the coma, you might not be able to see the results so clearly, but they would be almost as devastating.'

'Such as?' said Neil.

'The tides would all go wrong,' said Artemis. 'Tides are very important. Just ask Poseidon. Menstruation would go out of sync. Wild animals would roam the streets. And people would be having sex all over the place.'

'Sounds terrible,' said Neil, and Alice blushed.

Up until now the streets had been largely devoid of pedestrians, but as they walked down St Martin's Lane they could see the edges of the crowd that was gathering in the Square. A few stragglers were heading that way alongside them, bundled into heavy coats, hats and scarves, and if anyone thought that the sight of a beautiful woman effortlessly carrying a body over her shoulder was odd, they didn't show it. It seemed that people's tolerance for the bizarre had shot up in the past few hours.

'Good,' said Artemis, noting the scrum of mortals, looking to her eyes like scrabbling termites on a mound. 'The more witnesses, the better. Right, we need to get to the column.'

'We'll never push our way through that lot,' said Neil.

'Oh ye of little faith,' said Artemis.

In a deceptively casual gesture, she waved the arm that was not holding Apollo. The crowd gently parted before her, apparently unaware of what they were doing.

'Just like Moses and the Red Sea,' commented Alice.

Artemis winced. 'Enough of the biblical allusions, please,' she said. 'They got the idea from us – not the other way around.'

The three of them walked up the channel between the seething crowds towards Nelson's Column.

'Now remember,' said Artemis to Alice, 'they can see Neil but they can't see you.'

'Yes, I remem—' Alice broke off. 'That's my cousin. Neil, that's my cousin. That's Emma. What's she doing here? Can I talk to her? Artemis, can I talk to her?'

Artemis shook her head. 'She can't see you,' she said. 'Keep moving. We haven't got much time.'

'That's one of the other cleaners from the agency,' said Alice, pointing into the crowd. 'And there's my old boss!'

'Everybody here knows Alice,' said Artemis, 'either personally, or because they saw her in the newspaper or on the news. Hermes is very good.'

'Hermes?' said Neil.

'Yes, he gathered them all up. That's why I called him from the palace.'

'Oh my God,' said Alice, clapping her hand to her mouth. 'There are my parents. Please, Artemis, please. You've got to let me talk to them. Neil can see me, why can't they? Can't you make them see me?'

'Not yet, Alice,' said Artemis. 'You need to be patient. And please don't say "Oh my God".'

'Mum!' called Alice, waving. 'Dad! It's me, it's Alice!'

They were only a few feet away, but her parents didn't turn towards her, just kept facing ahead, unseeing. Alice's mother looked thin and drained, her drawn face swamped by her thick scarf and hat. Alice's father stood with a protective arm around her, holding her close against the cold and who knew what else.

'I just wish I could tell them I'm OK,' said Alice.

'Soon,' said Artemis. 'Right then. Here we are.'

They had reached the centre of the square, the famous tall column flanked by enormous lions – a strangely threatening presence in the gloom. A barrier had been erected around the column itself, holding the crowd back. Behind it, Alice recognised the faces of all of the gods that she used to clean for gathered at the base of the column, as well as several people she had never met before but who seemed to be part of the group. Artemis led them through a gap in the barrier and closed it off behind her.

'Hello,' said Alice to the gods.

They ignored her.

'Can't they see me either?' she said to Artemis.

'They can see you,' said Artemis. 'They just don't care.'

Artemis laid Apollo's body carefully down on one of the steps in front of the column. Aphrodite was the first to run forwards, with Hephaestus loyally following close behind. She knelt by her lover.

'Are you all right?' she said to him, but he didn't move. 'Artemis, where was he? Where did you find him?'

'Anyone would think you have a guilty conscience, Mother,' said Eros, sidling up behind her.

'You with your guilt,' said Aphrodite. 'I can see you're back to your old self.'

Suddenly, all of the gods were talking at once.

'Are you going to do something to help him?' said Demeter to Artemis. 'What are you going to do?'

'Wait and see,' said Artemis.

'Hello you two,' said Ares, walking over to Alice and Neil. 'Nice to see you both here together. I was a bit worried after the argument that I might have taken it a little too far.'

'Don't worry,' said Neil, 'we're fine.'

'Did you have a nice holiday?' said Ares to Alice.

'Not really,' said Alice.

'Oh well, at least you had a break,' said Ares. 'I can't ever go on holiday myself. Everywhere I go ends up as a war zone, and then it's just work, work, work.'

'I see you've found your cleaner,' said Hermes to Artemis.

'How did it go down there? I'm glad to see all of you back here in one piece.'

'The cleaner's in no pieces,' said Artemis, 'and she won't be until we can sort this mess out. I really owe her a body.'

'Hades and Persephone?' said Hermes.

'They refused to come,' said Artemis.

'And Cerberus?' said Hermes.

'I fought him,' said Artemis, 'and I won. I swapped him for the girl.'

Hermes raised an eyebrow. 'Nice work,' he said.

'Your hero helped,' said Artemis.

'Am I still mad?' asked Zeus of nobody in particular.

'Yes you are, dear,' said Hera, gripping him tightly by the arm.

'Hang on, didn't I kill that girl?' said Zeus. 'Should I kill her again?'

'Once is quite enough,' said Hera.

'Artemis,' Athena said, 'it is imperative that I emphasise the indispensability of whatever outward-focused public unfurlment of display you have strategised being calibrated for utmost exposure and accuracy, thus maximising its impact –'

'It's fine, Athena,' said Artemis. 'I know what I'm doing.'

'Does anybody fancy a drink?' said Dionysus.

'Yes, please, me,' said Artemis.

'You?' said Dionysus.

'For once I think I need one,' said Artemis, and she took the bottle out of his hand and took a deep swig.

'OK,' she said. 'I'm ready. Let's go.'

Artemis climbed up to the top of the steps in front of Nelson's Column and signalled for Alice and Neil to follow her.

'The two of you believe in me, don't you?' said Artemis.

'Of course,' said Alice.

'After everything that's happened?' said Neil. 'I believe in you completely.'

Artemis inhaled the force of their faith like a hit of pure oxygen. Then she addressed the crowd.

'Mortals,' she said.

She didn't make any effort to raise her voice, and yet every human being in the sea of mortality before her heard her, and turned to face her. Seeing their thousands of curious eyes, she did for a moment wish that she had chosen something a little more impressive than an old tracksuit to wear for the occasion, but it was too late to worry about that now. And in any case, it was the kind of thought that Aphrodite would have, and, as such, it was beneath her.

'These are strange times,' Artemis told the crowd. 'Your sun is gone. You have been plunged into darkness and cold, and you may be wondering if your last days are upon you.'

A loud murmur began to rise from the crowd, but Artemis silenced them with a gesture of her hands.

'They may be,' intoned Artemis. 'Or they may not. It is up to you.'

Now the murmur came from the gods, who preferred to think of things like the end of the world being their decision.

'Shut up,' hissed Artemis at her family. 'I know what I'm doing.' She addressed the crowd once more. 'It is up to you,' she said again. 'The choice is yours. You must decide whether or not you are going to believe.'

'Believe what?' shouted someone from the crowd.

'I believe what I can see,' shouted someone else, 'and I can't see much.'

'Where's the sun?' came a third voice.

Other members of the crowd picked this up as a refrain. 'Where's the sun?' they chanted. 'Where's the sun? Where's the sun?'

Artemis held up her hands again and the chant died down.

'Neil will explain,' she said.

'What?' said Neil.

268

'Who the fuck is Neil?' someone in the crowd called out.

'Go ahead,' said Artemis. 'Tell them everything that's happened. They're not going to listen to me.'

'But,' said Neil. 'But I can't.'

'Yes you can,' said Artemis. 'You're a natural preacher.'

'A preacher? Me? Artemis, you know how much I hate that kind of thing.'

'Exactly,' said Artemis. 'Look, up until I met you, I thought, like all the other gods, that we were losing our power because we were getting old.'

'Aren't you?' said Alice.

'No,' said Artemis. 'Neil, you were the one who figured out that we were losing our power, not from old age but because nobody believed in us any more.'

'You didn't know that?' said Neil.

'It may have been what Athena was trying to tell us all this time,' admitted Artemis, 'but she's not the clearest of communicators. But anyway, because you and you alone know the truth, and because you were one of the least likely people ever to have believed in us in the first place, you are the perfect person to get those mortals to believe in us again. There's no point me telling them I'm a god. That's never going to work. It has to be a mortal. It has to be you.'

'But I can't,' said Neil. 'I'm terrible at public speaking. Look at me. I've got no presence. And there must be hundreds of people here. Thousands. And listen to what they're saying!'

The crowd was chanting, 'Who the fuck is Neil? Who the fuck is Neil?'

'It'll be easy,' said Artemis.

Neil raised his eyebrows.

'Believe me, I will do my part,' said Artemis. 'But first you have to explain to them about Alice. You were there when she died. And you were with her when we brought her back.'

'But –' said Neil again.

'Neil,' said Artemis, 'you're the hero. Do your job.'

'Neil,' said Alice. 'Please. Do it.'

'OK,' said Neil. 'I'll do my best.'

'You'll be amazing,' said Alice. 'I know it.'

Neil turned to the crowd. He swallowed. There were an awful lot of people out there, and they weren't very happy. He could feel himself trembling, and, despite the cold, his palms were soaked in sweat.

'Hello,' he said. 'I the fuck am Neil.'

Some people in the crowd laughed, and the chanting died away.

'You don't know me,' said Neil, 'but you know my friend Alice.'

Alice whispered something.

'My girlfriend Alice,' said Neil, and he smiled over at her, or, as far as the crowd were concerned, at empty space. 'Alice Mulholland. She was the girl who died a few weeks ago, when she was struck by lightning.'

His words were travelling as effortlessly as Artemis's had. He glanced at Artemis, and she smiled through the look of concentration on her face.

'I was there,' said Neil. 'It was the worst day of my life.'

Neil caught sight of Alice's parents in the front row. Her mother had curled into her father's shoulder and was weeping.

'I loved her so much and I knew I'd never see her again.'

The crowd was perfectly silent and still. Even the drumming had stopped.

'But as it turns out, I was wrong about that.'

'What are you talking about?' shouted someone in the crowd.

'He means he's going to see her in heaven!' replied another voice.

'We're all going to die!' yelled another.

Somebody screamed, and the people in the middle of the crowd started pushing to the sides. The noise rose as panic began to take hold.

'Run!' shouted someone.

'Where to?' yelled someone else.

'No!' called Neil, waving his arms. 'No! That's not what I meant. Calm down, please! Listen to me! We're not all going to die! Not yet, anyway.'

Artemis was grimacing behind Neil, working hard to help settle the crowd. Eventually they became still again and waited, though their faces showed confusion and agitation.

'I'm sorry,' said Neil. 'I'm not very good at this. But please stay here and listen to what I have to say.'

He paused. The crowd was listening, so he continued.

'When I said I was wrong about never seeing Alice again, what I meant was, that I have already seen her again. Today. This afternoon, after the sun went out, I went with Artemis – this woman here – well, we went into the underworld. The land of the dead. I know you won't believe me. I wouldn't believe it myself. I went to look for Alice, and I found her. And I brought her back. You can't see her. But she's standing right here next to me.'

Neil smiled at Alice, and Alice smiled back. The crowd, though, weren't smiling. The chanting was starting up again.

'Bollocks! Bullshit!'

'Where's the sun? Where's the sun?'

'Who the fuck is Neil?'

'I know it's hard to believe,' said Neil over the noise. 'But think about it. Who could have imagined yesterday that we'd lose our sun? Things aren't the way we thought they were. What I'm telling you is that there really are gods, actual gods, and they're walking here on this earth with us. I've met them. So have you. They're the people standing right here in front of you. Trust me. Trust them. They brought Alice back and they're going to bring the sun back.'

The crowd started to boo and hiss. People started drumming again, aggressively this time, and missiles were thrown, coins and empty bottles.

'Well done, Neil,' said Artemis. 'That's perfect.'

'Perfect?' said Neil. 'Are you joking? Look at them!'

A beer can sailed past his head, only narrowly missing.

'You can step down,' said Artemis. 'It's my turn. I really hope I've got the strength for this.'

She addressed the crowd.

'It's true,' she said. 'Alice is here.'

She stepped forward and reached out a hand to where Alice was standing. For a couple of seconds, nothing happened. Then, suddenly, the crowd went silent.

Artemis turned to Alice. 'They can see you now,' she said.

'Can they hear me?' said Alice.

'Yes, they can.'

'Mum!' shouted Alice. 'Dad! It's all right! They brought me back! I'm OK! I'm alive, I'm fine! I love you!'

The crowd exploded into clamour. Alice's friends and family started pushing their way forwards to the barrier, calling out her name and crying, while other people shouted, screamed and applauded.

'Don't let them get too close,' said Artemis. 'You haven't got a body yet.'

But it took a huge effort to speak. The tidal wave of belief was flowing from the crowd, and it knocked her backwards with its force, filling her parched body to the brim with its power, making her feel renewed again, reborn, alive. Immortal. Around her, she could hear the gasps and groans of the other gods, as they, too, were overwhelmed with an ecstasy greater than any of them had ever felt. Artemis felt her skin tautening, saw the lines and wrinkles disappearing from her hands. Her muscles gripped around her bones, and her blood shot around her body, carrying vigour and energy to her limbs, clarity to her mind.

'There it is,' she moaned. 'Ahhh . . . It's starting.'

With some difficulty she looked at her family at the foot of the column. White hair turned dark, muscles bloomed, wrinkles smoothed out. They seemed to be exploding with light. A new Zeus burst out of his ancient shell like a butterfly from a seemingly dead chrysalis, the crumbled living skeleton giving birth to a muscular, gleaming, handsome man with shining eyes and flowing hair.

'My family!' he cried. 'I have returned!'

Around him, all of the other gods were blossoming like flowers opening.

'This is what I kept saying,' gasped Eros, 'about mortal belief . . .'

'It's amazing,' cried Aphrodite. 'It's better than sex! Artemis, you bitch, is this what you've been hoarding all along?'

Artemis pushed herself up and turned to the crowd, who were watching the transformation of the gods agog, mouths open, eyes wide.

'And now,' she announced, 'the sun!'

She hurried down the steps towards the rest of the gods.

'Aphrodite,' she said. 'Give that mortal her body back quick before the humans get to her. They can see her, but if they try to touch her before she's solid they'll think it's an illusion and they'll stop believing. The rest of you: let's wake up Apollo.'

Aphrodite broke away from the group and hurried up the stairs to where Alice was standing, her parents only a few feet away now. She was crying tearlessly, reaching her arms forward, calling out messages of love to all the people who were so desperate to reach her. They would cross the barrier any second, and Neil was standing a few steps ahead of Alice, ready to step in if anybody got too close, but unable to keep from turning back to look at her face, which was glowing with happiness and gratitude.

'So, Alice,' said Aphrodite. 'Exactly how pretty do you want to be? Any lumps and bumps, cellulite you'd like to get rid of? Now's your chance . . .'

'No thanks,' said Alice. 'I'm happy as I am.'

Aphrodite reached out and touched her – actually touched her. Alice gasped and staggered under the weight of gravity as she suddenly felt her body returned to her, in all its imperfect perfection. Then she ran forward to Neil, throwing her arms around him and kissing him, hard, on the mouth. As he kissed her back, her parents finally pushed through the barriers and rushed up the steps to their daughter, laughing, crying, arms outstretched. Keeping hold of one of Neil's hands, she fell into their arms, real tears pouring down her face, sobbing 'I'm back, I'm back, I'm back!'

Meanwhile the rest of the gods had gathered in a circle around Apollo.

'That's what I was attempting to inform you!' Athena was saying. 'The information was already in place!' But all the other gods ignored her.

'Are you sure this is going to work?' said Hermes. 'The life force of a god – that's a lot of power.'

'Can't you feel it?' said Artemis.

'Yes, I can feel it, but . . .'

'I told you so!' Athena screamed, but nobody was listening.

'Take hands,' said Artemis.

They all held hands around Apollo's prone body.

'Together now,' said Artemis. 'On three. One . . . Two . . . Three –'

Apollo opened his eyes. And the sun came out.

Epilogue

'Do we have to invite all of them?'

Neil was sitting up in bed, the pile of invitations on the mattress beside him.

'Of course we do,' said Alice.

'Even Hades and Persephone?'

'Hades won't come,' said Alice, 'which is just as well, but it would be nice if Persephone did. She always thought we made a sweet couple, remember?'

She put down her toothbrush, came back into the bedroom and climbed onto her side of the bed.

'You look very sexy in that nightdress,' said Neil, running a hand up over the satin.

'Neil. Invitations first. Concentrate.'

Alice took Neil's hand and returned it to his side of the bed.

'OK,' said Neil, picking up the pen and the next invitation. 'Aphrodite and Hephaestus.'

'Make a note on theirs that she should leave her mobile phone behind.'

'Is she still doing phone sex?'

'She does it for free now,' said Alice. 'She considers it to be a public service.'

'Hermes,' said Neil.

'He's already said yes,' said Alice.

'But we haven't even sent the invites yet.'

'He always has to get his reply in first.'

'Zeus and Hera,' said Neil.

'We'll have to keep Zeus away from the bridesmaids,' said Alice. 'But we can't possibly get married without him.'

'But if he comes, all the paparazzi will come. He's the king of the gods!'

'Hermes will keep them away.'

'OK,' said Neil. He addressed the invitation. 'Demeter's doing the flowers, so she's definitely coming, and Eros is too, of course.'

'Did you speak to him about the wording of the ceremony?'

'Yes, I called him this morning. He's happy for us to write our own vows, but he's still struggling with the service itself – he said he's finding it hard not being a Christian any more, all the Jesus stuff keeps creeping back in.'

'I'm sure he'll do a great job,' said Alice. 'What about Dionysus, have you heard from him about the music?'

'Yes, he said he can bring his own turntables, and he asked whether we wanted him to supply some wine for the party as well.'

'I hope you said no.'

'I said no,' said Neil. 'But I did ask for one bottle for the wedding night.'

'Oh dear,' said Alice, 'that's very naughty.'

'I can tell him to keep it if you like.'

'No, no,' said Alice, 'there's no need to do that . . .'

'Who else, then?' said Neil.

'Athena. And we should do one for Ares, though he isn't coming, he said, as a favour to us. Besides which, he's still got a lot of wars on. It's a shame, I thought all of that would have stopped now.'

'With this lot in charge?' said Neil. 'Hardly likely. What about Artemis? Has she agreed to be your matron of honour?'

'Yes, but she's being very fussy about the dress. And she wants to bring the dogs.'

'Tell her to leave them at home. She's got a big enough garden these days.'

'Oh Neil,' said Alice, 'don't be mean. She loves those dogs. Maybe she can just bring one, to head the procession.'

'You're soft,' said Neil.

'That's why you love me,' said Alice.

'OK, Artemis and one dog. So that just leaves . . .'

'Apollo,' said Alice.

'The world-famous Apollo,' said Neil. 'Celebrity clairvoyant. Rock singer. Raconteur. International playboy.'

'Invite him,' said Alice.

'Are you sure? After everything he did?'

'Of course I'm sure. Anyway I spoke to Eros. I thought maybe we could help him find a new girlfriend at the ceremony.'

'Alice . . .'

'Come on Neil! What could go wrong? I was thinking about your sister, actually. She hasn't been out with anyone in a long time, how about it?'

'Alice!'

Neil dived onto her, kissing her mouth as she laughed, and sending all of the invitations flying onto the floor. And Alice blushed pink, all the way down the back of her neck, and to the very tips of her ears.